THE SECRET KEEPER UP ALL NIGHT

(THE SECRET KEEPER SERIES #3)

BREA BROWN

WAYZGOOSE PRESS

Cover design by Keri Knutson at alchemybookcovers.com

Second edition ISBN: 978-1-938757-63-1

CONTENTS

For the three stinkers in my life who have each kept me up all night at various times, for various reasons.
Love you guys!

ADJUSTING

"*L*et's see here. You're out of wipes, big guy. Where does Mommy keep the new ones? Here? No. Hmm, that's where I'd keep them, but anyway— OH! Well, I guess I deserved that. Rookie mistake, leaving your little man uncovered. No matter. Baby pee never hurt anyone, right? Except now we're going to have to change your clothes, too."

Wait for it…

"So, are these the right onesies? They look kinda small. Hey! I found the wipes. Yay, me!"

Sleep deprivation to the point of nausea is my new normal, so I'm not alarmed that I feel like I'm about to barf when I swing my legs over the side of the bed. Smiling tiredly, I breathe the feeling away, fumble for my glasses on the bedside table, and lurch to my feet.

When I round the door frame to Max's room and come into view, Brice glances up and startles. He looks at me with wide eyes and a round mouth before smiling unsurely and saying, "Hey. Uh, what's up? I've got this, if you want to keep sleeping."

Before I can say anything, he holds up a tiny onesie. "Is this the right size? It looks so small!"

It's astounding to me how chipper he is only five minutes after being woken from a deep sleep.

"He's small," I say. "And they stretch. It should be fine."

"Okay," he says with a slight shrug. "Then I think we're good. Unless there aren't any bottles made."

"They're in the fridge."

"Oh, so?"

To explain my presence, I nod at the baby monitor less than a foot away on the dresser.

He follows my nod and winces. "Oh, man! Sorry."

I can't help but smile at his sheepish expression. "It's okay. I was already awake. You sounded like you needed help, though."

When I take a step toward the changing table, he blocks my way with his body and returns his attention to Max. "I thought I did, but now I've got it under control. I promise."

"Okay, but—"

Undressing and re-dressing the infant, he says, "I want to do this. He was already asleep when I got home last night. And you still have a couple of hours to sleep before you have to get up for work, so you should take advantage of it."

"I know—I look like shit."

His shoulders stiffen and drop. "Peyton, that's not what I said."

"I know you didn't *say* it."

"I wasn't implying it, either. Go get some sleep."

The way he says it with such finality pisses me off. But then everything pisses me off lately. Probably because I net about three hours of sleep per night and then work all day and then pick up Max at my sister's house and then come home to do everything by myself while my husband, the good reverend, works late at the church. Whew. Bitter much?

I'd quit my job, but we have to pay rent on this house, thanks to current budget cuts at the church that resulted in Brice agreeing to forego his housing allowance, which was a decent chunk of his compensation. It's still lower rent than we could ever imagine paying on any other remodeled, renovated house this nice, but with a new baby, we wouldn't be living as comfortably as I'd like without both of our incomes. Anyway, I don't want to quit my job at the art gallery. I like my job. Most days.

When I don't move or say anything, he pauses while snapping up the front of Max's pajamas and glances at me over his shoulder. "You're tired," he says, stating the obvious. "There's no reason for both of us to be up."

Yeah, except this is one of the first times we've been home and awake together in several days. Anyway, I can tell he doesn't want my sour company, and I can't blame him. Despite my exhaustion, I try to be upbeat and positive, but it doesn't come naturally to me like it does for him. It's work. And work is difficult when you're tired.

Grudgingly, I mutter, "Thanks," even though I know I won't be able to go back to sleep. Unlike him, I can't turn myself on and off, like I have a switch in the middle of my back.

Nevertheless, I shuffle back to bed and burrow under the covers. A normal woman would be glad that her husband is so cheerfully willing to get up with their three-month-old son in the middle of the night when they both have to work the next day. And I am. Glad, that is. Normal, not so much.

I don't know what my problem is. To pinpoint it would

require thought. Thought would require a fully functioning brain. I haven't had one of those for thirteen weeks.

Don't get me wrong; I love Max. He's such a good baby (when he's being held). He has a great personality already, and I'm positive that he's a genius. He looks exactly like his dad, so you can't get much cuter than that. And I can't remember what my life was like before he was born. Well, I vaguely remember sleeping sometimes. And not spending so much time (or any time at all, for that matter) trying to express milk from my breasts. But for the most part, my life has been enriched by the addition of Max to our family.

I also love my husband more than I can possibly express (no pun intended). Despite his chronic workaholism, he's a wonderful husband and an even better father. And *because* of his chronic workaholism, he's a fantastic pastor to our church family. I'd have to be an ungrateful bitch to utter a single complaint about him. And I don't have any complaints about *him*, necessarily. However, life isn't going exactly as how I imagined it would go.

I'm not such an idiot that I thought things would be idyllic and utopic and all those other words that mean "perfect" and end in "-ic." No, I have an older sister with kids, so I had an idea what I was in for. But I *am* enough of an idiot that I thought it would be a bit different (a.k.a., "better") for me than it was for Nicole. I mean, *my* husband is wonderful. Her husband, Lonnie, is not. Between their three children, I don't think he changed a single diaper. And she told me once that he'd get angry at her if she let Caleb, Everett, or Sadie cry long enough that it would wake *him* up, because he had to go to work the next day, but she was a stay-at-home mom and could "sleep all day," if she wanted to. So I thought, more involved, supportive husband/baby daddy equals sweet, tranquil new family and home life. Wrong.

Because I didn't take into account an important factor: the baby, whose job it is to make life complete chaos, no matter how many people are doing the work to try to keep him happy.

Sweet, sweet Max. The baby who wants to be held at least twenty hours a day. That would be fine with me, because I love holding him. Except it's difficult to do so while using the bathroom, taking a shower, eating, or sleeping, which comprise more than four hours in my ideal day. So when I'm with him, I do everything that requires two hands very quickly. I am now an expert in speed-showering and speed-peeing. However, I haven't yet mastered the speed-sleeping.

But I think the biggest time-taker in my current life is the feeding. I feel like I always have one of my boobs in his mouth or attached to a pump. If it was more of the former, it would be a lot better, because I could justify that as bonding time, but since he's not fond of breastfeeding (and I'm trying not to take that personally), I've lately submitted myself to many hours of the sort of torture I'd only heretofore read about in books featuring medieval dungeons or POW camps. Pumping breast milk hurts. And the nurse in the hospital who told me it would stop hurting was a flat-out liar. I told myself I'd do it for six months. I only have three more to go. Gulp.

Anyway, it's wrong for me complain about any of it. I'm incredibly blessed, and I'm 100 percent aware of that fact. But being aware of it and having the energy to be grateful for it aren't the same things. And right now, in addition to being blessed, I'm very tired. And a little disillusioned. That's all. Wah me.

All this is internal monologue, however. I'd rather pump breast milk 24/7 than utter a single complaint to Brice or my mom or Nicole or my best friends, Jen and Mitzi. No way. As far as they know, my life *is* idyllic and utopic. It's rare that I let my guard down and slip like I did with Brice just now. I mean, he obviously knows I'm tired, but he is, too. There's no use moaning about it all the time. Plus, this isn't forever. I'm sure I'll look back on this time fondly someday and miss it. Probably. Maybe. At least, that's what all the veteran moms have told me will happen.

A shift in the mattress next to me jostles me awake. It takes me a second to figure out where I am. I'm so accustomed to sleeping on the couch or in the rocking chair in Max's room or in my car on my lunch break that it's rare to wake up in a bed. I live in fear of waking up behind the wheel of my car while I'm crossing the median toward oncoming traffic, so every time I wake up, my heart hammers until I'm sure I'm in a safe place.

Right now, I'm in a very safe place. Brice hooks an arm over my waist and pulls me up against him.

"All settled," he whispers next to my ear when I ask how it went. He kisses the spot where my neck meets my shoulders. "I think he's down for the count."

My eyes closed, I reply with an affectionate grumble, "For twenty minutes, anyway." That's Max's modus operandi. He loves to do the sleep fake-out. He'll lead me to believe that this time, he's going to sleep on his own, so I'll do something impulsive—like run a hot bath—after putting him down in his crib. As soon as my toe hits the water, the crying starts.

"Twenty minutes is long enough," my husband murmurs against my shoulder, squeezing me even more tightly around the waist.

Oh.

"I'm so tired," I whine, hating that it's true.

I can hear the smile in his voice when he acknowledges, "I know. Me too, but it's been a while. Maybe it'll perk us up."

"Let's shoot for Saturday," I suggest instead, lying perfectly still and trying hard not to make any encouraging noises or moves during this critical negotiation.

He groans. "You're penciling me in three days from now?"

Resisting the urge to make a dirty pun about penciling, I chuckle. "Maybe." When he persists with his efforts, which are—amazingly enough—working, I bluff and say, "Can't we just cuddle? Cuddling is nice."

"I already got my cuddle fix with Max. I want to do more than cuddle with you."

Damn him for being so sweet and persuasive.

I open my eyes, turn over to face him, and smile. "What's gotten into you?"

He looks surprised by my question. "I love you!" he answers earnestly, sneaking his hand up the front of my t-shirt.

"Well, I know that, but usually you're good about taking no for an answer." I flinch when his knuckles make contact with my tender breasts.

"There haven't been many occasions for me to have to take no for an answer," he points out accurately before wheedling, "C'mon, you used to love this."

"I still do!"

"But you're tired." He raises his eyebrow as if he doesn't believe me.

My eyes flutter closed. "Yes, I am."

"And you want to wait until Saturday, even though we have a perfect opportunity right now."

I nod but scoot closer to him and make tiny circles on his hip with my index finger.

"You're a liar."

"I've never denied that."

Lifting his head a few inches from his pillow, he softly kisses my lips. Then he presses his mouth against mine again, more lazily. I thrust my body against his chest and hitch a leg over his hip.

The baby monitor behind me squawks to life. I can tell by the ratcheting nature of Max's crying that it's not the product of a short gas pain that will subside so he can go right back to sleep. No, he's discovered he's not sleeping in someone's arms, and he's gearing up for a wailing session.

"Fuck me," I grumble.

Instead of chastising me for my potty mouth like he normally would, Brice quips, "Well, I tried, but…"

This cracks me up and makes it slightly easier to throw back the covers and leave the bed to go tend to the baby. Less than a minute later, I'm back, sliding between the covers with a now-quiet Max against my chest.

"He's never going to sleep alone if you always give in to him and hold him at the first little cry," Brice states. But he scoots closer to us so he can kiss Max's nose.

"At least he's quiet. Maybe we can get some more sleep," I defend my coddling.

To Max, Brice says softly, "Stinky! You promised me some alone time with your mom. That wasn't enough time, just so you know."

Settling on my back, I close my eyes and absently rub my fingers down the baby's back, between his shoulder blades, to his diapered bottom, and up again. Sleepily, I say, "It's okay. Saturday. We'll try again then."

Brice sighs toward the ceiling. "Yeah. Saturday."

2

CALLING

When I wake up on Saturday, feeling amazingly refreshed and *human* for the first time in three months, the house is still and densely silent. And I'm alone in bed. I'm not as disappointed as I probably should be. It's safe to say I'm craving peace and solitude more than sex. Never thought I'd say *that*.

After a few minutes of languishing in bed, though, I start to feel guilty. How many times did Brice get up during the night with Max, and what time did he get out of bed for good? I must have been out of it; I didn't hear a thing. I look over at the baby monitor, and part of the mystery is solved: it's turned off.

Well, he didn't have to do *that*.

I creep downstairs but walk more normally when it's apparent the house truly is empty. In the kitchen, the coffeepot is full and on. There's a note propped on the counter in front of the small appliance:

Took Max to the park for a jog. I'll bring home donuts.
XO

--B

Mmm, donuts. Yes, please!

I sit down at the kitchen table with a cup of coffee, for which I have a newfound appreciation, but almost immediately spring up once more. I feel so great that I decide to put on some clothes and try to catch up with the guys.

After snagging the diaper bag, which Brice was either brave or clueless enough to leave behind, I go to the garage and hop in the Jeep. I back from the driveway and cruise along the route I know Brice would take to get from the donut shop to the house. No sign of the pair of them, so I continue along to the park across the street from the church.

There, I see them in the distance, on the other side of the duck pond. Brice is moving at a good clip, pushing the jogging stroller along the paved path. While I park, I watch him wipe his forehead on his t-shirt sleeve, near his shoulder, keeping one hand on the handle of the stroller. I imagine what the muscles in his legs look like as they flex and contract while he runs. With that picture in my head, I close my eyes and take a deep breath through my nose, inhaling the scent of him trapped in the warm interior of the Jeep.

Maybe I *would* rather have sex than sleep in and have coffee and donuts. Now that I'm not as sleep-deprived, it strikes me as appalling that I can't remember when the last time was. I think it was two weeks ago. I think. Or has it been longer? The weeks are flying by and blurring together.

Dwelling on it too long seems crass, so I pull the keys from the ignition, pocket them, and set off around the pond in the direction opposite to which Brice is running. In no time, he's a few yards away, grinning at me and slowing to a walk.

"Hey! I figured you'd still be snuggled up in bed," he says breathlessly when we meet up.

Peering down into the stroller at a sleeping Max, I say, "My body didn't know what to do with all the sleep I got. My batteries are so full, I feel like I could…"

"Jog the rest of the way with me?" he suggests hopefully.

He smiles while I laugh at that idea, before saying, "No. Not quite *that* full. Ever. If you want to keep running, I'll take over pushing the stroller and meet you at the Jeep."

He seems to consider it for a second but then chuckles. "Kidding. No, I'm finished."

He already has his breath back, I notice with a mixture of admiration and jealousy. I wish I could run for longer than two minutes without preferring death. If only exercise were as fun as eating.

Fantasies involving custard-filled donuts dissolve as he clears his throat and says suddenly, "I've received a call."

I blink and fall into step next to him when he starts walking. "A call? While you were jogging? From who?"

His smile is patient and oddly sad. "No. A *call*. From another church."

It takes a second for that news to sink in, but when it does, I'm thankful for my full night's sleep. I know my reaction to this statement is very important.

Controlled and noncommittal is how I'm going to play it until I have more information. "Oh, I see."

"Actually," he qualifies, "the Synod President is the one who told me that a church in southwest Missouri, Peace Lutheran, sent him a request for a Senior Pastor. He gave my name and the names of four other candidates to Peace's call committee, and after reviewing all the information, they chose me."

"Wow." I swallow and smile shakily. "Missouri. Well. That's… great."

His face lights up. "You think so? Because I think I want to answer it."

My eyes bug out before I can moderate my response. "Wait. What? Whoa, whoa whoa."

"I know. It's kind of crazy. And impulsive. Neither of which are anything like me. But I've been praying about it—"

My brain immediately picks up on the words *been praying*. "How long have you known about this?" I ask.

My tone puts him on guard. "Um… Well… For a couple of weeks. But—"

"A couple of *weeks?*"

"I mean, the Synod informed me two weeks ago that it had recommended me to Peace, but I found out yesterday that they chose me from all the candidates." He stops walking and grabs my hand. "This could be wonderful, Peyton."

"B-but what about Messiah?" I ask, feeling more like one of the soon-to-be abandoned members than I do the wife who would accompany him to his new life.

He narrows his eyes at me and tilts his head as if he's not sure exactly what I mean. Uncertainly, he explains, "Well, they'll have to call a new pastor, if I leave."

I'm relieved when he uses the word *if*, but I can tell by the look in his eyes that he wants it to be a *when*.

My shoulders slump as I simply say, "Right. Of course," and continue walking toward the car, determined to hide my rising panic.

It's time to show him what I'm really made of. So far in our relationship and marriage, I haven't been tested too much on this "pastor's wife" thing. In most instances, our challenges have been similar to those any other married couple would face. We've learned to balance our professional lives with our personal lives; we've gotten used to living together as a couple and dividing the household labor between the two of us; and we've integrated fairly seamlessly into each other's families. And now that we're parents, we've entered a new phase in our relationship, but it's still pretty standard stuff.

I'm not gonna lie, though; I've been dreading this. A call. This is what separates us from laypeople.

If Brice were an architect, for example, and he were offered a job in a different state, I would expect him to talk to me about it immediately and extensively. We'd weigh the pros and cons together; we'd research schools and real estate; we'd discuss salary and benefits packages and moving expenses. I'd be part of the decision-making process from the very beginning. But that's not how it works, because Brice isn't an architect. He's a pastor. He consults God first. Apparently, he consults Him for two weeks before he says a peep to me about it.

After he catches up to me, and I don't say anything else while I mentally put the most diplomatic spin on his motives for not telling me sooner, he says, "It's a very nice church. A big congregation, a large staff comprised of ordained ministers *and* laity, no major upsets or conflicts in more than ten years, situated in an affluent area."

"Why do they need a new pastor, then?" I quickly ask when he trails off.

He looks straight ahead. "Their Senior Pastor is retiring."

"Do they have an Associate Pastor?"

"Yes."

"Why don't they promote him, then, and call a new Associate Pastor straight out of Seminary?"

"The Associate Pastor's not interested in being the Senior Pastor. He's nearing retirement, too."

Oh, I see. So this church is going to poach Messiah's young, dynamic pastor as they put their own pastors out to pasture. Of course, I don't say this to Brice (it's kind of a tongue-twister, anyway). To him, I simply say, "Hm."

We're nearing the parking lot. I keep my eyes trained on Brice's sparkly red Jeep while he persuades, "Listen. The thing is, we'd be closer to my mom, which is important to me as she gets older—you know that; we've talked about it a lot."

I nod.

"And Peace is solvent. Extremely solvent."

Now I jerk my eyes toward his. "Unlike Messiah, you mean?"

He has the grace to look somewhat embarrassed. "Yeah. And trust me, I know it sounds bad that I care about that, but it's important! A few years ago, I would have told you it didn't matter, but I was naïve and idealistic. Now, I'm tired of beating my head against a brick wall with the elders and the treasurers, who dismiss every idea I have to get things going in the right financial direction. I yearn to know what it's like to be able to focus on the ministry and not worry about what's in the offering plate every week." Next to the Jeep, he waits while I lift Max from the stroller and continues while folding the apparatus, "This is the next logical step, Peyton."

Without so much as a glance over my shoulder at him while I strap Max into his car seat, I say dully, "I understand."

He opens the back hatch, slides the stroller in, and looks at me over the back seat. "You don't sound pleased."

Am I supposed to be pleased? *Supportive* I can do. But I can't seem to muster *pleased* or *excited* at this juncture. Too busy fighting off *panicked*. Chicago is the only place I've ever called home. Messiah is the only church home I've ever had. I have a newborn baby and a relatively new husband, and I'm still not close to being what I know I should be as a pastor's wife, but at least here, people know me (and know not to expect much). With a bunch of strangers, the stakes are a lot higher.

"I'm sorry," I say, paying an unnecessary amount of attention to Max's car seat harness. "I'm still trying to process the information. I don't know what to think or feel."

Shutting the hatch, he walks around the side of the vehicle and rests his hand on my shoulder. I turn to face him, and he pulls me against him in a sweaty hug.

"Come on. What happened to the woman who, while sitting with me on a freezing dock, told me she always figured it was who she was with, not where she was, that mattered?"

"Dirty pool," I say petulantly. "It's not fair that you remember everything I say and use it against me when it suits you."

He laughs. "It was a bold statement. It definitely caught my attention, too, considering how likely relocation is in my line of work."

"Maybe I was just saying what you wanted to hear."

"I think you're scared, so you can't isolate any of your other feelings on this topic. When you have time to pray and think about it logically, you'll find it's not such a terrifying prospect. We'll be together, the three of us. And my mom will be only a couple of hours away." He rubs my shoulder blades with his thumbs. "This is my third call. I know what to expect, so there won't be any surprises for us."

I pull away from him, looking up into his eyes. "But your decision isn't final yet, right? We're going to talk more about it and do some research and look at things from every angle. Right?"

He nods. "Of course. Absolutely. We can even take a trip there to visit the church and drive around the town to get a firsthand view of everything. Would that make you feel better?"

"I don't know. But it's worth a shot."

"Then that's what we'll do."

"And what if I hate it?"

He grins. "I don't think you will."

"But what if I do?"

"Then we'll stay here in Chicago," he says after a deep breath.

"You promise?"

"You promise to give it a chance?" he counters.

I nod sincerely. "Yes. I do."

"That's all I can ask, then. Now, let's go get some donuts. Unless you'd rather go home and take advantage of Stinky's current sleepiness." He wiggles his eyebrows at me.

I pretend not to catch his suggestion. "I need donuts."

"Donuts it is, then," he says with a good-natured slap to my backside as I walk away from him and around the Jeep to the passenger side.

Yeah. I definitely need to allay my worries with fried dough and custard.

～

The red wine swirls in front of my unfocused eyes. I blink

and accept the large bowl-like glass from Brice as he lowers himself onto the floor next to me with his own goblet.

We've had a lovely, relaxing Saturday, until now. Max's bedtime is never lovely or relaxing. And I think I'm expected to deliver on my Saturday sex promise, but there's no way it's happening with that squalling going on in the background.

"Drink," he commands gently.

In my head, I finish his statement with, "'This is my blood, shed for you for the forgiveness of your sins,'" which is what he always says in the Words of Distribution before Communion at church. A psychological trick like that would normally make me laugh, but laughing is the furthest thing from my mind. And my throat is too tight for me to drink without choking.

Brice takes his own advice, nearly downing his entire portion in four long swallows. When he sets down his glass, he says, "He's okay, you know. He'll settle down in a few minutes."

"He's *not* okay," I counter. "*Listen* to him. He's beside himself. And he probably thinks we don't love him." That last sentence chokes me up for real.

"No, he doesn't! He has a full tummy and a dry diaper, and he's warm in his bed."

"His crying is killing my boobs," I announce bluntly, pressing my free hand to my chest.

Brice smiles tenderly. "I'm sorry."

I make a move to stand. "I'm going to go up there and hold his hand. Or something."

With a warm hand to my knee, my husband keeps me in place. "Not yet. Please. Give it a few more minutes." He holds eye contact with me. "Please."

I'm torn between his wish (and mine, too!) to have a

baby who can sleep for longer than thirty minutes outside of our bed and Max's want for a comforting parent. In the end, Max wins out.

As I rush up the stairs to his room, I tell myself that Brice is a grown-ass man with the ability to reason, an understanding of what's going on around him, and the capacity to process disappointment. Max isn't. As far as he knows, he's all alone in the world, without anyone listening to his cries or caring that he's distressed. I can't allow that!

Navigating the nursery by nightlight, I sidle up to his crib and reach down into it to scoop him up. "Shhhh. It's okay. Mommy's here. I'm so sorry you're upset. It's okay." Within seconds, his lusty bleating pulls back to the occasional whimper and tapers down to nothing as he balls himself up and snuggles sleepily against me. "That's right. You're fine now."

Brice's silhouette appears in the doorway, but he doesn't say anything. Since he's backlit by the bright hall light, I can't see the expression on his face, but I imagine it's not a happy one.

"I can't do it," I say. "I can't."

"I know," he says in a resigned tone.

"I'm sorry."

"I know," he repeats. "Uh, I'm going to run up to the church and do some last-minute stuff for tomorrow. I may be late."

Confused, I say, "Oh. Okay." This is the first he's mentioned having anything to do there. As far as I knew, his plan was to spend the evening with me, after Max stopped crying.

As I'm thinking all of these things, he explains quietly, "You're sort of preoccupied with him. So, I might as well…"

My heart sinks when I get where he's going with this. Remorseful, I begin, "Brice, I'm sorry, but—"

He puts up a hand. "No. Don't apologize. I understand. But if we're not going to spend the evening alone together, then I'm going to get some work done." The shrug in his voice is heartbreaking.

I hear his footsteps on the stairs, his keys jingling as he pockets them, and the front door closing behind him as he sets off on foot toward the church.

I sigh as I look down at Max's peaceful, sleeping face. "Oh, Stinky. This will never do."

3

GOING PUBLIC

I feel a pair of warm lips on my forehead and a slight lightening of weight from my chest. Blinking sleepily, I gaze up from my position on the couch to see Max being lifted what seems like a great height from this vantage point.

Brice settles the baby in the crook of his arm. "Good morning," he says softly. I'm not sure which one of us he's talking to. Both, maybe?

"What time is it?" I ask with a grunt as I stretch the tense muscles in my back. He's already dressed for church, but I hope it's not too late.

"A little before seven," he answers. "I'm getting ready to head out the door. You want me to feed Max while you get a shower?"

I readily accept, practically sprinting for the stairs at the prospect of a rare, guilt- and stress-free bathing experience, knowing Max is in his father's capable hands.

In the shower, while I don't have time to let the water beat against me as long as I'd like, I do have time while I lather and rinse to ruminate about the current unsatisfactory state of affairs in the Northam household.

For the hundredth time, I try to tell myself this is temporary. Max isn't going to be an infant forever. But I think of all the articles I've read about "family beds" and "co-sleeping," and I wonder, *How temporary is temporary?* Are we talking weeks, months, or years here? And what permanent effect does something even as temporary as a few weeks have on a marriage? Is Brice starting to resent the way I've chosen to deal with Max's refusal to sleep alone? Because I'm not *choosing* this. I don't have a choice but to respond to my child's cries.

I've researched methods for shifting his sleeping patterns, but they all have the same basic strategy: let your baby cry while you helplessly listen. Like I told Brice last night, I can't do it. But I can't sleep on the couch with a baby on my chest for very many more nights, either. And I can't stand to have Brice annoyed or unhappy with me. I feel caught between the two of them.

It's like the time Robby Marshall and Sam Dixon both asked me to the senior prom. Okay, maybe not *quite* like that, but it elicits a similar mixture of emotions: guilt at having to disappoint one of them and dissatisfaction with my eventual decision. In the Robby versus Sam situation, I was pressured by my mom to say yes to Robby, even though I preferred Sam, because Robby went to our church, and his mom and my mom were friends.

In this current case, biology and psychology are working against my desire to accommodate my husband's reasonable request that we figure out a way to make Max an independent sleeper. No matter which side I choose, someone's going to be hurt. I think. Do babies have the capacity for hurt feelings? Hmmm.

Either way, the situation seems hopeless.

I jump at the soft knock on the shower door. "Hey. Uh, I have to get moving," Brice says from the other side.

"I'm finished," I inform him. "Just give me two minutes to dry off."

A towel attached to a hand appears over the top of the door. "No rush. Max is in his crib. Seems okay with it for now."

Yeah. I'm sure. That'll last barely long enough for me to pick out something to wear. I grab the towel and rub down in double-time.

Brice loiters on the other side of the door. Finally, as I'm opening it to step onto the bath mat, he says quietly, "I'm going to tell everyone at today's services about the call from Peace."

I pause in the middle of wrapping the towel around myself before continuing with ultra-precise movements.

When I don't say anything, he fills the silence. "The elders know already, of course, since Messiah has to put in its own call for me, to counter Peace's. They're waiting—within reason—for me to tell the rest of the congregation. I don't want to keep it from people any longer, though. They deserve to know before I make my decision, so they can pray about it and—"

"Hound you mercilessly?"

His serious expression softens, and he chuckles as he looks down at his shiny dress shoes. "Um, probably. The only solution to that problem is making a decision."

Message received. However, considering we haven't had a chance to talk about it as a couple, and he promised me a trip there to scope out the church and town, making a decision isn't something I expect to happen quickly.

All that aside, I step forward and kiss his smooth cheek.

"Well, good luck with your announcement in the early service. I'll be with you in spirit then and physically with you in the late service."

And I'm dreading every second of my life from this day until he announces his decision—and possibly beyond.

As expected, it was pandemonium after the 8:00 announcement. Usually, people are either attending Sunday school classes or have not yet arrived when I get to the church thirty minutes before the second service, so the narthex is quiet and empty. Today, however, the area right outside the sanctuary is buzzing with activity. It's wall-to-wall people, clumped in groups of two to ten, everyone wearing similar expressions, like they all bought the same *Scream* mask from the costume shop.

When I walk through the doors, weighed down by Max's infant carrier on one arm and balanced by an equally behemoth diaper bag on the opposite shoulder, the roar of conversation immediately dies down. There's some whispering and nervous coughing.

I give the assembly a shaky smile. "Good morning," I venture.

"Not really," I hear from a distance too far away for me to tell who said it.

Mom steps from the throng and relieves me of the baby carrier. "Hi, honey," she says, trying to act is if this is a normal Sunday. Even though she fails, the rest of the people around us take their cues from her and at least go back to their own conversations, albeit a lot more quietly so I can't hear what they're saying about my husband.

Since my dad is an elder, I'm sure Brice's announcement

wasn't news to Mom this morning. Hell, she might have known before *I* did, given how long it took Brice to tell me about it. I can't think about that, though, without feeling the variety of anger that's unbecoming of a proper pastor's wife.

While she coos over Max, I mutter sarcastically, "Looks like everyone's taking the news in stride, as usual."

Sadly, she replies, "It *is* a bit of a shock. To all of us. Brice… er, Pastor, has only been here for a few years. When we called him, we hoped it would be a long-term arrangement."

A thousand defenses and excuses spring to mind to counter her justification of the congregation's surprise and dismay, but I hold them all back. This is definitely not the time or the place to discuss it. Plus, I'm not sure I want to defend Brice's consideration of this call. Actually, I'm tempted to ask for everyone's attention and tell them I'm on *their* side. I know I can't do that, either, though. I have to remain silently supportive of my husband. As a matter of fact, I should have been here for the 8:00 announcement, I realize with a belated sense of guilt and shame that's all too familiar. It seems I always realize the correct thing to do after it's too late.

"I take it Brice is in his office?" I say to Mom now.

She nods. "We could hardly hold a productive Bible class after that bombshell, now could we? The kids' classes are still going on, as usual, but none of the adults seemed interested in continuing our study of the Book of Acts."

I leave Max in her doting possession and wend through the mob to get to the hallway that leads to the church's offices. Away from the hubbub, it's eerily quiet in the dark outer office. Brice's office door is closed.

I knock and open the door at the same time so that he

doesn't have to worry for more than a second about a potential confrontation with an angry church member.

He visibly sags behind his desk when he sees it's me. I softly close the door behind me and lean with my back against it.

"Yo," I greet him briefly.

After a weak wave, he asks, "Where's Max?"

Nonchalantly, I answer, "I left him out in the car so we could have some time alone." When he seems to believe me, I roll my eyes. "He's with my mom. Der."

He laughs at himself. "Of course. Der. Sorry. I'm not thinking very clearly."

"Could it have anything to do with the chaos out there?" I point in the direction of the narthex. "Because everyone's acting like you cancelled Christmas."

Running a hand through his hair, he says, "I know. I wasn't expecting that reaction."

"What were you expecting?"

He flaps his lips. "I don't know. Not that, though. I guess I thought everyone would keep their wits about themselves, if nothing else."

"Are you new around here?"

With a rueful smile, he answers, "Apparently. I think that's one of the biggest objections to the idea of my leaving."

It may seem to him like he's been here a long time, but to lifetime members like ninety-plus Mrs. Hanson and my parents, he's still "the new guy," especially compared to his predecessor, Pastor Niedermeyer, who was with the congregation more than twenty years. They've worked hard to break him in, and now, when it seems they've finally broken him, he's considering leaving. And they're going to have to go through the call process all over again, so soon after going through it to call him, someone they assumed would be with the church for another twenty years.

"I'd think they'd be relieved to be rid of me. Some of them, anyway."

"My dad, yes. But for the most part, people here love you. They have a mean-older-brother way of showing it sometimes, but…"

I walk around his desk and perch on his leg. Repairing the damage he's done to his hair with his distracted tousling, I continue, "You know, the possibility of losing you may turn things around enough here that you won't want to take that call, after all. Maybe this is God's wake-up call to them, that they'd better stop taking you for granted and making things so difficult all the time."

"It's not only about that, though," he insists. "I'm not running away from a challenge. I feel like I've done all I can do here. I'm ready for *new* challenges and *new* experiences. I want to take what I've learned here and start fresh with new people, people who don't have a history with me, people who don't have a history with *us*. People who can get to know us without any biases coloring their judgment."

I stiffen at this revelation and what it implies, but before I can ask him exactly what he means, he stands and practically dumps me from his lap.

"I have to get ready for the second service. That means wading through the multitudes out there, which may take a while."

I give him an encouraging hug. "Hey. Don't let the bastards get you down," I advise.

He groans at my word choice but says, "I won't. I mean, silver lining: when I make the announcement during the sermon at 10:30, I won't be telling anyone anything they haven't already heard on their way into the building. So at least I won't have to hear gasps, like in the early service."

"People gasped?" I ask, pulling away and looking up at him.

He sets his jaw. "Yup. Like I'd told them we were going to have a Harry Potter theme for Vacation Bible School, or something."

I can't help but laugh at his reference to one of our former vicar Jared's most disastrous and controversial ideas last year.

With one last kiss and a side-hug, he strides to the door, opens it, and steps aside for me. "Let's do this," he says grimly.

I now have an idea of how celebrities feel when they have to push through a wall of paparazzi. Getting to my car after church was harrowing. *Harrowing!* I've never seen Lutherans behave so savagely when Jell-O salad wasn't involved. They were even raising their voices! And more than one person touched me! But their questions were the most intrusive part of the ordeal. "What are *your* thoughts on this?" "What does this new church have that we don't?" "How can you guys be leaving already?" "When will he be making his decision and letting us know?" "Do you have a say?" "Can you convince him to stay?"

By the time I get home, my ears are ringing, and my head is swimming. All I want is a sandwich, then a nap in my own bed alone. But between Max and my phone, neither will be happening. I'm half-heartedly playing on the floor with the baby and considering turning off my phone when it rings again. I can tell by the ringtone that it's my sister, Nicole, so I deign to answer it.

After the usual pleasantries are out of the way, she says, "I was wondering when he was finally going to say something."

I stop shaking the rattle in front of Max's face. "What?"

"Well, he's known for weeks. It's not like he has to have an answer, but—"

"Wait. How do you know he's known for weeks?"

As if I'm an idiot, she snaps, "Mom told me weeks ago! Thank goodness, too, since it's obvious *you* weren't going to tell me."

I blurt, "I couldn't tell you, because I didn't know until yesterday!" before I can think better of it.

There's stunned silence on her end of the line. Then she says, "Oh. I mean— Wow. I just assumed…"

"Yeah, well you assumed incorrectly!" I cover my eyes as my emotional Berlin Wall crumbles like hordes of people dressed in Members Only jackets are beating on it with sledgehammers. The tears aren't only about this latest development—although I'm pissed off that everyone else in my family knew about such a potentially life-changing occurrence for my husband and me before I did—but they're a culmination of all the disappointments of the past couple of months, disappointments that I've been keeping to myself and holding inside for so long that it physically hurts to release them now.

Probably the biggest frustration, though, is the knowledge that I can't really be angry at anyone in particular. I can't be mad at Max for keeping me awake every night; he's a baby. I can't be mad at Brice for not telling me right away about being a candidate in Peace's search for a new pastor; he was right not to freak me out unnecessarily, and he was smart to wait to tell me after I'd had a full night's sleep. I can't be mad at my dad for telling Mom about the call; he was simply sharing important information with his spouse. I can't be mad at Mom; gossiping with Nicole is second nature, and she can no more resist it than I can let Max "cry it out." I can't be mad at Nicole; she was the recipient of the news and thought I already knew, which was a logical assumption.

I've been robbed of any basis for my specialty, righteous anger. That doesn't mean I'm not allowed to be upset, though. I never have to have a legitimate reason to be upset. Justification is for sane, rational people.

While I blubber incoherently into the phone, Nicole tries to soothe me. "Oh, come on now, Peyton. It'll be okay."

"I know!" I wail.

"He was only protecting you."

"I know!"

"It's probably been very difficult for him not to have you as a sounding board the past couple of weeks."

"I know!"

"If you know all this, then why are you so upset?" she challenges quietly. "What's really wrong? Is it something else? Something worse?"

For once, she doesn't sound like she's hoping that's the case, hoping for some juicy drama to keep things interesting in her otherwise dull life. She actually sounds concerned. Great. I knew I was right all these months to hold everything inside and not let on what I've been feeling. Why didn't I trust the secret-keeping instinct that's been my trusty friend all these years? On top of everything else, I can't handle worrying about her concern for me.

I sniff wetly and take a deep, shuddering breath. "I'm fine. Everything's fine. I'm tired. That's all. I'd be handling this a lot better if I could string together some consecutive nights of decent sleep."

She sounds relieved when she assures me, "All couples go through this when there's a new baby in the house. It's one of the most stressful things you'll ever experience. You have to remember that it's fleeting, and you need to lean on each other for support. Don't try to do it all yourself."

"Yeah. Okay."

"I always wanted to divorce Lonnie when we had a new baby."

"I don't want to divorce Brice!" I manage to sputter.

She laughs. "Well, see? You're ahead of the game, then."

I know she's trying to make me feel better, but her making light of everything is making me feel worse somehow.

"I have to go," I say when Max shows signs of being bored with his tummy time.

"I hate hanging up with you when you're so upset."

"I'll be fine," I repeat none-too-convincingly. I try to take another deep breath, but it only produces a painful sob that leads to hiccups. "Max needs to eat, and Brice will be home soon."

"Why don't I come over and watch Max so you two can go out to dinner alone?"

"No. I'm too tired. I don't want to go anywhere."

"Then I'll take Max for the night. He can have a sleep-over here—Sadie would love that—so that you and Brice can have a quiet evening and a full night of uninterrupted sleep."

I'm literally drooling while I stare off into space and listen to her describe such a beautiful concept.

When I don't answer right away, she prompts, "Huh? Doesn't that sound nice? And since Max'll already be here, you'll even get to sleep in tomorrow morning, because you won't have to stop by here on your way to work, unless you want to."

"You'd do that for me?" I ask, hating how pathetic I sound and how much I crave being away from my baby for a few hours that don't involve going to work.

"Absolutely!"

"If you're sure."

I'm hesitant because I'm ashamed at how good her offer sounds to me, and, I have to say, I'm not used to the new Nicole yet.

There's been a definite shift in her behavior and personality since she and Lonnie went through marriage counseling with Brice. Every once in a while, I get a peek at the old Nicole, the one who never talked about anyone but herself (and her problems), but for the most part, she's a different person. A better person. I've thanked Brice for it a hundred times, but he always dismisses my gratitude with a humble, "Only the Holy Spirit can bring about change in a person; I was merely the conduit," or something equally self-effacing. I hope he accepts more credit tonight, when we're enjoying a quiet house for the first time in more than three months.

"I'm sure," she insists. "When do you want me to come get him?"

Already springing into action, I breathe into the phone, "I can have him ready in thirty minutes!"

4

PARENTS' NIGHT OFF

I wish I could say that I put on some sexy underwear, tossed a simple dinner together, and lit some candles so that the backdrop for a romantic evening was set when Brice got home.

What ended up happening was not nearly as glamorous or organized. I collapsed on the couch as soon as Nicole left with Max and half the contents of his nursery. While I was brainstorming all the ways I could make the night special, Brice arrived home, and I practically tackled him in the kitchen, right in front of the garage door.

I'm afraid it wasn't pretty, but neither of us cared. We weren't going for style points.

Now that it's over, Brice holds his clothes in a bunch in his lap and sits with his back against the cold oven door while he catches his breath.

I grin up at him from my flat-backed vantage point next to him.

He laughs. "Okay, then. I, uh… What's going on?"

"Are you really asking questions?"

"I am. Oddly enough. Where's Stinky?"

Suddenly it occurs to me how oblivious he is and how random this all must seem. I have a quick debate with myself over how much to share. Finally, I decide on, "He's spending the night at Nicole's, because we need some alone time."

That receives a raised eyebrow and what looks like mild concern at first, but both expressions disappear so quickly that I wonder if I imagined them when he resumes smiling down at me.

"Is that okay?" I think—belatedly—to check.

"Yes!" is his quick reply, followed by the speedy qualification, "If it's okay with you. I mean, I love him to death, but a break will be nice."

"And it's only one night, right?" I seek approval. "It's not like we're giving him up for adoption or—" The thought of that makes my smile falter. "Although, *he* doesn't know that. Oh, no!" I sit up and gather my clothes. As I frantically get dressed, Brice looks on, confused.

"What are you doing?" he asks.

"We need to go get him," I state firmly, rising to pull up my shorts and button them.

He stands, letting his clothes drop to the floor at his feet as he uses both hands to grab my shoulders. "What? No. Just calm down a second."

"No! Oh, crap. He probably thinks I don't love him. You should have seen how quickly I fed him and pushed him out the door with all of his stuff. He probably thinks he's going to live with Nicole forever!" I shrug away from his hands, but he persists, managing to grab my wrist as I turn toward the garage door and reach for my car keys on their peg.

"Peyton. Stop!" He yanks gently but firmly, spinning me back toward him.

I look down at his nakedness and blush.

"Yeah. I'm lettin' it all hang out here, so listen to me for a second."

Forcing my eyes upward, I widen them and attempt to obey him, despite the panicked mama bear in my head, worried that her precious angel bear cub feels abandoned, and the admittedly prudish pastor's wife (standing next to the bear), competing for attention as she keeps pointing out that there's a very naked, very adorable man standing in her kitchen.

He squeezes my hand. "Take a deep breath for me, all right? Let's keep things in perspective."

"I am!"

"No, you're not. You're giving an infant way more cognitive credit than he deserves. He has no clue where he is or who's holding him or—"

"That's not true! He recognizes how we look and sound and smell!" I spout like a Dr. Spock audio book.

Sighing, he acknowledges, "Fine. I'll grant you all of that. But he doesn't have the capacity to feel anything as complicated as abandonment, as long as someone's taking care of his basic needs. He may feel like something's not quite right or normal, but—"

"Exactly! I don't want him to feel anything but perfectly content and happy."

This makes my husband throw back his head and laugh at the ceiling. When I object to his laughter, he puts a hand on his hip and says, "Too bad! You don't have control over that."

"I do when he's here."

"No, you don't. You may feel like you do, but you don't. At all. The sooner you learn that, the better off you'll be."

My eyes wander south again. "Will you please put some clothes on? I can't concentrate or take you seriously."

"Only if you promise to take some of your clothes *off*. And leave Max at your sister's."

We stare each other down for a few seconds before I relent and say, "Okay. Fine!"

He grins. "Atta girl." Extracting his underwear from the jumble of clothing at his feet, he slides them on and spreads his arms. "Better?"

I remove my shorts so that I'm only wearing my t-shirt and panties. "Much. How about me?"

"Still too many clothes." He pulls me up against his chest. "But I guess it's okay for now."

"Do you really think he's okay?" I ask, enjoying the feel of Brice's arms around my back.

He puts on his most earnest face. "I do. If I didn't, I'd drive you over there. But your sister's very capable. And we're very tired."

I chuckle sheepishly at that. "Yes, we are."

"So, what's next? Sleeping or eating?" he inquires.

After thinking about it for a few seconds, I say, "How about eating in bed? Then sleeping for a while. But not for too long."

While he dials to order a pizza and listens through the rings, he says, "That's sort of the point, isn't it? To sleep for a long, long time?"

"Later," I answer suggestively.

He wiggles his eyebrows at me. "Ahh, I see. You want to test out my shower-singing claims, that I have the moves like Ja— Uh, yes! Delivery, please." A blush blooms across his cheeks and the bridge of his nose.

I crack up at his embarrassment at being caught talking "dirty." He waves a hand at me and rubs the back of his neck while placing our order. At the end of the call, he says to the person who took his order, "Yep, that's the address..

Oh, hey, William! I thought you sounded familiar…!" Now he turns nearly purple. "Yeah. Huh-huh. Just a boring night in. Your parents finally made you get a job, huh? Good. You can't be a slacker your whole life, you know. Ha! All right. See you at church!"

When he ends the call, he closes his eyes and rests his phone against his forehead.

"William from the Youth Group?" I barely manage to say through my giggles while I hold onto the kitchen counter for support. "William heard you describe yourself as having moves like a Rolling Stone?"

He nods sickly. "Sure did. That poor kid will never look at me the same way, I bet."

"If for no other reason than that you talk in song lyrics, like a big dork."

He opens his eyes, flattens his lips in a tight, white line, and reaches out to smack my butt. "Looks like we have no choice but to move away now."

I hope he's not truly factoring that in to his decision.

"I miss Stinky," I admit in a surprised tone of voice the next morning while we're cuddling in the minutes before the alarm.

Brice smiles sleepily at me. "Me, too. Not as much as I missed this, though."

"Really?"

He suddenly looks adorably guilty, but he justifies his claim with, "I've known you a lot longer than I've known him."

Despite being pleased with his confession, I tease, "He's your flesh and blood!"

"I know. But—"

"I'm totally messing with you. I'm glad you've missed me."

Now he raises an eyebrow. "I didn't say I missed *you*. I said I missed *this*. Meaning, sleep. And other things."

Mock indignant, I flounce onto my other side and show him my back. He laughs while hugging me to his chest. "Just kidding. I missed spending time alone with *you*." He kisses my shoulder blade.

"That's better," I accept.

"And since it went so well—you know, being away from him for a night—I was wondering if you'd like to do it again sometime soon." He presses himself against me. "Very soon."

With a flirty tone, I reply, "Sure. I bet we could trick Nicole into one more sleepover before she realizes that he *never* sleeps by himself through the night."

"Not Nicole," he corrects. "My mom."

I grunt a confused, "Huh?"

"Yeah! Let's go visit Peace next weekend. The elders can cover the services for one Sunday. We'll road trip it to Mom's, leave Max with her, and continue on. That way, we can explore and get a feel for the area without worrying about sticking to his schedule."

When I say nothing, he continues, "It'll be like old times, when we'd take trips in the Jeep and listen to the radio and have long, philosophical conversations, talks that had nothing to do with the color or consistency of someone's last dirty diaper. Remember those?"

I grin. "Yeah. Vaguely."

"You won't even have to miss any work. We can leave early Saturday morning, be at Mom's by noon, and be in Springfield by early evening." Now he murmurs, "We can eat dinner in a nice restaurant and drive around a bit, find somewhere to take a romantic, nighttime stroll, maybe. Then we'll go back to the hotel and…"

"Test out your moves?"

In a silly basso profundo, he says, "Oh, yeah."

I giggle, then inhale sharply when he rubs my shoulders, digging his thumbs into the tense muscles near my neck.

"We'll sleep in, go to late church and meet some of the people at Peace, then we'll eat lunch and hit the road. What do you say?"

"Sounds nice," I mumble distractedly, unable to think about much more than what his hands are doing.

Soothingly, he says, "I'll take care of everything. You don't have to worry about a thing."

That sounds really nice.

5

ROAD TRIP

*A*nd that's the best way to describe Peace and its neighborhood and the town that encompasses both the church campus and the neighborhood. It's also the best way to describe the people in the congregation. Nice. The service we attended was nice, too. Nice, nice, nice. I can't find a single thing technically "wrong" with any of it.

Except it's not home. It's this foreign land that's nice to visit, but do I want to live here all the time? Where will I work? Who will watch Max during the day? What if I get a craving for a Cozzoni's calzone? And those are just the important questions. I have so many other petty things swirling through my head as we speed down the highway toward St. Louis. We got a later start than planned after attending a prolonged lunch at the invitation of several (*nice*) families after church.

Suddenly, Brice cranks up the radio and starts singing along ultra-dramatically to "Somebody That I Used to Know," by Gotye. He curls his fist around his invisible microphone and sing-yells the chorus at me, glancing back and forth from me to the road.

I laugh but half-scold, "Keep your eyes on the road, Reverend Rock Star!"

He returns both hands to the wheel and looks ahead but continues belting out the lyrics. Then he says during an instrumental part, "It's almost your turn. This is a duet, remember?" He waits a beat then points to me. "Go!"

Kimbra's reedy voice fills the car. I hesitate but decide to play along, even though my singing voice is terrible. I don't want to ruin Brice's fun. Plus, we both got a solid eight hours of sleep last night after a romantic dinner at a quiet restaurant and some fun back at the hotel. So, sure, I'll sing his duet.

When my (blessedly short) part is finished, he grins over at me, grabs my hand, and finishes the rest of the song alone. I go back to looking out the window at the passing fields (and fields... and fields), strange billboards with religious messages, and small towns peppered near the interstate while thinking about how lucky I am to have a husband who knows how to cut loose and have fun and not care about being a goober. He's *my* goober.

At the end of the song, he turns down the volume. "Great tune," he declares. "Funky." In a terrible Australian accent, he adds, "Thanks for singing along, mate!"

I roll my eyes at him. "Any time. Anytime you want an earache, anyway."

He laughs. "Your voice isn't *that* bad."

"Love is both blind *and* deaf, apparently."

With a shrug, he says, "I guess so. Speaking of singing, Peace's choir is outstanding! Did you hear them today?"

I would have had to have been in a coma not to hear the choir, but I answer with a straightforward, "Yes. It's pretty awesome." Then under my breath, I add, "Like everything else at that church."

He squeezes my hand. "How do you manage to make that sound like such an insult?" he asks, with his grin still firmly in place.

Now it's my turn to shrug. "It's just a talent I have."

"Tell me what's so bad about Peace being awesome, then."

I think back to our lunch less than an hour ago and try to put my finger on what's bothering me. Is it that I don't want to like Peace and Springfield, because I'll feel disloyal to Messiah and Chicago? Maybe a little bit, but I'm a grownup and can separate those unreasonable feelings from justifiable misgivings. No, there's something else, something deeper, that's giving me pause.

Recalling some of the interactions from today, I finally say, "It's not natural for people to be that friendly."

When he laughs at my cynicism, I defend my statement with, "C'mon! Hear me out! It's like an entire congregation of Justine Heidekers! I can't handle that."

He thinks about it for a few seconds and says, "Well, they're not being *phony*."

It's the first time he's ever hinted that he thinks Justine's not genuine when she fawns all over people. I can't help but smile at that snippet.

"I think you're so used to the malcontents at Messiah that you don't even realize that people can be *happy* at church. They *should* be. Church should be a welcoming, warm place. I think it's wonderful that the people at Peace seem to know that. It's refreshing!"

I say nothing, so he glances over expectantly at me. When he continues to wait for my response, I say, "What?"

"Is that the only complaint you have? Everyone's too nice?"

"You make me sound like such a bitch. It's more than

that they're 'too nice.' They're like Stepford parishioners." I blink my eyes robotically and put on a glassy smile. "'How can we be a blessing to you today, Pastor Northam? We don't even know you, but we already love you so much!' Something's not right." Before he can chastise me for being uncharitable, I say, "And maybe it's that they're trying too hard to impress you, and they're not *always* like that, but it's creepy."

He sighs. His smile has faded quite a bit. "You're unbelievable sometimes."

"Thanks."

When he doesn't laugh with me, I say, "Anyway, it's such a small town."

"Oh, here we go!"

"It is!"

"First of all, it's not. I mean, compared to Chicago, I guess it is, but so what? I like it. I think it's the perfect-sized place to raise a family. Sometimes the city worries me."

"Since when do you worry about anything?"

"Since Max."

"Bullshit. We live in a nice neighborhood."

"We'll live in a nicer neighborhood if we move to Springfield."

"Where? They don't provide a house," I point out.

"The housing allowance they're offering is more than generous. And it goes a long way there. Cost of living is ridiculously cheap." He rubs his forehead. "Plus we have some money saved. Plenty for a good down payment on a place in a safe neighborhood. Maybe not the church's neighborhood, but close."

The houses around Peace are ridiculously large. I can't believe he'd stoop to exaggerate his housing allowance in an effort to bribe me into moving to that cow town! I don't want one of those silly mansions, anyway. They're obscene, and I tell him so.

He bites his lower lip and makes a frustrated noise. "Now the houses are too nice, too?"

I'm beginning to hate the word "nice."

"I didn't say that. We don't need a big place, though."

"Then we'll get something smaller. I'm sure Springfield has smaller houses, too."

"Well, der!"

He looks sharply over at me. "Don't 'der' me! I'm not the one being completely irrational and difficult and negative!"

I can tell he's seconds away from calling me "ridiculous," which never goes over well, so even though I'm fuming and think that I've made some valid points to counter his full-blown euphoria over the prospect of moving more than five hundred miles away from all of my friends and family, I take a deep breath, swallow my pride, and say calmly, "I'm sorry. I'm just scared."

If he knows how hard it is for me to admit that, he doesn't acknowledge it. "Of what?" he blows up, decidedly not catching on that I'm trying to mollify him. "Are you afraid that I won't have to work as hard, so I'll be home more, and we'll get to spend more time together? Scary, I know. Or are you worried that we'll make so many new friends that we won't have time for them all? You know, friends like *us*? Couples who have kids the same age as ours? People of faith who go to church and want to raise their children according to the teachings of Christ? Terrifying! Or maybe you're leery of the prospect of my liking what I do and feeling fulfilled, as opposed to always feeling like I'm not good enough and that I'm fighting a losing battle."

"That all sounds great, but…"

"Oh, my *mpphhh*." He clamps his mouth shut and rubs his index finger along his upper lip before shaking his head and barking out a sarcastic laugh.

Oh, gosh. I shudder to think what he caught himself about to say. I think he's the closest to his cursing point that I've seen in a long time.

"Brice."

"I want to take this call," he says with finality.

"I know you do."

"And I think God wants me to take it."

The earnestness with which he says that makes me soften. "How do you know He does?" I ask gently. "How do you know it's not just your own desire to take it, to get away from all the hard work and difficult people at Messiah?"

"He wouldn't want me to want it so much if it wasn't the right thing."

"That logic is flawed, and you know it." It sounds like something I'd say to justify one of my vices.

"I don't care." When all I do is blink rapidly at his uncharacteristically immature declaration, he repeats, "I don't care. All right? Trust me on this. This is good; it's right; it's—"

"Salutary?" I joke, at the expense of our church liturgy.

He shoots me a dirty look. "Very funny."

"I'm simply trying to lighten things up," I explain with a nervous laugh. "I feel bad that I got you all worked up, when I was only trying to balance out the decision-making process so that we don't rush into something that may be too good to be true. I don't want us to be blindsided by something that we—*you*—were too excited to consider. I mean, *is* it a good thing for Max—and any other children we may have —to grow up in such a culturally homogenous community? Springfield is *not* diverse. It was shocking to me how *white*

Peace's congregation is. Lack of exposure to other cultures breeds ignorance."

"That's where we come in. You know, parenting? We'll teach them about other cultures."

"It's not the same as experiencing it firsthand and seeing it regularly enough that it's not foreign and—on some level —frightening."

"Oh, come on!"

"I'm serious."

"I know you are; that's what's so crazy."

"Excuse me?"

His anger gives him the courage to expound, "You'll come up with any reason not to disrupt your little corner of the world, which is alarmingly small. You'd be perfectly content if you never had to stray more than twenty miles from our current front door. You're complacent. And you preach to me about diversity and exposure to new people and experiences? Puh-lease!"

After staring at his profile for several miles, I finally say, "Maybe we should stop talking about this."

"Maybe we should," he readily agrees. "There's really nothing to discuss, anyway."

The way he says it immediately puts me on guard. "What do you mean? There's a *lot* to discuss, but it would probably be better if we both thought more about it individually before talking about it together."

"Whatever."

He reaches over and turns up the radio. But he doesn't sing a single note the rest of the trip.

When we get to his mom's house, it's nearly 5:00. Mary meets us at the front door with Max.

"I was about to feed him," she announces cheerfully.

Brice plucks his son from her arms and says tersely, "I'll do it," before disappearing into the house.

She gives me a confused look.

I respond with a quick head-shake just say, "I pissed him off.

Pulling the corners of her mouth back so far that her neck muscles twitch, she says on a wince, "Oh. Yikes. That's not good, kid." When I sit down on the top step of her tiny front stoop, she says, "You want to talk about it, or do you think I should go inside with him and pretend like nothing's wrong?"

I wave her inside. "I'll be fine. He needs you to soothe his ruffled feathers, I think." Half-turning, I smile sadly and say, "Just go in there and agree with everything he says. Do you have any pie or cake?"

She nods. "Of course. Cinnamon crumb cake."

"That oughtta do the trick."

Placing a warm hand on my shoulder, she says, "You're a good wife." Then she turns and goes into the house before I can list all the reasons she's wrong.

That doesn't stop me from listing them for myself, though.

Here are the Ten Commandments of pastor's wifedom:

1. Thou shalt know how to cook, not only for thine family but for other families who need good home-cooked meals during difficult times.
2. Thou shalt know how to crochet, knit, or quilt.
3. Thou shalt know how to play the piano (or organ) or sing.

4. Thou shalt always put thine husband's needs before thine own.
5. Thou shalt always put the church's needs before thine own.
6. Thou shalt, preferably, have no needs.
7. Thou shalt enjoy spending all thine free time in the service of others.
8. Thou shalt know exactly what to say in any given situation.
9. Thou shalt not think negative thoughts about others nor gossip.
10. Thou shalt not curse.

I don't meet any of the requirements. Not a single one. I have no desire to do what it takes to meet half of them, either. And the other half… Well, let's just say, I'm not built that way. I have needs. Lots of them. No matter how much I try to focus on others' needs, my own seem to always take precedence.

I'll be the first to admit that I'm more worried about how Brice's accepting the call from Peace would affect me than I am about what it means for him and for his ministry. So sue me! He fits in anywhere he goes. He gets along with everyone (almost). I don't. I can't leave the only two friends I've ever had and move to a strange town and make a bunch of new friends. That's not how I operate.

Plus, he's right: my world *is* small. And I like it that way. He's lived in several different places, oftentimes alone. This relocation business isn't new to him, but it's very new to me. If my mother didn't drive me so crazy, I probably would have lived at home well into adulthood. Change is *not* my friend. And this personality trait is getting worse the older I get. At least when I was young, I was somewhat adventurous. Adulthood—and lessons learned from poor life choices —have beaten that out of me. Adventure-seeking only brought me trials and tribulations—and an unwanted pregnancy. So couching this as an "adventure" isn't going to make it more attractive to me.

I need reassurance that this experience is going to be perfect, and no one can guarantee that. Not even Brice.

Not for the first time, I privately lament how unsuited I am to be a pastor's wife. Why did he choose me? Of all the other women who would have been glad to be his wife, why did he choose me, someone who struggles so much with her faith? What even attracted him to me to begin with? My cynicism, my negativity, my selfishness? Let's assume for argument's sake that it was purely superficial; he liked the way I looked. Once he got to know me, why didn't he see right away how utterly wrong I am for this job?

To put it bluntly, I suck at this. And when Max isn't keeping me awake at night, that inescapable fact is. Add to that the fact that I'm not sure I *want* to be good at it, and I have the kind of problem on my hands that makes me feel hopeless.

6

SHAKY TRUCE

*W*e strike a shaky truce in time to decide to stay at Mary's for the night and head home in the morning, rather than driving five hours late into the night, when we're both tired and irritable and toting the only baby I know who doesn't like riding in a car. It's the smartest, most cooperative decision we've made all day.

Crammed together in the full-sized bed in Brice's old bedroom, we can hardly harbor grudges about things said—and left unsaid—earlier today. Well, I guess we *could*, but it would make for a long, tense night. It's uncomfortable enough, as it is.

"Do you have enough room over there?" he asks.

"Why, am I crowding you?"

"No. I was just making sure you had enough room."

"I'm fine."

"Are you sure?"

"Yes."

"Then can I have another inch or two? I'm about to fall off the edge."

"I'm as far up against the wall as I can get."

"Oh."

"Sorry."

"No biggie."

I take a big breath. "I'm sorry about earlier in the car, too."

"No biggie," he repeats, shifting a bit and catching himself right before rolling off the edge of the mattress. "Oh, Chicago," he mutters, righting himself. "Is it me, or is this bed smaller than it was last time we were here?"

I think the issue is that we're bigger. Or at least I am. But I don't say that. Instead, I press my back harder against the wall behind me and straighten my legs so that I'm taking up as little room as possible. I feel like a Popsicle stick.

He turns onto his side, facing me, his eyes closed.

Unsatisfied with his flippant response to my first apology, I try again. "Really. I'm sorry about being such a killjoy today."

He's so still that I think for a second that he's broken the world record for quickest drop-off time in a dinky bed (I'm sure it's a real record). I blow in his face.

He flinches and gripes, "Hey!"

"Just making sure you're alive."

Eyes still closed, he replies dully, "I am. And I'd like to be asleep as soon as possible."

I almost say, "Too bad," but reconsider at the last second and merely reply, "Okay," when I remember how I'm supposed to put his needs before mine. It doesn't matter that I need closure on our argument. Or that I need reassurance about so many things—the call, his feelings for me, and his belief that I can handle this wife-and-mother gig, to name a few. He needs sleep. And sleep he shall get.

"Goodnight," I mumble, bobbing my head forward a couple of inches to give him a peck on the lips.

Half-heartedly and after the fact, he puckers his lips to return it. I watch his placid face for a few more seconds before resigning myself to closing my eyes and trying to get some sleep before Max's first cry. Mary insisted she'd get up with him, but I'm not sure I'll be able to lie here while my seventy-five-year-old mother-in-law spends a sleepless night with my baby. I mean, I'm crap at this, but I'm not sure I'm *that* bad.

"You're not," Brice says barely above a whisper.

At first I think he's read my mind, so my eyes fly open as I stutter, "W-what?"

His eyes remain closed. "You're not sorry," he clarifies mildly.

This statement is nearly as disturbing as what I originally thought was a response to my unspoken thoughts. "Yes, I am!" I insist.

"You're sorry I got mad at you, and you're sorry you didn't win the argument, but you're not sorry for what you said, and you're not sorry for wanting to stay in Chicago."

I blink against the gentle puffs of minty-fresh breath that hit me in the face with every syllable he utters. They may as well be slaps.

"How can you say that?"

"It's true." There's a shrug in his voice, as if it's patently obvious, and I'm simply being obtuse.

Rather than engage in an "Is not/Is too" argument, I say, "I thought you wanted to sleep."

"I do. But first I wanted you to know that I know you're not sorry, and you're convinced you're going to get your way."

I poke him in the chest so he'll at least open his eyes when he's leveling such harsh accusations against me. "What?"

He finally looks at me but appears bored.

In a low voice, so his mom can't hear us across the hall in her room, I tell him, "For your information, I've already figured you're accepting Peace's call, and moving to Springfield is a foregone conclusion. You've made it clear that my input isn't necessary in this decision-making process."

When he scoffs at that, I continue, "Yeah. It's obvious that my opinion means dick to you. But it was a mistake for me to be honest with you about my feelings. Especially because they're not going to change anything."

"See?" he says triumphantly. "That's what I mean. You're not sorry!"

"In that case, I'm sorry I apologized, if you're going to be such an asshole about it."

He shuts his eyes. "Oh, good. At least that's a genuine apology. I believe that one."

My Irish temper is high now. "You can believe this, too: I want us to want the same things, but—"

"It's not about what we want!" Anger flashes in his eyes, which are wide once again.

"You're right; it's about what *you* want."

Jaw clenched, he replies, "No. What I want just happens to coincide with what I think God wants for us. For Peace. For Messiah."

"Well, as long as I'm the only one unhappy in this situation. Majority rules, right?" I fight hard against the tears of frustration stinging my eyes and nose.

"Don't play the victim."

Suddenly the entire argument seems ridiculous and pointless, and the only comeback I can conjure is, "I love you." It comes out sounding more like an insult than I mean it to, because my brain hasn't caught up to my heart, but I mean it in the traditional sense, no sarcasm or irony intended (for once).

My non-sequitur brings him up short. He opens his mouth to say something but stops. At his confused expression, I say with a wobble in my voice, "That's all that matters. I'd follow you anywhere. To Hell and back."

"Well, you won't ever have to do *that*," he mutters.

I can't help but smile at the way he says it, befuddled, as if he's worried I actually think it may be necessary. "It's a figure of speech, dork."

"Oh. Right."

"But that's the bottom line. Period."

He wraps his arms around my back, crisscrossing them and stacking his hands on the small of my back. Pressing firmly, he pulls me against him and smiles crookedly. "I love you, too. So, I'm glad you're willing to go to such extremes. Springfield will be pleasant in comparison to that worst-case scenario."

I'm not sure about that, but for the sake of argument, I say, "Exactly. So stop trying to pick a fight when I'm trying to make up with you. I was thinking out loud in the car, and we both know that my thoughts are rarely suitable for public consumption."

"So true." He looks immensely relieved at the quick turnaround of this latest argument.

"I trust you," I state. "More than anyone I've ever known." After he kisses me, I touch my nose to his. "So you know what that means."

He shakes his head.

"You better not screw this up."

I've never seen him look as confident as he does when he replies, "I won't."

∼

He's not looking very confident this morning as he faces the congregation from the pulpit, waiting for us to finish singing the final words of the hymn before his sermon. I say, "us," but I'm not singing. I haven't been able to do anything more complicated than sit and stand when told. It's all I can do not to drop Max, who's like a sleeping sack of potatoes in my arms (he sleeps so well during church that I've often wished we could have all-night marathon services, so I could simply drop him off and go back home to get some uninterrupted sleep). I'm trembling, that's how nervous I am for Brice to tell everyone his decision! *Our* decision. In a way. At least, that's how I'm looking at it. I decided to stop being a brat about it, anyway, so I guess I should get partial credit. Or blame.

There was no announcement or warning that he'd be giving his decision today, but I think my attendance at the 8 a.m. service is a dead giveaway that something's up. I haven't attended this service since... ever. In my world, there's no such thing as being dressed and out the door by 8:00 on the weekends. 'Til today.

The music stops, and Brice says the pre-sermon prayer. Then he looks up and begins, "The Lord's will versus man's will. How do we know the difference? When faced with an important decision, what's the surest way to know we're doing the 'right' thing? So often, people say, 'It *feels* right.' But Satan is good at tricking us into thinking something feels right, when it's anything but. How can we know the difference? Or maybe less dramatically, how do we know the difference between what we want and what the Lord wants? How do we drown out our own impulses so we can hear His commands? And what is the point of free will? Is that just a tricky thing God's equipped us with to confuse us and muddy the waters? I've puzzled through these questions for weeks, and I keep coming back to one thing: prayer.

"Jesus prayed in the desert. Jesus prayed in the Garden of Gethsemane. Jesus prayed continually. And He urges us, His followers, to do the same. Much wiser men than I have also given this advice. In his Epistle to the Colossians, Paul exhorts us to 'continue earnestly in prayer, being vigilant in it with thanksgiving.' Prayer. It's as simple as that. Or is it?

"Because before you roll your eyes at me and say, 'Sheesh, Pastor, we could have told you that and saved you the busted brain cells,' let me explain. I think we take prayer for granted. I think we get complacent about it. Or we treat it like our personal soap box with God. Or, worse, like a magic lamp or wishing well. We resort to prayer when all else has failed or when we can't be bothered to worry about something or when we think it would take nothing less than a prayer to get what we want.

"I'm not talking about that. I'm talking about something closer to meditation. I'm talking about an open, frank dialogue with God, the One Who knows us better than we know ourselves. No use sugar-coating our intentions or motivations, anyway, since He knows everything in our hearts. Hebrews chapter four, verse twelve states, 'For the word of God is living and active. Sharper than any double-edged sword, it penetrates even to dividing soul and spirit, joints and marrow; it judges the thoughts and attitudes of the heart.'

"We have no choice but to be honest with Him. It's being honest with ourselves that's the tricky part. After we've done that, the next challenge is to clear our minds, the better to *listen* to what's being said to *us* in response to our prayer. *That's* the variety of prayer I'm talking about.

"Most of us don't engage very often in prayer like that. It's time-consuming. It requires a lot of energy and concentration. We're busy. We're frantic for answers. We already know what we want to hear. We're not asking for God's will to be done; we're demanding that—for once—He answer our prayer the way in which we'd like it to be answered. He owes it to us, right? After all, we offer up hundreds, thousands, *millions* of prayers and petitions, and we don't get bent out of shape when the majority of them seem to go unanswered, or we get an answer that's the opposite of what we'd hoped. Right? Sometimes we pray to thank Him for something, and we don't even ask Him for anything in return. Or we selflessly pray for others. So, when something's important to us—and could affect a number of other people—it may be tempting to *plead* with God, to ask Him to short-list our prayer, to make it a priority."

He shakes his head. "Ah, silly us. Because the truth is, all of our prayers are a priority to Him. Some are easier to answer than others. Many of them—'Please, Lord, make this lottery ticket a winner'—are quick no's." He pauses for the nervous, guilty laughter. "Conversely, many others are quick yeses. And others are not yet's. Those are particularly frustrating; it's hard to tell if we're getting an answer at all."

He pauses to allow us to relate to what he's said so far. "But perhaps the most difficult answer we receive is, 'You know what to do.' Oh. When He leaves it up to us, that's scary. Sometimes the fear stems from the overwhelming number of options we have. How do we narrow it down? And from there, how do we know which option is the best? What if we choose incorrectly? Other times, there are only two choices. Easier, right?" He chuckles mirthlessly. "Not necessarily."

He takes a sip of his water and clears his throat while

my heart rate picks up, and the butterflies in my stomach go into panic mode.

"Well, you all know where this is going, I think. You know why I'm veering from the Lectionary series, discussing choices and God's will and prayer, rather than what we read about in today's Gospel. I don't do that often. Has to be a special occasion. Has to be important. And I think you'll agree with me that this is. It affects you, my church family. It affects my wife and son. It affects me. It affects people you've never met, hundreds of miles away."

He shoots a shaky smile at the congregation, looking last at me. I beam back at him and nod, even though my heart is breaking at what he's about to say, not only for myself, but for the others gathered here. Even the few who will be glad to see him go will feel understandably rejected on some level.

"After much prayerful consideration, I've decided to accept the call from Peace Lutheran in Springfield, Missouri. I believe this opportunity is God's will for Peyton, Max, and me, although I didn't receive one of those definitive answers to my prayers that would make the decision easy. I don't think I've ever gotten one of those, come to think of it. There were no beams of light or an audible voice from above or peals of thunder. I really had to listen."

I hear a nearby sniffle and stretch my peripheral vision to glance down the pew at my mom, who's dabbing at her eyes. Even Dad's mouth is doing this strange twitchy thing, like he's fighting his emotions. My stomach drops. Oh, shit. I can't handle witnessing my parents choking up. I'm okay, as long as everyone holds it together.

But that's when I notice more sniffs and general fidgeting around me. A few coughs, some throat clearing. I'm fairly close to the front, but the people in the rows ahead of me are digging through purses for tissues. Husbands are putting their arms around their wives' shoulders. One little boy named Gage innocently and loudly asks, "Mommy, why are you crying?"

Brice blinks but doesn't look in Gage's direction. Instead, he looks down at his notes on the pulpit and gives his head a tiny shake. "The thing is… The thing is…" He falters, as if he's lost his place, but I know he's stalling to compose himself. "Uh, the thing is," he says more confidently, stepping down from behind the pulpit and walking closer to the pews, "that it doesn't necessarily take a long time for people to make an impact on each other's lives. I may not have been here as long as you'd hoped when you called me to be your pastor, but that doesn't cheapen the work we've done here. Together. If anything, it's made more remarkable by the short amount of time we had to get to know each other and to do God's work. We're a family."

Now he has to stop. I'm used to his becoming emotional during sermons, since it happens with such regularity, but it's especially poignant this time. I feel like he's talking to me as much as he is to everyone else. I'm simply the lucky one who gets to go with him when he leaves. Actually, that makes me feel worse, like I have some form of survivor's guilt.

An audible sob startles me. I'm one of several people who looks to see who made the noise, and I'm not shocked when I see it's Justine. I am, however, astonished when she picks up her son and Brice's godchild, Isaiah, climbs over the legs of the people in her pew, and rushes from the sanctuary.

Clearly troubled, Brice watches her go and chokes, "We've made what I hope are life-long bonds. Just because you move away from your family doesn't mean you lose touch. But sometimes something bigger than us requires the separation."

He sniffs and takes a deep breath. "And this isn't solely my opportunity. This is Messiah's opportunity, too, an opportunity to inject new life, new energy, new ideas, and new experiences into this ministry. I know many of you aren't a fan of the concept of 'new' anything, but it's my prayer that you see this for what it is: a blessing, God's gift for you to start fresh with the next person called to enrich your lives. It's an exciting time, a time for you to grow in your faith, if you'll only allow it."

After another deep breath, he says loudly and with less of a quiver in his voice, "Which brings us back to prayer. I'll be praying for you, as I hope you'll continue to pray for me. And pray for my family. And pray for my new church home. And I look forward to the day when I'll be back here as a visitor, sitting out there, listening to the man God chooses to put in your midst to bless you and who you'll bless in return, as you have blessed me for the past few years. In Jesus' name. Amen."

He quickly utters the post-sermon prayer and retreats to his chair, where he recovers during the offering.

It's going to be a long day.

Heck, it's going to be a long month.

7

FAREWELL BARBECUE

*N*icole and Lonnie's backyard is already packed with friends, family, and church members by the time we arrive at our going-away cookout. Kids are running around, music's playing, Nicole and Lonnie are bickering by the grill, and everyone else is laughing and talking. It's so loud and crowded that not a single person has any clue we're here.

"It's Messiah-palooza," I mutter through my tight smile, which I pasted on my face before we even got out of the car.

Brice laughs loudly, drawing everyone's attention to us.

"Pastor's here," intones one little boy unnecessarily, sounding somewhat like Lurch from *The Addams Family*.

That earns a big laugh, and Brice points down at the five-year-old. "Thank you, Reese. I was wondering who was going to officially announce me."

Nicole hands off the meat platter she's holding for Lonnie so she can rush across the deck to greet us. She hugs me first then Brice. He gives her a one-armed squeeze, since the infant carrier occupies his other hand.

"Wow. Thanks for coming, everyone!" he says to the

people in the yard. "I, uh, guess you all wanted to make sure we're leaving, huh?"

They laugh. Gus calls out, "That, and we heard there'd be food! You know us Lutherans can't pass up the chance for a good potluck."

Nicole interjects, "And the food's almost ready, too, so everyone, make your way up here. The line starts over there." She points to the far side of the deck. "And ends at the grill, where Lonnie will load you up with your choice of hot dog or hamburger. Condiments and toppings are on the tables in the yard." When people start milling around again, she turns to me, "Whew! This is quite the production."

"Thanks for doing it," I say, even though being the center of attention isn't something for which I'm usually thankful. I feel a lot more comfortable doing this here than I would at Mom and Dad's house, though, or—worse yet—at the church. And I do appreciate the trouble she's gone to. I grasp for something complimentary to add to my somewhat lackluster statement of appreciation. "The yard looks great. Very festive."

"Yeah," Brice says, nodding toward the paper lanterns and Tiki torches. "I'm torched."

"Oh, gosh! I forgot to have you say the prayer!" she suddenly gasps.

He sighs, visibly disappointed that she's not acknowledging his corny joke. When it's clear she never will, he shrugs and produces an ear-piercing whistle that gets everyone's (especially Max's) attention. "Uh," he says sheepishly to the upturned faces, "we almost forgot something relatively important. Let's say a quick prayer over the food. Then we can get back to business."

He swings Max's carrier in an arc to settle him down and bows his head. As soon as the baby's quiet, he closes his eyes, says a simple prayer, and ends with "Amen. God's neat, let's eat."

"That one never gets old," I say sarcastically.

"Gets a laugh every time," he points out.

"Polite laughter. You need some new material."

"Not the way I see it. By this time next week, I'll have a whole new audience who's never heard it."

Before I can retort, Jason and Dustin walk up to us. Jason reaches for the infant carrier. "Here. That looks heavy. And even if it's not, I want to hold my nephew," he says without preamble.

"Good evening," Dustin says with exaggerated pronunciation. "How are you guys doing? I'm the one with the manners, as you can see."

I chuckle at them both and give Dustin a quick hug. "Hi, Dustin. Jas—"

But he's already gone, making his way down the four steps to the yard. He parks Max's carrier in a bag chair next to one of the picnic tables and extricates him from his straps.

Dustin rolls his eyes, but there's an affectionate twist to his smile when he says, "Are you sure you don't want to take him with you? He'd be a fabulous live-in manny."

Brice raises an eyebrow. "'Manny?'"

"Yep. A male nanny."

Laughing and nodding, Brice says, "Ah, yes. Of course. How slow of me. I think we're all set for childcare, considering Peyton will be Missus Stay-at-Home-Mom Extraordinaire."

"You're going to be an SAHM?" Dustin gushes, widening his eyes in disbelief. "No!"

I try to inject some enthusiasm into my nod, but I'm

afraid I wind up looking more deranged than excited. "Yessir. Gonna see what that career path is like."

"I hear the benefits are excellent," Brice quips. "Not much room for advancement, though; the glass ceiling's pretty low. But your boss *is* cute."

"I hope you're referring to Max."

"Of course I am. I'm not your boss."

"As long as you know that."

"Now the janitor, *he's* hot." He wiggles his eyebrows and points to his chest.

Dustin lets loose with one of his characteristic eardrum-bursting laughs, which draws the attention of everyone—in the neighborhood. I think he may have set off a car alarm.

My dad grumbles nearby, "For crying out loud."

Mom hisses, "Kent! Shh!"

"I'm not going to miss *that*," I murmur to Dustin and Brice while nodding toward Mom and Dad.

They're nice enough not to call me on my obvious lie. I have to talk tough if I'm going to get through the next couple of days. I'm going to have to tell myself a lot of lies, in the hopes that they'll eventually become the truth. You know, things like, "I love Springfield; it's dandy!" and "Meeting new people is fun!" and "The most rewarding job I've ever had is being a wife and mom!"

Anyway, how many times have I wished I didn't have to leave the house to go to work? This is going to be great. It won't matter if Max never sleeps at night; I can sleep whenever he does during the day, right? Nicole never complained of him being a bad napper, so he must simply have his days and nights confused. Therefore, since I won't have a day job to go to, problem solved! I'll start getting sleep again and become as normal as I can ever hope to be, considering I'll still be me.

Brice interrupts my exhaustion-induced fantasy with a gentle hand on the small of my back. "Since Max is in capable 'manny' hands, maybe we should get in line for food."

Before I can tell him I'm not hungry, Jen and Mitzi arrive.

"You go ahead," I tell him, gladly relinquishing my place in line so I can run to my best friends and pull them to me in a group hug.

Mitzi giggles next to one ear while Jen grouses, "Seriously? I'm having flashbacks to the last day of high school."

I take a step back, laughing through my tears. While wiping my face, I say, "Yeah, that was an emotional day, too!"

Jen straightens her shirt and makes sure her long blonde hair is still sleek and lying just so against her shoulders. "You two cried like you were never going to see each other again, even though we were already enrolled at the same college. *And* we went to the lake together the very next day."

"Are you breaking the story that high school girls are dramatic?" Mitzi asks, pulling out her phone. "Hang on. Let me tweet that."

"I'm going to miss you two so much!" I say, diving in for another hug so I can hide my crumpling face.

Patting my back, Mitzi says, "Now, now. Don't make me cry. We'll still talk just as much as we do now!"

"Yeah," Jen says. "It's not like we see each other all the time anymore, since you're Super Mom now."

I snort at that ludicrous description. "Shut up. Anyway, I'm not the only one too busy to get together more often." I look pointedly at Mitzi, whose new relationship with Jared, Messiah's former vicar, is moving along quite nicely. She blushes but accepts partial responsibility before reminding us that Mitch, Jen's boyfriend, also takes up a lot of Jen's time.

"Where is Jared, anyway?" I ask when it occurs to me that he should be with Mitzi.

She explains, "He'll be by later. He has an exam tomorrow for one of his graduate summer classes, so he's cramming right now."

"Then it sounds like we're all busy," I say, leading them to a table down in the yard, where we nearly instinctively take our usual positions: Mitzi on one side and Jen and me on the other. Brice stares after us, shrugs, and keeps his place in the food line. The man's not going to give up grub so he can sit in on our girl talk. I don't blame him.

Jen begins with the important question: "Do you guys have a house yet?"

I sigh. "Yes and no. Our offer has been accepted, but we don't close on it until a week after we've been in Springfield. We'll stay at a hotel that week."

"A whole week in a hotel room with a baby?" Mitzi breathes, wrinkling her nose. "Ugh. That doesn't sound very fun."

Shrugging, I reply, "It is what it is. It's an extended stay hotel, so it's more of a suite, not just one room. Plus, I plan to spend a lot of time out and about, becoming familiar with our new surroundings and looking for things to do. It'll be fine."

Yep. I can still lie with the best of 'em. Good to know.

Although I can tell Jen's not buying it. Uncharacteristically, she refrains from commenting and merely gives me a skeptical look as Brice sits down next to Mitzi with his plate piled ridiculously high.

"Hey, Preach. Did you save some for everyone else?" Jen comments sardonically.

He barely looks up as he answers earnestly, "Plenty. You can't believe the amount of food up there. Everyone decided to bring their uber-Lutheran potluck skills to this thing."

Mitzi laughs at that. "Well, then, I'm going to go up there and see what that means. I'm curious now. And starving. You guys coming?" she asks Jen and me.

Jen stands up, but I keep my seat. "You go ahead. I'm not hungry."

I haven't had any interest in eating since Brice gave his sermon about accepting the call from Peace. My appetite left the building with Justine. Silver lining: Brice and I fit a lot better nowadays in the guest room bed at his mom's house. Drawback:

"You need to eat something," Brice states quietly, after Jen and Mitzi are gone. He concentrates on his food so he doesn't have to receive the dirty look I'm shooting him.

"I will."

"No, you won't. But you need to."

"It's counter-productive to eat when I'm not hungry."

"Your body needs fuel."

"I don't want to talk about this now. Why don't you go find Justine and— Oh, never mind. She's on her way over here right now," I observe, pretending to search for something in the diaper bag so that she can't see me rolling my eyes at her imminent arrival.

Brice stops eating and half-turns to greet Justine as she approaches our table.

"Hey!" he says as if she's the most important person at the barbecue. "Where's I-man?"

Without asking if the seat is taken, she slides in next to Brice. He puts a friendly arm around her shoulders and gives her a half-hug while she gives him a kiss on his cheek (I know!!!) and answers, "Oh, he's running around with the other kids. Now that he's walking, he thinks he's a real big shot."

Going back to his food, Brice says, "Well, I'm going to have to steal him from them for a while as soon as I'm finished eating."

"Steal away," Justine replies, but her tone isn't nearly as bright and cheery as it usually is. Turning to me, she says after a sigh, "Hey, Peyton. You all set for the big move?"

I start to smile politely and open my mouth to answer her question, but the sadness in her eyes brings me up short. It nearly knocks the wind out of me. Suddenly, I get the strangest, most disconcerting flash of what she's feeling, and I have a hard time forming a coherent sentence.

At my lengthy pause, Brice looks across the table at me and raises an eyebrow.

Eventually, I manage to stutter a generic, "For the most part," but it comes out all choked. I clear my throat and try again. "We haven't lived very long in our current house, so we haven't had time to accumulate too much junk, thank goodness," I say. "Not that either one of us is a packrat."

She nods. "Well, that's good." Then she picks at the vinyl tablecloth, seeming to be at a loss for words.

My eyes tear up as another wave of compassion hits me.

Ohmigosh! What is wrong with me? I mean, this is a woman who's been throwing herself at Brice since the day she met him and didn't find it necessary to stop doing so once he became *my husband*. This is a woman who not only made my husband her adopted son's godfather—and snubbed me, his *wife*, in the running for godmother—but she made my husband's first name her son's middle name and didn't think it at all inappropriate to do so without checking with me. She's been an ever-present pain in my ass for as long as I can remember; I've thought horrible things about her for years (since way before Brice and I were ever married, even); I've wished she'd either get married or move away (or worse).

But now, for the first time, I'm glimpsing what unrequited love at this level must be like. Because we all know she's in love with Brice. That in itself makes me feel bad for her. It must be humiliating for such private feelings to be so apparent and widely known. Of course, she's mostly to blame for that, due to the way she acts around him; but I of all people know that sometimes you can't control the way you act and react in certain situations, especially when emotions are involved.

And look at her! Sitting as close to him as she possibly can without it being considered "cuddling;" glancing at him surreptitiously through her eyelashes; laughing at all his corny jokes, even though she's probably heard them a hundred times. She's still as in love with him today as she was when she initially fell in love with him, whenever that was (probably the first time she laid eyes on him).

How would I feel if the roles were reversed? If she were Brice's wife and I were the woman in the background, watching him leave, how would that feel?

It's a good thing there's nothing in my stomach, because the empathetic stone that just dropped into it would certainly have sent its entire contents up the chute and onto the table between us. How is she functioning?

And why am I worrying myself with it? Her inappropriate (albeit likely uncontrollable) feelings for my husband are none of my business, as long as she doesn't act on them. If I'm not going to resent them, as I've been doing for the past few years, then I should ignore them, which I've also managed for some of that time. I definitely shouldn't be relating to them. And I shouldn't be overwhelmed with compassion to the point of nausea and tears. I mean, I'm used to Justine nauseating me, but this is out of control!

"You okay, hon?" Brice stops talking to her to ask me.

Justine's goofy smile fades as she pulls her eyes away from him and looks over the table at me. "Wow. You look pale," she says, before I can answer.

I'm about to reassure both of them that I'm fine when it occurs to me that I should leave the two of them alone. (Huh? Did I hear my thoughts correctly?) Because no matter how improper she's been in the past, she's never crossed The Line. And even though that may not have been entirely her choice (Brice would never let her), the least I can do is give her a few minutes alone to say goodbye to him.

"I do feel sort of weird right now," I answer accurately. "Maybe I'll grab some Jell-O salad and take it inside, in the air conditioning."

Brice starts to rise from his seat, but I wave him down. "No. I'm fine. Really. I'll be back in a few minutes."

After all, I don't want her to think she has an unlimited amount of unsupervised time with my husband to say whatever she needs or wants to say. She should worry that I could be back at any minute. (Ah! There's the feeling I'm used to having around her! Whew! I thought I'd lost myself down a rabbit hole.)

Inside the cool house, away from the noise and the people, where I'm able to think, I'm also able to justify my sudden uncharacteristic diplomacy toward Justine. Not only are we about to be hundreds of miles removed from her, but I'm sick of disliking her. It takes a lot of energy. And I haven't had enough sleep to sustain the level of energy my dislike for her generally requires. My greatest wish for her, I realize now, is that she finds someone—someone attainable —who is as devout as she is, who can be a good father to

Isaiah, and who will make Brice fade from her memory. I don't wish her any ill will (that would be mean and spiteful at this stage of the game), but if she could stop having my husband feature in her happy family fantasies, that would sure be appreciated.

Oh, and I lied about the Jell-O salad. That's the *last* thing I want to eat right now. Fruit floating in fruit-flavored animal collagen? Guh-ross! The thought of it is setting off my gag reflex.

I'm emerging from the upstairs bathroom after a close call with *le vomi* when I hear sniffling and the unmistakable sound of crying coming from Sadie's room. I peek through the crack between her door and its frame to see her lying face down on her bed, her head buried under her pillow.

Now, *this* is someone for whom I have deep, unconditional love. Seeing *her* upset immediately makes my chest hurt and my eyes well, before I'm even sure what's causing her tears.

After a slight hesitation (mostly to compose myself before approaching her), I push open her door, cross her pink zebra-striped room, sit on the edge of her bed, and place my hand on the small of her back. "Sadie Lady, what's the matter, sweetheart?"

The nine year old merely shakes her head beneath the pillow and continues crying.

"Did something happen outside with one of the other kids?" I posit hopefully. At least that's something I can possibly remedy.

Again, she shakes her head.

I bite my lower lip. Wincing, I ask, "Is this about..." I can't bring myself to say it, though. I don't want to be the one to say anything out loud that will make her cry harder. Instead, I proceed on the assumption that our moving away is the cause of her distress and say, "Hey. Why don't you take your head out from under there before you smother?"

She does as I suggest, tossing the pillow aside and sitting up so that she's facing me, her arms wrapped around her bony knees. Within seconds, she resumes crying and has to put her forehead against her knees.

I scoot further up on the bed and pull her against me in a hug. "Come on, now. It's going to be okay."

"No, it's not!" she wails.

"Yes, it is. I promise. We're not moving *that* far away."

In the grand scheme of things, it's true. I mean, what's eight hours of driving on (mostly) four-lane highways? Nothing. Sure, she can't come over on a whim like she does now. We can't have regular girls' nights or sleepovers or spa days, but…

"You and your brothers can come visit us as soon as we get settled, before you have to go back to school. Our new house has lots of bedrooms, so you won't even have to share with those stinky boys." I'm being quite liberal with reality, but she's nine. I don't think it matters too much.

"I want to come all by myself."

I take a deep breath and promise, "Sure," even though I'm *not* sure how I'm going to swing that without hurting Caleb's and Everett's feelings.

My quick acceptance gets her attention. She raises her head and asks on a sob, "Really?"

Not wanting to have to go back on something like that later, I admit, "Maybe not. It wouldn't be very nice to exclude your brothers, would it? But they can hang out with Uncle Brice and do boy stuff, and we can go off by ourselves and do lots of girlie things, just the two of us."

"Okay." After a few shuddering breaths, she asks quietly, "Why do you guys have to go away, though? Why doesn't

Uncle Brice want to stay here? Grandpa said it's because he doesn't like our church anymore."

I can't hold back the gasp at this information. "What?"

She nods emphatically. "Uh-huh. He said something about it being too hot in the kitchen. But the church has air conditioning. Why doesn't Uncle Brice just make it colder in there? Then you guys can stay."

If I weren't so furious with my father and so close to crying, I'd laugh at her literal interpretation of one of Dad's favorite clichés. Instead, I stroke her hair and say, "It has nothing to do with the church air conditioning, or you. Or anything, except that Uncle Brice thinks it's time for us to do something different, to meet new people."

"I hate the new people you're going to meet!" she cries. "It's not fair that they get to be with you, and I don't!"

"I know." My lack of argument makes her look up at me and blink.

"Does that mean you won't go?"

I wipe the tears from her cheeks. "We still have to go," I tell her regretfully, bringing on a fresh round of sobs. "I'm sorry! But we already promised. We can't break our promise. Plus," I improvise, "Springfield is a neat town. It's not as big as Chicago, but there's still a lot to do, and when you come to visit us, which I expect to happen *a lot*, we'll do everything you want to do."

This doesn't console her at all. She's finally figured out that I'm talking from my ass. She can probably also sense I'm trying to convince myself as much as her. And now I'm out of ideas. I don't know what else to say, except, "I'm sorry, Sadie. It doesn't mean I love you any less. It doesn't mean Uncle Brice loves you any less. We're going to miss you every single day."

Now I'm crying almost as hard as she is. Shit.

A soft knock on the doorframe indicates someone's presence. We both look up quickly at the newcomer. Brice tilts his head at us and smiles sadly. "Hey. What's going on in here?"

"A pity party," I confess, dabbing at my eyes, sniffing, and trying to smile back at him.

Sadie vaults from the bed and flings herself at him. Wrapping her arms around his waist, she presses her face against his belly. He pats her back while I give him a *What're-ya-gonna-do?* look.

"I wanna go with you guys tomorrow!" she insists.

He chuckles at her. "We don't have a house yet, Sades. Not a good time for a visit."

"I don't care! I'll sleep in the car!"

Pushing her away slightly, he drops to one knee so they're eye-to-eye. He holds her upper arms in his big hands while he says playfully, "Pull yourself together!"

Amazingly, she giggles at him.

"There. That's more like it." He grins. "Anyway, even after we have a house, you're sleeping in the garage, so that's not the issue."

"Uncle Brice!"

"Now, stop making your Aunt Peyton cry."

Tears instantly dry, she signals her complicity with a quiet, "Okay."

"Thank you. And if you're brave for the rest of the evening, I'll come back and get you in a couple of weeks, so you can go to Vacation Bible School at our new church in Springfield. Okay?"

Her whole face lights up. "Okay!"

"Go play," he demands gently, rising to his feet and steering her toward the door with a hand on her head.

When she's gone, I stare at him and shake my head in wonder.

"What?" he finally asks. "I came in here to check on you. I had no idea I was walking into a boohoo-fest."

I scoot off the bed and glide over to him, accepting his hug and the kiss he plants on the top of my head. "She was inconsolable. And in two sentences, you had her laughing."

He replies, "That's kind of how jokes work. They make people laugh. And sometimes all someone needs is some motivation (a.k.a. 'bribery') to do the right thing."

"What do I get if I'm brave for the rest of the evening?" I flirt in a small voice.

He pretends to think about it and says, "Oh! You're so lucky. You get to follow me 500-plus miles, while I tow my Jeep from the back of a moving van that's carrying everything we own. Including frequent stops for things like fuel and sanity, it should be about nine hours of pure excitement."

"Can Max ride with you?"

"I'm not sure he'd enjoy my habit of singing along to every song on the radio. He'll be happier with you."

"This isn't the brand of motivation to induce me to bravery tonight."

Ultra-enthusiastically, he adds, "But wait! There's more! You'll also have the pleasure of six days and seven nights at the luxurious Extended Stay Radisson in beautiful Springfield, Missouri, minutes away from outdoorsman's paradise, Bass Pro Shops, and the always-entertaining Branson, Missouri. Amenities include soap wrapped in paper, unlimited free ice, undoubtedly loud neighbors, a hair dryer that's permanently attached to the wall (ooh!), and a fully stocked mini bar."

"Stop it!" I say when I've caught my breath after laughing at his pitch.

"Is all that enticing enough?"

I consider it for a second. "I guess. As long as you'll be there."

He looks down into my face and lowers his lips to mine. "Absolutely. I love"—he pauses dramatically before whispering against my mouth—"those tiny bath towels."

8

CULTURE SHOCK

*C*W*e may as well have moved to a different country. This town is… weird. And it's super-duper proud of a "Chinese" dish called cashew chicken. The dang stuff is everywhere! Have I tried it yet? No. And I'm not going to. It looks gross, and I'm protesting the locals' obsession with cramming it down my throat.

Cashew chicken isn't the only unpalatable thing about this place, though. No. I wish. The lack of diversity that was somewhat unnerving at Peace the Sunday we visited is downright unnatural and creepy when magnified across the entire population of a town this size. It's not that I haven't seen *any* people who don't look exactly like me, but 98 percent of people here look pretty much exactly like me. Okay, that's a slight exaggeration. The meth heads don't look like me, so that bumps it down to about 90 percent. However, I don't want to speak too soon. Too many more days in this hotel room, and I may look just like them.

There's so much more, including a seeming utter lack of a middle class, a disturbing pride regarding redneckery, and a systematic disregard for basic rules of the road (i.e., the use of turn signals), but once I get started, I won't be able to stop. And I'm trying so hard to turn over a new leaf and *not* be the complainer that I've been my whole life. I also realize that I run the risk of sounding like a *huge* snob if I make any of these observations out loud, even to Brice. Especially to Brice.

So, the biggest secret I've ever kept (and I've kept a few whoppers) is that so far, I hate it here.

But things will change once we move into our own house. Right? Right? I'll meet our neighbors (oh, gosh!), and I'll become involved at the church (double-gosh!), and soon I won't feel so much like a fish out of water. And not because I'll be a redneck meth head. That's surely a small (yet highly visible) segment of the population. I'll feel more like a part of the community, because I *will* be. I won't be holed up in a hotel room or scheduling my life around the housekeeping crew's hours. I won't be driving aimlessly around town, alternately depressed by the poverty and awed by the wealth in neighborhoods that are amazing close, geographically, yet worlds apart in every other regard.

I'll have a life. A real life. With real things to do. Like, um… Hang on. I'm trying to channel Nicole now. She wrinkles her nose and shudders any time someone suggests that now that all three of her children are in school, maybe she'd be interested in getting a part-time job to fill the hours when they're out of the house. Her first response is always, "Then what do I do in the summer, when I need to be home with them? Quit my 'real' job?" Her second reaction is probably closer to the truth: "Anyway, I've earned this time. Why would I start a new career now?"

And that's just it: being a mom *is* her career. She got so mad at me one time when I innocently asked her what she did all day while the kids were at school. She went on what felt like a five-hour rant about laundry and housework and grocery shopping and meal planning. Then there was the detailed account of her personal maintenance regime, including mani-pedis, waxing of unmentionables, and exercise-based torture on borderline-dangerous machinery at the gym. "Part of my job is making sure I look good for Lonnie. You know, like an actress!"

I remember thinking, *What is this, 1950?* followed by, *Where do you do the most acting?* but I voiced neither question. I'd already pissed her off enough by making my original query, which was the last time I ever tried to make idle conversation with her about her daily routine. Plus, I really didn't want to know the answer to the second question and was disgusted with myself for even thinking it.

I'm also sure I'll have a better attitude about things when I get to sleep in my own bed. It doesn't matter how nice this hotel suite is; it's still seen a lot of people. I have a very hard time sleeping when I think about all the bodies that have been in that same bed before me. That thought leads to itching, which leads to tossing and turning, which leads to Brice grunting at me, which leads to my feeling like I have to lie motionless, which leads to muscle spasms, which leads to no sleep during Max's nighttime catnaps.

By the time Brice gets up to get ready to go to work, I'm nearly delirious. And I live for the time he returns to the hotel room, so I can doze as I listen to him enthuse about his day before I grab a couple of hours of coma-like sleep while he cuddles with Max on the sofa in the "living room."

This evening, Max and I have just returned to the hotel after a boring afternoon of walking the town's one mall for the umpteenth time, and I'm longingly imagining Brice driving "home" to rescue me, when his ring tone plays from my phone.

"'ello?" I slur after hurrying to pick up before it wakes Max.

I can tell by the intermittent whooshing in the background that he's driving. "Hey, hon. How was your day?"

"Delightful," I answer, lying on my back and closing my eyes.

"Good. Good," he replies, obviously not really listening. "Hey. Uh, good news. We've been invited to dinner at the Denmans'."

The fact that I have no idea who that is doesn't alarm me, considering I don't know anyone. Mustering as much cheer as possible, I say, "Oh. That's great. When?"

"At 6:30."

My eyes pop open. "Tonight?"

Sinking dread fills my tummy when he answers, "Yeah! I thought, 'That's perfect!' because we're getting so burned out on restaurant food, right?"

"This town has more restaurants per capita than any other place I've been. We haven't even scratched the surface of places to eat," I point out, knowing I'm wasting my breath but feeling the need to lobby for a night alone nonetheless.

"Yeah, but doesn't a home-cooked meal sound good?"

You know what sounds good? Three to four hours of oblivion while he quietly entertains Max in the other room. That sounds heavenly. Putting on my pastor's wife's smile for an evening? Not so much.

"You're tired," he finally declares at my silence.

I keep it simple to avoid whining. "I am." It's hard to work up a good whine with only two syllables. I almost manage it, though.

"I understand."

Relief makes me verbally incontinent. "You do? Because

I am *so* tired. And the thought of socializing with strangers makes me want to cry and puke at the same time. Max didn't take a nap today, not even when I tried to hold him the whole time. And I have the layout of the mall completely memorized. Try me. Ask me to name all the stores from the food court to JC Penney, in order. I can do it. Both sides. Oh, kiosks, too!"

He chuckles. "I believe you. But the thing is—"

"You have no idea how I've been counting the minutes until you get here. I just need three hours of sleep. Maybe three and a half. Max ate about thirty minutes ago, so he should be content to sit with you on the couch while you eat and watch anything you want. What day is it? Thursday? Friday? Oh, well, everything's reruns, anyway, but still."

"Honey! Whoa, whoa, whoa!" He laughs nervously. "Goodness! Where is Max right now?"

"I left him at the mall." Pause. "He's right here next to me, of course!"

"Oh, well, he's so quiet." He takes a deep breath. "I already told the Denmans we'd be there tonight."

When I groan, he rushes on, "But that's okay. I'll swing by and get Max, and we'll go without you, and I'll explain the situation and how you haven't had any real sleep for a few days. I'm sure they'll understand. Then you can go to bed and get a few hours of sleep before we get back."

"I love you," I say emotionally.

"I know you do, hon." His tone is full of affection and amusement.

"No, I'm serious. I'm not being silly."

"You're exhausted."

"But serious."

"Okay. Hang on for two more minutes. I'm pulling into the parking lot right now."

I have my pajamas on before he makes it to the room.

And that was my one "Get Out of Dinner Free" card. Especially now that we're mostly moved into our house, and I still do a fairly spotty job of putting dinner on the table (and when I do manage it, it looks like something a college guy whipped up in an Easy Bake Oven), and Brice blindly accepts nearly every invitation that comes his way. And I'm expected to accompany him. Fair enough. I get it. This *is* my job now. No more, "Well, my husband's a pastor, and I work at an art gallery." Nope. Now it's, "My husband *and I* serve at Peace Lutheran Church in Springfield, Missouri." Blink, blink. Smile, smile.

Plus, it'll slow down once the novelty of us wears off. We're new, and people want to get to know us. Anyway, it's not like it's a huge imposition to be fed by a different family nearly every night of the week. Saves me from cooking and cleaning up the kitchen. Saves Brice (and me) from eating my admittedly uninspired and sometimes inedible dinners.

Tonight we're the guests of a couple roughly our ages, who are also first-time parents to a daughter, Jessica, who's a couple of months older than Max. For the first time, I feel almost hopeful we can get to know these people on a personal level. They seem *genuinely* nice, down-to-earth, and funny, but they're not trying too hard. And I haven't felt once that they invited us to dinner with an agenda, other than to get to know us and to make us feel welcome.

On a more shallow level, their daughter's name is normal, which leads me to believe they may be normal, too. You wouldn't believe how many families we've met with virtuously named children, as if they worried more about how it would sound on the kid's baptism day than about how their kid would have to live with that name for the rest of his or her life. Greeting the congregation's younger members is like a sermon on the Beatitudes. Patience, Serenity, and Peace (talk about sucking up!) top the List of Bizarre and round out the usual Angels, Hopes, Faiths, Chastities, and Charities. There's even a Zion. Really, people?

But Clark and Marianne Pryce have a Jessica. And that's so refreshing!

After dinner, when we're seated in the living room, Clark asks, "When did you decide to go into the ministry, Pastor? It's always fascinated me to hear the various reasons. Is it a family tradition, or...?"

Brice laughs and rubs his eyebrow with his thumb. "Well, no. There are no other pastors in my family, especially not Lutheran ones. My mom was raised a Baptist, so it was a big deal when she married my dad and converted. But that's another story. No. I, uh... Well, it's a little embarrassing," he reveals, suddenly squirming next to me on the couch.

I sit up straighter. What is he talking about? When I asked him this same question while we were dating, he gave me some blow-off answer, something to the effect of, "I was called. It's not something I decided to do."

I'm not about to admit I don't know the whole story, though, especially not to a couple of near-strangers. I tickle Max's toes and pretend this is something I've heard a hundred times.

Marianne says, "Oh, boy. This sounds juicy."

Now he's definitely blushing. "No, not juicy, really. The opposite. I, uh, had no idea what to do with my life, and I couldn't think of anything I was interested in that would translate into a career, so…"

He fidgets some more and takes a deep breath. "I figured I would either join a branch of the military or go to Seminary and see what that was all about." He grins at the Pryces. "Since I don't enjoy having someone yell into my face and call me names, I didn't think I'd fit in very well in the armed forces. So, here I am."

He chuckles sheepishly at their dumbfounded expressions and says, "It was slightly more complicated than that, but that's what it boils down to. I didn't know what else to do. And theology and history always interested me. But, no, there was no beam from Heaven that shone down on me one day, no voice that said, 'Brice, my son, you will preach to many nations.' I was a normal college guy, trying to figure out how to stall as long as possible before entering the grown-up world. Four years of Sem fit the bill."

Oh. My. Gosh.

"Anyway," he continues, obviously still uncomfortable, "it may not be the most altruistic reason for joining the ministry, but it was God's will, all the same. There's nothing like desperation as motivation. And here we are!" He glances over at me then quickly away.

I nearly have to use my fingers to prod the smile onto my face, but somehow I manage to make it happen. Then I look down at our dozing child.

Clark rubs his chin. "Wow. Sounds a lot like how I decided to be a CPA. Process of elimination."

Marianne adds, "And you obviously love what you do, so it's not like it was the wrong choice."

"Exactly," Brice says. "It wasn't a choice at all. It was a calling. I may not have recognized it at the time—I probably would have resisted it, anyway, if I'd thought that's what it was —but that doesn't mean it wasn't. God knew I was a stubborn young guy who had to think everything was his own idea."

That makes the two of them laugh and leads to their own stories about having to learn things the hard way. Or something. I don't actually listen for the next several minutes as I try to envision the person my husband described, someone who was aimless and resistant to maturing, possibly even irresponsible. It doesn't jibe with anything he's previously told me about himself. It does fit with some things his mom's hinted at, but she's never come right out and talked about it. Anyway, I always assumed she was embellishing in an effort to embarrass him. Now I see she was, in fact, holding back, protecting him, leaving it up to him to tell me. But he never has. I'm as ignorant as anyone else who's met him in recent years, in his "new" life.

Brice shifts on the cushion next to me and places a hand on my knee. "Should we get Stinky home and see if we can parlay his current state into something more sustained, possibly in a crib-like apparatus in his very own room?"

I smile weakly while he and the Pryces commiserate about baby sleeping patterns. By the time the three of them have come to the wholesome conclusion that "They're only babies for a short time," I have the diaper bag on my shoulder, and I'm ready to get the heck out of here.

We say our thank yous and goodbyes and climb into the Jeep for a ride so tense that I'm sure the other motorists sharing the road with us can feel it, too.

9

UNASKED, UNTOLD

*D*elicacy isn't one of my fortes, so as soon as we're home and I've deposited Max (however temporarily) in his crib and have joined Brice in the kitchen, where he's downing a glass of milk, I decide to dispense with it altogether and blurt, "How come you've never told *me* how you decided—or, more precisely, avoided deciding—to become a pastor?"

He takes the final swallow, lowers his glass, looks down into it, and licks his lips. After several seconds, he says, "You never asked."

"Yes, I did! Maybe not in so many words, but I know I inquired about when you knew you wanted to be a pastor."

"That's a different question, though."

"And your answer was, 'I was called.' You left out all the stuff about being rudderless and—"

He frowns and closes one eye. "I'm not sure I was ever 'rudderless.' Simply unsure of my future. Which is the perfect opportunity for God to step in and fill in the blanks."

I glare at him. "You know what I mean. You've always

made it out to be that you knew exactly what you wanted to do with your life."

With one shake of his head, he barks a short laugh, puts his glass in the dishwasher, and says, "I think you've been making assumptions. I never said that. Because that would be untrue."

I point out the highlights as if on an invisible timeline in the air between us. "College, Seminary, vicarage, prison chaplain, associate pastor, senior pastor. You never said anything about considering military service or treating Seminary as another way to be a professional student."

He opens and closes his mouth several times and makes soft choking noises that I think are supposed to make me laugh, but they fail. Finally, he repeats, "You never asked."

"I didn't realize I had to ask in the *exact* right way to get you to tell me."

"Are you seriously angry at me about this?"

"'Angry' isn't the right word. Surprised, maybe? Disappointed?"

"Oh, not disappointed! Come on! How can this be disappointing?" When I don't reply, he walks past me, exiting the kitchen with me right on his heels.

"Don't go upstairs. I don't want to wake up Max."

Stopping with his right foot on the bottom stair, he holds onto the newel post and turns to face me. "Are you planning to speak about this in tones that would wake a baby?"

"Maybe," I acknowledge. "It depends on how you answer my question."

He sighs. "What question?"

I take a deep breath. "Have you been deliberately leading me to believe that you're better than you really are?"

"What are you talking about?"

"I mean, all your talk about your job being a 'calling.'"

"It is!"

"When truthfully, you basically fell into it, because you couldn't think of anything better to do."

"Oh, for Pete's— No! *That's* what you got from what I said at the Pryces'?"

"That's what I got, because that's what you said."

"Well, I didn't mean it that way."

"Yes, you did. You were even embarrassed to admit it. But for some reason, you felt obligated to tell *them*. I guess because they used the secret password. Or whatever."

He puts his hands on his face and presses his fingertips into his eyes. "What is happening here?" he asks no one in particular.

"I'm making you tell me the truth about why you became a pastor. Or what led you to become a pastor. Or how you decided to become a pastor. I can't remember exactly how I'm supposed to ask to get the truth and not some half-assed, cockamamie bullshit *pastor's* answer."

Pinching his lips together, he waits until I finish with my rant and retorts, "How did you decide you wanted to work in an art gallery?"

I snort. "Uh, I had no one in my life who cared enough about me to tell me that art history was a completely useless major, so when I graduated from college, I was up shit creek. I looked in the want ads, saw the posting for a gallery attendant, applied, and made half of a career out of it. But I was hardly in the business of saving souls."

"Neither am I."

"You know what I mean."

"No, I don't. *I* don't do anything. The Holy Spirit does it all. And so what if I was more curious than convicted when I entered the sem? Does that make you think less of me, that I didn't always *know* I was being called?"

My morbid curiosity piqued, I ignore his annoyingly logical question and ask instead, "Did you curse and have casual sex in college, before you decided to go to Seminary? At what point did you fully commit yourself to being who you are today?"

"I wasn't born a pastor. Is that what you're getting at? You're disillusioned because I had a different life before the ministry, a life that I left behind?"

"A life you've never felt the need to share the details of with *me*!"

"I haven't hidden anything from you, either," he insists. "You knew I wasn't a virgin when we got married; I told you that. Is that the issue here?"

I'm losing the thread of my argument. What *am* I getting at? What *is* the issue? Feebly, I reply, "Maybe. You never talk about any of that stuff."

"I didn't realize you wanted to talk about it."

"I don't, I guess."

He looks toward the ceiling and takes a big breath. "I don't either. So, that explains why we've never talked about it."

"It doesn't mean we *shouldn't*."

He sits down on the third step, as if he doesn't have the energy to stand for another second. "I find it highly irrelevant," he claims. "Plus, I don't want to talk about *your* past; why do you want to talk about mine?"

"My *past*? You make it sound so sordid and seedy and shameful."

"You're projecting. I have a past, too. Everyone does. It's not healthy to dwell on it, though. Your sins are washed clean, just like mine."

"Only yours didn't take quite as much scrubbing, probably."

His eyes widen. "They most certainly did. And do."

Oh, crap. Now I've pushed one the great, big, red button that never fails to activate the Pastor Sequence. Three, two, one...

"Are you kidding me with that nonsense? You may think you have the monopoly on sin or that your transgressions are somehow deeper and worse than anyone else's, but we all have Christ's blood on our hands in equal measure." He comes away from the stairs and backs me into the living room.

I'm tempted to stand on the couch so I'm not forced to look up at him, but I realize that would be ridiculous, so I stand my ground on the ground, like a normal person. Anyway, his destination is the couch, where he sits and plants his elbows on his knees, looking up at *me*.

"What do you want from me, Peyton?" he implores. "Would it make you feel better if I told you every immoral thing I ever said or did? Because I'm not a fan of bragging about those things, but if it somehow made you feel like we were even, I'd hash it out with you. Gladly."

I shake my head and mouth, "No."

It wouldn't make me feel better. It would make me feel terrible, as a matter of fact. I *don't* want to know about his sex life before I came along. I *hate* that he knows so much about mine. On the other hand, I'd feel worse if he *didn't* know. I needed him to know and understand and still tell me he loved me, in spite of it.

He pats the sofa cushion next to him. Like a loyal dog, I eagerly take the seat. After he straightens, he puts an arm around me and leans back, pulling me back with him. I put my head on his shoulder.

"I don't like finding out things about you at the same time as strangers. That was a horrible feeling," I tell him, working hard to keep my tone neutral. Sulking is so unattractive at my age.

"Ah. Now, we're getting somewhere," he murmurs against my hair. "And that makes sense. I'm sorry."

"You're forgiven," I say with a sigh. As if I have a choice to forgive him. I can never stay mad at him. He's too damn reasonable. And humble. And cute.

"Praise God for that."

I do. And a whole lot more. But I can't help but wonder what else I don't know about my husband.

10

PARENTS OF PEACE

*I*t's time to stop hiding. It was fun while it lasted, I guess. But I have to admit, now that the boxes are unpacked, and Sadie, Caleb, and Everett have returned to Chicago, I'm going stir-crazy, and the only cure for that is to get out and get involved. The most logical place for me to do that is at Peace. Sigh. I mean, yaaaaaaaaaay.

To hold me to last night's weak agreement to attend Peace's stay-at-home-parents' group (Parents of Peace, or PoP—I wish I were kidding), Brice called me this morning and told me the church staff was expecting me to drop into the office with Max before the meeting started. I've met everyone briefly, of course, and I've seen them at church every Sunday, but this will be the first time I've stopped into the church during the week. This will be when everyone will feel me out to see what my interests are, so they can decide how to use me in the various ministries and groups at Peace. It's like my "coming out" party.

I'd rather stay home.

I'm sure that's why Brice committed me to this meeting without checking with me. He knows I'm a flaker and will find any excuse (sometimes, I must say, they're pretty creative) to get out of doing things I don't want to do.

So now I'm sitting in the church parking lot, steeling myself to be one of my very least favorite things to be: the center of attention. Ugh.

"It's okay," I reassure myself. "They're not judging you. They only want to get to know you. They want *you* to like *them*. You're the pastor's wife. The *Senior* Pastor's wife. He's the head honcho. And he loves you. And he'll defend you to anyone. And if they want *him* to like *them*, then they have to be nice to *you*. So, stop being a chickenshit and get in there. Otherwise, you'll be late for PoP, and you'll be the center of attention *there*, when you walk in late."

That thought makes my stomach lurch and puts me in motion. I pop the trunk and rush around to the back of the car to unload the stroller, which is unwieldy but a lot easier to manage than that clunky car seat/carrier thing that weighs a ton. After the stroller is properly unfolded (I hope), I retrieve Max from the back seat and transfer him to it. Then I spend precious minutes untangling the safety harness straps (why must everything be so complicated?). When everything is straightened out, I go about fastening the clips, being careful not to pinch his chubby little thighs, and feeling like I'm preparing my six-month-old son to do something a lot more dangerous than lying in a stroller. Like rappelling, for example.

I'm literally sweating when this process is complete. Well, I guess that's not too surprising, considering it's 90 degrees in the second week of September. (Ick, Missouri!) By the time I make it into the office—after an embarrassing false start in the parking lot resulting from my forgetting to release the stroller's "parking brake" and proving the need for all those straps—I feel and surely look like a disgusting, sweaty mess. I can only hope I don't smell like one.

Sure enough, when Brice steps from his office to greet us, the first thing he says after a chaste kiss on my cheek is, "Are you okay?"

I blot sweat from my forehead and upper lip. "Fine!" I say in my brightest voice, which I'm sure is a tip-off to him that I'm anything but. Before he can press me on it, I turn to the church secretary. "Hey, Lucy. How's it going today?"

She smiles back nervously and replies meekly, "Good, thanks. And you?"

"No complaints," I lie to the thirty-something brunette, Brice's appointed assistant and gatekeeper.

She sucks at both, by the way, according to what little he's told me. She's so nice, though, that she can't say no to anyone who drops by to see him, even if his door is closed, and he's specifically asked not to be bothered. Plus, she doesn't have a highly developed sense of humor, which is a major disadvantage for someone who works with Brice. Or maybe it's Brice's disadvantage, in this case. Either way, it's been one of his biggest reported challenges with getting settled and acquainted with everyone. He'd never complain, of course, and the few times he's said anything about it, he's put the blame on himself, but suffice it to say, she's no Marilyn.

She stands up and looks over the edge of her desk to see into the stroller. "Aww! What a cutie!"

"You want him? He's not as cute at 3 a.m." Brice claims.

Looking uncertain and somewhat aghast, she replies, "Uh, no. I don't think so."

He almost manages to hide his sigh while he undoes all the difficult strap-up work I did in the parking lot and picks up Max. "I was only kidding, Lucy. He's cute at any hour."

While Max excitedly slaps and grabs at Brice's face, he blinks and says around the chubby hands, "Pastor Long should be here any minute. He had some shut-in calls to make this morning, so he hasn't been in yet." Nodding over my shoulder, he adds, "But here comes Ben," referring to Peace's Director of Youth Ministries.

Ben Eiffler rushes in, apologizing for being late. "Lost track of time in my office, planning out my lesson plan for Catechism." Sheepishly, he tacks on while running a hand through his reddish-blond hair, "And listening to Coldplay."

Brice laughs. "Man after my heart. You've met Peyton, right?"

"Briefly," he answers, stepping forward to shake my hand. I'd put him at mid-to-late-twenties. He's only an inch or two taller than I am. "There's always quite the crowd around you after church, but I think I got through once to say hi."

I blush. "You make me sound so popular. I think they're mostly trying to get a look at Max. They're shocked by how much he's Brice's Mini-Me, and everyone has to see for themselves."

He looks over at the two clones and sizes them up. Brice puts on a vacant baby stare and pretends to be drooling. (Or filling his pants. I'm not sure which.)

"Oh, yeah. Wow! That *is* kind of crazy. There's no denying that one, Pastor."

Brice resumes his usual posture and grins. "Right? I know. You should see us when we're watching TV together. I taught him how to put his hand down the front of his diaper." He bites down on his knuckle. "So precious."

Lucy's looking back and forth between the three of us and grinning vacantly while we laugh. "Y'all are silly," she declares. "Did you really teach him how to do that, Pastor?"

Six eyes land on her. All laughter ceases. Finally, Brice says, "Uh, no, Lucy. He's usually wearing a onesie and doesn't have access to the front of his diaper."

Ben snorts.

Lucy looks over at him. Then she finally seems to get it. Or she pretends to. "Oh. Oh! Huh-huh." She sits down and goes back to whatever she was doing on her computer when I arrived.

My back to her, I shoot Brice a wide-eyed wince.

He stifles a smile and says, "Anyway," with a laugh in his voice. "Oh, here comes Pastor Long."

When the older gentleman enters the office proper, he smiles warmly at the sight of Brice with Max before beaming down at me (the man is a giant; he makes Brice look short!). "Ah! Peyton. I was wondering when we were going to get the chance to visit with you. I'm glad you had time to stop by this morning."

My genuine smile falters a bit and freezes into something resembling the expression Lucy was wearing seconds ago. Was that a dig? I glance at Brice, but he's oblivious, making faces at Max in an effort to elicit one of his elusive giggles, which always seem to startle the baby, as if he can't believe the sound has come from him.

I push down the paranoia and reply, "Thanks." I can't think of anything to add that isn't a lie.

He drops a slip of paper on Lucy's desk. "Some additions to Sunday's bulletin, Luce. Sorry they're on the late side. But I thought of a better hymn to sing before the sermon. It's more familiar, anyway."

She takes the paper and nods earnestly. "Not a problem, Pastor. I'm putting the finishing touches on the bulletin now, but I haven't printed yet."

After barely acknowledging her, he looks over at Brice.

"Uh, Pastor Northam. You're comfortable with the liturgy I've chosen? Have you given it a look? I know it's not one you're familiar with. And since you're leading the liturgical portion of the service…"

Brice keeps his eyes pinned on Max's face. "I've got it. And anyway, if I flub a few 'lines,' God will understand." He smiles. "Right, Max?"

Pastor Long frowns. "Yes, that's true, but it makes the congregation uncomfortable when we're unsure of ourselves. And this is a liturgy they're very used to, so it will be obvious to them if you're lost."

My internal jaw drops, but Brice's smile remains fixed. "I won't be lost. I've practiced. It'll be fine, Wayne."

I have to avert my eyes. *Man, my shoes are… well, they're dirty. But interesting!* I try to keep from letting loose with a nervous giggle at his use of Pastor Long's first name in mixed company. I think that's as close to "Step off!" as I've ever heard him say to someone. But he's right. What the heck is Pastor Long's deal? I'll have to remember to ask Brice about this later. Not that he'll give me any dirt. I can hear Reverend Diplomacy now as he eats his dinner: *"He only wants everything to go as smoothly as possible."*

To cover the suddenly awkward silence that's descended on the room, I reach for Max and say, "Well, I guess I'd better get to PoP."

While I put the baby back in the stroller, Pastor Long says, "Peyton, we're eager to hear what your pet projects are going to be."

"Oh, I'll pitch in anywhere I'm needed," I respond easily and vaguely.

He chuckles. "Well, that goes without saying, but we have a rich tradition of women's ministry at Peace. Your predecessor was a tireless advocate at the Family Violence Center and was a wonderful witness in the community."

I straighten and look blankly at him. "Oh. Right. Well, I haven't given it much thought."

His laughter indicates that he thinks I'm either joking or being humble. I laugh along with him, but I'm freaking out on the inside. What is he talking about? I thought I'd lend a hand at events for the church, *at* the church, but I never considered that I'd be expected to be Peace's ambassador in the greater community.

This appears to be news to Brice, too, but he recovers more quickly than I do, as usual. "I'm sure we'll think of several possibilities, as soon as we're more familiar with the area and where the need is strongest." He smiles reassuringly at me. He knows I'm having an internal meltdown.

Pastor Long's expression can only be described as condescending when he says, "Yes, well, the most important thing is that you get out there and do *something*."

When my eyes widen enough to pop from my skull, Brice steps forward and gives me a kiss, full on the mouth, and squeezes my shoulders while turning me toward the door. "Hey. So. Uh, when you're finished with the group, let's grab some lunch, huh? Yeah. I'll be thinking of where to go, since I know you don't like making that decision."

Before I can react to anything that's been said in the past two minutes, I'm standing outside the office in the hall, facing the direction in which I need to walk to get to the room where PoP is taking place. Max looks like he's surer of what's going on than I am.

～

I wish I wore a watch. Then I could glance at it to see

precisely how long this Paul dude has been going on and on about sugars and high fructose corn syrup. Seriously. My husband has to limit his sermons to twelve minutes, but this guy has carte blanche to bore us to death with his self-righteous preaching about the evils of sweets? And anyway, duh. It would be like Brice preaching an entire sermon on the theme, "The devil is bad."

Unfortunately, the only timepiece I have is my cell phone, which I was asked to turn off upon entering the "parents' circle." More unfortunately, the rest of the parents —all women—seem to be hanging on Paul's every word and adding to the discussion, therefore encouraging him to go on and on and on. And on.

I was hoping Marianne Pryce would be here today, but she told me at dinner that her attendance at these meetings is sporadic, since she's a freelance writer who works from home and can't always get a sitter for Jessica. I see that today is one of those days. I also see that I'm the only parent here who brought her child to the parenting group. I didn't realize it was "adults only."

Paul suddenly angles his body toward me. "Peyton? What are your thoughts?"

He doesn't want to know. In a span of two seconds, I consider the following honest answers:

1. "Is it lunchtime yet?"
2. "Who the fuck cares?"
3. "I think you all need to get a life and worry about bigger issues, like… anything."
4. "I'm only here, because I promised my husband I'd join this group to look more engaged."
5. "This is my first kid, so I don't have any opinions on anything."

6. "I'd need a lot more sleep than I've been getting to give you a nice answer."

Somehow, though, I manage to utter, "You all make good points. All things to keep in mind when Max is eating… stuff."

Paul blinks at me. "But, surely, he's already eating strained vegetables. Oh, don't tell me you're giving him that garbage they sell at the grocery store under the label 'baby food.'" He actually uses air quotes and laughs, looking to the other women in the circle for validation.

I have to resist the urge to swat at his hands.

Calmly, I say, "Well, he's still getting used to cereal. But he'd rather drink a bottle, if given a choice. We're laidback about it. He'll figure it out."

He glances at Max, who's wide awake but lying on his back in the stroller. "I notice he's a fan of lying flat on his back. I hope he gets tummy time at home. And plenty of time in his Bumbo, right?"

My raised eyebrow and skeptical expression (I think he's making words up now) are all the answer he needs.

"Oh, Peyton! I'll drop Pastor an email later with some pointers. You need to be strengthening those tummy and neck muscles to prepare him for crawling and walking!" He pats my knee condescendingly. "This is your first shot at this, though, so we understand. It's a lot to take in, especially if parenting hasn't always been your main focus."

I'd like to ask him what the hell he knows about my focuses (or is that "foci"?), but I'm saved from saying something defensive and inflammatory by one of the mothers across the circle from me. "Actually, Paul, I've read some recent articles about Bumbos that indicate they're not the best things for babies and that good old-fashioned Exersaucers may be more effective when it comes to strengthening a baby's core."

His head snaps her way. Instead of looking peeved at being contradicted, he appears genuinely intrigued. "You have *got* to send me hyperlinks to those articles, Amanda. I would be fascinated to see the evidence behind those claims."

At this point, I'm looking for the camera. Surely Brice is punking me. Or he's standing outside the door, watching all this, laughing hysterically at my reactions. He's definitely put these people up to this. Because they can't be for real. Especially this Paul character. He should have warned him not to be so over-the-top. He's an obvious plant. Looks like Brice has been a member of my family long enough that he's learning some of our favorite tricks and practical jokes. Well, I'm not falling for it.

Glancing at the door, I say, "Okay, okay. All right." All eyes focus on me. "You had me up until the 'Bumbos versus Exersaucers' debate. Very funny. And clever. Brice! You can show yourself!" I call.

When I get no response, I start to doubt myself a little, but I still stand and walk to the doorway, poking my head into the hall. There's nobody there. More doubt creeps in (along with the dread that proceeds embarrassment), but I retake my seat and say confidently, "Well, you guys can report back to him later that his trick *almost* worked. I'm sure he'll get a good laugh at my expense, especially when you tell him that I came close to punching Paul for insinuating that Max is developmentally stunted due to my lax parenting."

Paul tilts his head at me and shoots me a look that clearly conveys he thinks I'm insane when he says, "Um, we don't know what you're talking about, Peyton. Pastor dropped in one time, but other than that, he hasn't been part of our discussions. And I'm sorry if you thought that's what I meant when I commented on Max's development, but I don't joke about things like this. It's very serious, with serious consequences."

I swallow loudly and appeal to the other ladies in the group. "C'mon guys," I practically plead. "Joke's over. Tell Paul, here, to give it up."

A few of them shake their heads at me, but most of them fix their eyes on their laps, unable to make eye contact out of shame. For me.

"Oh," I mutter. "I see."

Paul says, "We consider ourselves a family here at Peace, and especially in this group. We rely on the assumption that we can be frank with each other so that we can provide loving support and encouragement in a safe setting. All advice given is done so with the utmost respect and with the ultimate goal of raising spiritually and physically healthy children of God."

My humiliation melts away with this last sentence, and I laugh, mostly from relief. "See? That! *That's* how I know you're putting me on. Who says that? Shi-oot! You almost had me again!" I point to the rest of the circle. "You guys are good! If it were up to you, I'd have fallen for it, but Paul!" I lean over and rap on his knee. "You always take it a bit too far and expose the gag. I'm amazed, though, at your ability to keep a straight face when you say some of those things. Are you active in Community Theater? I bet you are! You have a real gift."

He purses his lips and brushes at the spot on his knee that I recently touched, as if he's trying to remove the skin cells I may have left behind. Mumbling toward his folded hands in his lap, he says, "Mrs. Northam, I'm sorry you feel like we have nothing better to do with our time than play elaborate practical jokes on the pastor's wife, but…" Now, he looks up at me. His eyes are cold. "We are all *very* busy people. We come together once a week to share our experiences in the hopes that we can help each other with the most important job we'll ever have, raising children. Maybe you don't feel the same way. Maybe you think we're silly, with our talk of Bumbos and nutrition and exercise, but we're absolutely serious. And we don't appreciate being ridiculed and made to feel bad about that."

Before I can respond, Amanda stands up. "I'm sorry; I have to go. It's time for me to pick up Jonah from his morning playgroup."

The other mothers mutter their excuses, gather their purses, and make their swift exits, too. Nobody looks at me on her way out.

Soon, Paul and I are the only ones left.

Quietly, I say, "Please tell me this is a trick. Please."

He sighs. "I told you; it's not, although you've made a huge one out of something that's extremely important to a lot of people here at Peace."

My face flaming, I stand when he does and grovel, "I'm so sorry, Paul. Really. I mean, I only joked about it, because I thought you guys were teasing me. Because it's totally something Brice would do, to try to teach me a lesson about giving something a chance before passing judgment—"

"I find it disturbing—and hard to believe—that a pastor would take delight in making a mockery of a ministry such as ours, just to prove a point." He picks up the large stack of books and reference materials on the table behind him. "If you didn't want to be part of our group, then you shouldn't have come. And Pastor shouldn't have forced you."

I feel sick. Like I might puke all over Paul's sensible

shoes, perfect for chasing after children across mulchy play-grounds.

"I— I— That's not what I meant at all. No, Brice *isn't* in the habit of doing that, you're right. I don't know what I was thinking. I haven't gotten much sleep lately. Does that matter at all to you?"

Paul seems unmoved by my stumbling apology, but I couldn't stop talking if I tried. "I mean, I'm sure a lot of the other people in the group are in the same boat, but I also had insomnia during my pregnancy, so I think this prolonged lack of sleep is starting to affect my brain func-tion. It's been nearly a year and a half since I've had healthy sleeping patterns."

To my horror, I start to puddle up at the hopeless mess I've put myself in and how every person in this group is going to hate me and go home to their spouses and tell them how crazy I am, and they'll tell other church members who aren't part of this group. By Sunday, I'll be a pariah.

Finally, I choke, "I'm sorry, Paul. I would never have punched you."

My tears seem to have triggered some sort of sympa-thetic response in him, because his face visibly softens before he says, "Well, it's not very Christian-like to be unforgiving, now, is it?" When I can't answer, he continues gently, "Maybe this isn't the group for you. It's *not* for everyone. Granted, most people who feel that way simply stop attend-ing, rather than mocking us to our faces, but…"

The group most certainly *isn't* for me, and my gut reac-tion is to run away and never show my face here again, and that would be doable if this were a community group, but since these people are part of my church family, I can't really avoid them. If nothing else, I'll see these people on Sundays and at church events. Plus, I feel I have an obligation to continue attending PoP, if for no other reason than to try to repair the damage I've done today.

After a big breath, I say, "Again, Paul, I am sorry about that. And I promise it won't happen again. I'll be here next week. And thanks for the advice about Max."

He doesn't look overjoyed at the idea of seeing me here every Thursday, but he does a decent job of sounding mostly sincere when he replies, "We'd love to have you back, Peyton. And I'll make sure the other parents are aware of the misunderstanding before next week so that we don't have to waste time with any awkwardness. You'll find that we're a very forgiving bunch."

I swallow my pride and my defensiveness when I tell him, "Thank you," before pushing Max from the room and going straight to my car, where I text Brice that I have a headache (so true) and will have to take a rain check on lunch.

11

TO CALL OR BE CALLED

*T*here's still one thing I refuse to fake.

Propped against the headboard, I say, "I'm sorry."

"Why apologize?" Brice asks tersely.

"You're right. I'm not really sorry. The story wasn't funny." I'm referring to Pastor and Mrs. Long's epic tale, told at dinner a couple of hours earlier. "What was I supposed to do? Laugh anyway? One of those stupid, annoying, obviously fake laughs?"

When all Brice does is shoot me his *Work-with-me-here* look from his side of the bed, I say rather unapologetically, "Sorry. That's just not me."

"Their anecdotes are never funny."

"And they're never going to learn that if people like *you* humor them." I pull the covers up higher on my chest and open my book to its marked page.

From the corner of my eye, I see him smile. "It's Pastor Long. Are you really expecting the same level of finely honed material you get from me? No. But he and Vivian think they have this Christian comedy duo thing going. So in the interest of keeping the peace—"

"I don't want to keep the peace with him," I mumble, still pretending to read.

The more I've gotten to know him during the past three months, the more obvious it is that Pastor Long thinks Brice aimed way too low when choosing his wife. He refuses to give up trying to make me into what he thinks I should be, though. Prior to Christmas, I responded to his latest idea —"A blog about your experiences as a Christian wife and mother would be interesting, don't you think? Maybe that would be tech-trendy enough to catch your interest?"—with my usual polite smile and noncommittal, "Maybe. We'll see." If nothing else, he'll be pouting about that for a while as it becomes obvious there's no way in Hell I'll be broadcasting on the Internet what it means to be me.

First of all, who gives a shit? I can't think of a more boring blog on the planet than that. Second of all, I'm too busy dodging him and his creepy wife to have time to write a blog. Unless it's a blog about how to avoid creepy associate pastors and their wives. Hang on a minute. That actually sounds helpful, and Lord knows I have plenty of experience. Anyway, he shouldn't get too discouraged, because Brice snatches up every idea that I reject. He's tearing up the Internet, with his blog and Facebook page and Twitter account.

Reverend Social Media plucks my book from my hands and holds it aloft, away from my reach unless I want to resort to climbing onto his shoulders to reach his hand. I'm almost tempted, but I refrain and merely shoot him a dirty look while I watch him gearing up for a good mini-sermon.

"Now, Peyton."

"Don't 'now, Peyton' me," I say with a laugh. "He's a

subversive jerk. And their story was misogynistic. So, there are *two* reasons I don't have to humor him."

To ensure that my book isn't a distraction for the rest of the night, he tosses it across the room, where it lands with a flutter and a thud underneath the window.

"Hey!"

He pulls me closer to him. "If you don't want me to get frisky, then you know better than to use five-dollar words like that."

"'Misogynistic'?"

He moans and nips at my neck. "That's the one."

"You're so weird," I mutter, my eyelids suddenly feeling like they weigh a hundred pounds each. I push weakly at him. "Anyway, you're only trying to distract me, because you don't want me to badmouth or talk about Pastor Long."

"Not right now, I don't. Major mood kill," he acknowledges. His hand snakes up my t-shirt, and his fingers trace against my belly, and then higher.

"Are you sure you want to spend precious minutes of Max's three-hour night sleep on sex?"

"You were going to waste it on reading, so yes. I think this is a much better use of the time." He continues his aggressive efforts to disrobe and arouse me, but I'm too focused on Pastor Long to respond. And I don't even think Pastor Long's wife can get in the mood while thinking about Pastor Long.

Remaining motionless and keeping my voice passive, I say, "What's the deal with that guy, anyway? Does he resent you, because you're the Senior Pastor, and you're younger than he is? It was *his* choice not to be promoted when Pastor Wiseman retired. Or is it not about age but about your being an outsider?"

He stops what he's doing and looks up into my face. "I *really* don't want to talk about it."

"Right now, or ever?"

After considering it for a second, he answers, "Possibly never."

He cranes his neck to kiss me, but I pull my head away. "Too bad. This has been bothering me for months, so even if you don't need to talk about it, I do."

Groaning, he rests his forehead against my chest. "Can we talk about it *after* doing what I want to do?"

He doesn't sound hopeful that this is a possibility, so I know I'm not giving him a surprising answer when I say, "No. I can't focus on *that* while I'm thinking about him."

"That makes two of us." He rolls away from me and back to his own side of the bed.

I try not to feel too guilty when I say, "I want to know what's going on. And how you're dealing with it. And if there's anything I can do to help."

He sighs. "You're refusing to have sex with me so we can talk about Pastor Long. I'm not dealing well with it. And, yes, there's something very simple you can do to help."

I laugh at his self-pity. "See? Now, *that* was funny. You might get laid tonight, after all." When he perks up and glances over at me, I qualify, "*After* we talk about what's going on with you and Pastor Long."

"Sonofa-Bit-o-Honey," he grumbles. "I won't be in the mood *after* we talk about him."

"Why not?" I snuggle up against his arm. "What's happening? And why haven't you told me before now?"

"Why didn't you tell me what happened at PoP way back in September?" he counters.

I freeze, then blush. I'm sure he can feel my hot cheek

through his t-shirt sleeve. "Uh... Hmph. You know about that?"

"I do."

"How come you never asked me about it?"

"Because I'm sensitive to the fact that it's probably a painful, embarrassing thing for you to talk about. And you'd prefer that it would disappear without a bunch of reminders about it." He tries to look down at me, but I refuse to move my head so that we can make eye contact.

"Yeah, well, I've got that under control, I think." At least, I've suffered through months of weekly meetings without a single, solitary eye roll. It's a bigger accomplishment than it seems. "And this isn't about me. This is about you and your Associate Pastor, someone who works beside you on a daily basis and is supposed to help you. Why do I get the feeling he's not doing that?"

Absentmindedly, he rubs my arm for a few seconds and says, "I don't want to complain or gossip about Wayne. He's doing what he thinks is best for the church. I'm sure he's not being malicious or spiteful."

"But?"

"Well, he has a habit of undermining me. Sort of."

I tense. "Sort of?"

"More than sort of," he admits. "It hasn't been anything big so far, but it's a lot of little things. And they add up."

"Like what?"

Now he balks. "No. Never mind specifics."

"Brice!" I look up at him.

He grimaces down at me. "Please. It's nothing important. And the few times I've confronted him about the things that mattered to me, he shrugged them off and made me feel like I was being petty. I ended up looking like an idiot. Or worse, a control freak."

"Well, that's a neat trick!"

"It's not a trick," he insists unconvincingly. "He seemed genuinely confused about why I'd be annoyed with the things he'd done. So, I've stopped mentioning things. I go behind him and do things the way *I* want them done, and that's the end of it."

"That's not a solution. And that's not the way *you* handle things at all!"

"Not normally, no. But it's easier this way."

"Is it?"

"Maybe not in the long run, okay?" he snaps. "But for now, it's the only way I can think to handle it. I think, in a few instances, I've sent a fairly clear message."

"About being passive-aggressive?" I poke.

"No! About who's in charge!"

I don't bristle or stiffen at his outburst. Instead, I say, "I wish you'd give me some specifics."

"I don't want you holding grudges against him about any of this stuff."

"But it was okay for me to know about every conflict you had with my dad so that I'd hold grudges against *him*?"

Now he strokes my hair. "No. That's just it; I was wrong to tell you everything then. That's your dad."

"Well, too late now. And Wayne's not my dad. So, have at it."

He laughs. "No! I'm not going to sit here and give you a list of all the times I feel I may have been wronged by Wayne. Pastor Long, I mean."

I use his chest for leverage as I reach up to kiss his jawline. "Fine. I don't need specifics to hold a grudge. I already don't like him, anyway, because of the things he's said to *me*. Plus, I can't do anything right with that guy. Nothing's enough. And simply knowing that he's being a dick to you, in general, is enough to make me dislike him even more."

He rolls his eyes. "Come on, now."

"Oh, I'm so serious."

"I know you are! And it's not right."

"He and his Sasquatch wife—"

"Hey, hey, hey!"

"—should take their comedy routine elsewhere. It's not funny, and neither are his efforts to undermine your authority. Sounds like he wants all the influence of being a senior pastor but none of the work."

He sighs. "I would have been lost without him the first few months we were here, though. I *needed* him to show me what's what."

Nestling against his chest again, I say, "Yeah, well, now you're finished with the three-hour tour, and you're ready to do some things on your own, your *own* way. And as long as your way conforms to the ways of the Church with a capital C, then Wayne needs to step back. And if the people at Peace don't like *your* way, then maybe they should have thought of that before they called you and uprooted your family and—"

"I have no one but myself to blame for that, though."

Dismissively, I defend him. "Whatever. That's not how it works. They called you, not the other way around."

He's quiet for so long that I check to make sure he hasn't fallen asleep. He hasn't. As a matter of fact, he looks wide awake. And guilty. And nervous.

"What's wrong?" I ask, sitting up and turning myself to face him.

He shakes his head subtly. "Nothing. But..." I stifle every urge to prod him to hurry up and spit it out while he sits there, swallowing and looking miserable. Finally, he says,

"I *did* call them, in a way. Not Peace, specifically, but…" Now he looks up almost defiantly at me. "I put my name on the Synod's call list."

"Huh?" I grunt, my mouth too dry to form words.

With a half-shrug, he elaborates. "Three months before I got the call from Peace, I contacted the Synod and said I wanted to be put on the call list, and I specifically said I was interested in Missouri churches."

"Three months before?"

He nods.

I count backwards in my head and nearly gasp when I arrive at my own conclusion. "But that's— That was before Max was even born!"

"Yes," he says matter-of-factly. "Things were so bad. And I thought we needed a big change, something to—"

"Wait! Things were so bad with Messiah or with you and me?"

"Both?"

I stare at him for a few seconds and shake my head. "I can't believe you."

"Peyton, I—"

Turning my back to him, I flip the switch on the lamp on my bedside table and burrow under the covers. "Goodnight."

"Hold on. You can't just go to sleep. I understand you're upset, but—"

"'Upset' doesn't even begin to describe it. *I* wouldn't even know how to begin to describe it, so don't pretend like you have a fucking clue how I'm feeling."

Oh, man! That would have sounded so much scarier if I'd been able to hold back the tears for a few more seconds. I take a deep, steadying breath and tack on, "Anyway, I'm sure I *won't* be going to sleep, but I'd appreciate it if you'd leave me alone."

Despite probably dying to defend himself, he has the restraint—and the good sense—to honor my wishes.

I wish I'd had the good sense to honor *his* wishes before we ever got onto this topic.

How miserable was Brice in the last trimester of my pregnancy with Max? He couldn't stand his annoying, complaining wife (fair enough); his father-in-law was making his life difficult, both personally and professionally; and he was unhappy enough in his job (er, calling) that he basically did what us laypeople would call "requesting a transfer." Only when you're a pastor, you're rarely—if ever—told no by the folks at "Corporate."

Oh, but be careful what you ask for, Reverend. Because you could get exactly what you want. Plus, you have to take your tiresome wife with you, and you should know by now that there's at least one of *those* people (like your father-in-law) in every congregation. At least at Messiah, the malcontents were merely elders or members; here, he's dealing with a difficult colleague. I'd think that would be much worse. But maybe not. Maybe being five hundred miles away from my dad is a big enough improvement to make up for the other two non-improvements.

Hold on a second, though. I've improved *somewhat*. As far as he knows, anyway. I'm still the same Debbie Downer in my head that I've always been, but I've kept my promise to myself not to burden Brice with it. As far as he knows, with the exception of the PoP catastrophe, I'm fitting in just great here.

Everything else aside, though (and I mean *everything*), it doesn't change one thing: my husband made major decisions on behalf of both of us without a whisper about them to me. *That's* the issue here. If it were the first time, I might chalk it up to a brain fart, as if he were still thinking like a single man, making career decisions without realizing, *Oh, hey. I have a wife now.* But, no. This is a pattern. A very disturbing pattern. This is the type of behavior that women who have escaped controlling, abusive relationships say was the beginning of when things went horribly wrong.

I can hear the dark silhouette now: *"It started with little things, like switching our bank without telling me, but then he was taking out life insurance policies on me without my knowledge. Then he moved me away from all my friends and family. Before I knew it, I wasn't even allowed to decide which brand of toilet paper we used. I had absolutely no say in anything! Now I'm in a relocation program with a new name, and our children will never see their father again... for their own safety."*

Okay, maybe I've been watching too much *Lifetime* during the day. I can't imagine Brice ever going *that* far. But I'm sure those faceless, nameless women didn't imagine the men they married and promised to love and cherish for the rest of their lives ever going that far, either. Nobody fathoms it can happen to *them*. Until one day, it just happens.

But it *doesn't* "just happen," does it? No. It's a systematic taking of control over several years. When was the first time Brice made a unilateral decision regarding our life? Almost a year ago, exactly. He told the church governing boards that we'd forgo living in the house paid for by the church so that they could sell that house and free up some capital. I was furious with him for at least not telling me the decision was on the table. No, I found out after it was a done deal. Mere weeks before we were expected to move out. When I was *very* pregnant with Max.

Considering Peace's call for weeks before telling me was the next blatant offense that I knew of. Of course, now I know that putting his name on the call list was actually the next thing he did without consulting me. *Then* he considered the call before telling me about it, probably in an effort to conceal the fact that he solicited the call himself. I guess it only took him a couple weeks to remember that keeping that detail from me wouldn't be as difficult as he first thought, because his wife believes everything he says, since he's normally so gosh-darned honest. Honesty *does* pay off.

CRY IT OUT

"*I* know! You two, go sit outside on the back patio!"

Brice looks skeptically at his mother. "It's freezing out there. Literally."

"But it's quiet, kid. You won't have to be out there long; trust me."

I pull him by the hand toward the glass-paned back door. It's either that or run upstairs to pick up Max. And I promised Mary—and myself—that I wouldn't interfere with her efforts to straighten out our son's sleeping patterns while she's staying with us this week. He *will* sleep through the night before his first birthday. I can't take much more of things the way they are now.

After we've stepped onto the porch, Mary says soothingly, "I'll stay in here and make sure he's okay." Then she closes the door with a firm click. And locks it.

"Uh…," Brice opens his mouth but closes it again with a snap.

Despite feeling horribly guilty at what's going on in Max's room, I can't help but laugh. "Okay, then," I say. "That's that."

Stuffing his hands in his pockets, he agrees. "So it is."

"Maybe it would have been smart to grab some coats on our way out," I add, crossing my arms across my chest and tucking my hands in my underarms.

"She promised it wouldn't take long," he points out, stuffing his hands into his pockets and staring into the yard.

Under normal circumstances, he'd wrap me in a hug and offer to keep me warm. Under normal circumstances, he'd distract me with dad jokes. Under normal circumstances, he'd whistle or sing a totally inappropriate song to make me laugh. Tonight, we keep plenty of distance between us and keep to our own thoughts.

He eventually breaks the silence with, "I should have told you about the call list."

"And getting the call from Peace, *when* you got it. And putting the parsonage up for sale."

"You're still bent out of shape about *that*?" He sounds more flabbergasted than angry.

"I wasn't. Until I found out about the call list."

"What does one thing have to do with another?"

As if he's a simple child, I explain, "Uh, it's a pattern of behavior, your keeping secrets from me. And I don't like it."

"Three things!"

"I'm sure it's more than that. And they're big things. Big."

He rocks back and forth on his feet. "You want to start listing and comparing secrets? Are you sure about that?"

"I don't have secrets from you," I fib. Nothing he can prove, anyway. And nothing that would completely change his life.

He shrugs his shoulders up around his ears as a breeze picks up. Turning toward me, he says, "Oh? You wouldn't know how to be completely upfront and honest if your life depended on it."

"Excuse me?"

"Don't get all indignant on me. You know it's true."

Realizing I'm walking straight into a trap, I nevertheless bluff, "Try me."

He thinks about it for a second before asking, "How happy are you?"

"Right now? Not very."

With a dirty look, he clarifies, "With life as it stands, in general; not this very second."

I look away from him but reply more quietly, "The answer's the same."

He matches my volume when he asks, "Why?"

I start with the most selfless true answer on the long list of reasons. "Because you're not happy. And that was the whole point of coming here to this weird-ass town—"

"Oh, come on!"

"It's weird, Brice!"

"You haven't given it a chance. You're too focused on how it's different from Chicago, and…"

I talk over him. "Hundreds of miles away from my friends and family, and…"

"Even if you liked things about Springfield, you'd never admit it, because that would be uncool, or something."

"I *wish* I liked it. Don't you think that would be so much easier? But you don't like—"

"Because you *like* being unhappy, exactly like your father!"

I was about to accuse him of not liking it here either, but his last assertion stops me cold. Without even looking at him, I whirl toward the back door and run smack into it when the doorknob won't turn.

"It's locked," he states stupidly.

I close my eyes and count to five to prevent myself from yelling at him while stomping my feet.

Mary, having heard my collision with the door, walks up to it and puts her finger to her lips as she unlocks it and swings it open. "Shhh," she says, looking quite satisfied with herself. "He's been quiet for about two minutes now. I was about to come get you two."

I rush past her without a word.

Behind me, I hear Brice say quietly, "Thanks, Mom."

I'm halfway up the stairs when she replies, "No problem, sweetie. Is everything all right?"

From the top of the stairs, I hear him answer miserably, as I'm hurrying down the hall to our room, "No. Not really."

Like my dad, my ass! I'm not like my dad. Am I? No. My dad is difficult for the sake of being difficult. He works at it. I happen to be difficult without trying. Big difference. Right? Totally right.

Except it yields the same result: a difficult person who nobody—not even the most forgiving of people, like Brice—wants to be around.

Oh, shit! I have to fix this. Right now. I don't have the faintest idea how, and I can't exactly ask Brice how to do it, since we're not *technically* speaking to each other (and haven't been for four days and counting), and I don't have any friends here, nor can I think of any intrinsically happy people to ask how *they* do it. Except…

Jared and Mitzi! Once irrepressibly happy people on their own, they've become almost obnoxiously happy since they started dating each other about six months ago. When I talk to Mitzi on the phone, she gushes about Jared. When I talk to Jared, he practically waxes poetic about Mitzi. When I talk to Jen, even she—the eternal cynic—seems caught up in their web of joy. I need an infusion of one or the other—or both—right now.

While Mary's taking her daily walk during Max's nap, I plop down at the dining room table and try Mitzi first, naturally. I mean, she's been my friend since grade school, and she understands me better than almost anyone else, besides Jen. Unfortunately, all I get is her voicemail, because it's the middle of the day. On a Wednesday. Okay, so I didn't think much further than, "I need to talk to Mitzi."

Moving on, I scroll back up in my phone's address book to the J's. He answers on the first ring. "Why, Mrs. Northam! To what do I owe the pleasure of this call?"

It's working! I'm already smiling!

Without preamble, I ask, "How are you so happy all the time?"

He pauses, then replies, "Are you asking for a recipe, or…?"

I feel stupid but answer anyway, "Maybe. Or just some general pointers would be nice. Do you have a minute?"

"For you, I have hours. I mean. That's not what I meant! I didn't mean it would take me hours to give *you* pointers about being happy! It's just—"

I laugh at his typical bumbling. "Oh, Jared! Never mind. I'll call you whenever I'm down, and a two-minute conversation will cure everything. You don't mind being on permanent standby, do you?"

"Not at all."

"Great." I stare out the window at the sunny day that

feels more like spring than the middle of winter. My smile fades when I remember where I am, both literally and psychologically. "Really, though, I need help."

Gently, he says, "You're in luck, then. Because you called a sort-of pastor who has nothing on his schedule this afternoon but doctorate thesis research, which he didn't want to do anyway."

I can't help but tear up at his generosity. "Thanks."

"Now, tell me what's going on."

An hour later, I've soaked three tissues, and Jared's hardly said anything, but I still feel a lot better. I end my latest crying jag with, "Tell me what to do, Jared. I don't even know where to start!"

He sighs. "Well, you start with your own happiness. Which is good, because as you and I both know, I wouldn't know the first thing about how to make Brice happy. Pretty sure I managed to never do that during my entire vicarage."

Laughing through my tears, I have to agree.

"So! You have to figure out how to make chicken soup from the chicken poop that is your current situation," he states. "Simple, right?"

When he doesn't say anything else, I prod, "Yes? And how do I do this?"

Now it's his turn to laugh. "Oh! Well, *you* have to figure that out."

"What did you do when you were the vicar at Messiah? Maybe I can steal some of your strategies."

"Oh, yeah! Good idea. I had to work hard to stay happy there," he admits on a mutter. "I mean, you were a good friend, and so was Brice, when he wasn't annoyed at me about something stupid I'd done or said. Let me think a second."

I hear him tapping his finger against his phone.

"Oh! I remember one thing that worked okay. I made a list of the things that were upsetting me the most. Then I wrote down what I could do about my behavior that might change each of the things."

"I like lists," I mumble. "But what if there's nothing I can do? I can't change how Pastor Long looks down his nose at me and is constantly pressuring me to 'find a cause.'"

"No, but you can find a cause. Then he'll stop bugging you about it."

"Don't you think I've already tried?"

"How hard have you tried, Peyton? Honestly."

I pick at my jeans. "Um, okay. Not very hard, I guess. I've mostly only thought about it every once in a while and come up blank, so I give up thinking about it. Because it stresses me out."

"Go through the phone book," he suggests brightly. "And don't give up until you find something that really catches your interest. Probably part of your problem is that you need to get out of the house more often. You're not used to being cooped up."

"I get out! I go to the church's stupid parenting group once a week, and—"

"That doesn't count! You're there out of obligation."

I don't want to break it to him, but the community service I end up doing will most likely fall under the same category. Anyway, it's not fair to bog him down in all these details. He's given me some good advice; now it's time for me to shut up.

Taking a deep, bracing breath, I say, "You've been such a big help, Jared. Thanks for listening and for giving me some suggestions for change. I appreciate it so much."

"Hey, I owe you, like, a billion more venting sessions. So,

don't mention it." He pauses, and as I'm about to say goodbye (even though I don't want to), he blurts in what sounds like one continuous word, "I'm going to ask Mitzi to marry me. Do you think it's too soon to ask her to marry me? How do you think she'll answer? I don't want to screw this up!"

I nearly drop the phone; then I squeal so loudly that it wakes up Max, who's upstairs, several rooms away. Mary, who I thought was still out, pokes her head into the dining room.

"Are you okay?" she asks.

I nod, but I'm sure I don't look okay, with tears in my eyes from Jared's announcement and a red nose from my earlier crying.

She gives me a doubtful look but backs off with, "Okay. I'll get Max, then."

As soon as she's gone, I say, "That's the best news I've heard all year! Almost. No, definitely! And no, I don't think it's too soon, and yes, I think she'll say yes. Ohmigosh! I can't believe this!"

He sounds shy suddenly. "I know. Well, I *can*, but I didn't have much hope that I'd ever meet anyone who would understand me enough to want to, you know, be with me for the rest of her life."

"Oh, Jared."

"No, I'm serious. But she gets me. It's amazing."

Now it's my turn to pepper him with questions. "When are you going to ask her? Can I tell Brice? Do you think you'll get married soon or wait a year or two?"

His answers are, "Sure"; "Please do. He'll need to know before I ask him to perform the ceremony"; and "I think that's more up to her than me."

I squeal again but have mercy on his ear, ending the call

and making him promise that he or Mitzi will text me as soon as he pops the question.

I'm so happy right now that I won't even *think* about my problems for a long time.

FAIR'S FAIR

*T*hat was the plan, anyway. But you know what they say about best-laid plans: well-meaning mothers-in-law have a way of screwing them up. Isn't that what Robert Burns wrote? No? Well, maybe I should try to get my own quote to catch on. I'm sure it's an experience that's universal enough, even among the lucky ones, like me, whose husbands' mothers are wonderful.

Basking in the afterglow of my conversation with Jared, I walk into the kitchen to find Mary putting Max in his high chair for his dinner. I tell her I'll feed him, but she responds with a good-natured, "No, no, no! You get to feed him all the time. Why don't you sit across the table, put up your feet, and let's get caught up?"

At first, I don't think much of it. "Sure!" I say, following her instructions to a tee.

When she's settled in front of Max with a bowl of pureed green beans, and I'm comfortable in my chair, she says, "Now, this is none of my business, kid, so if you'd rather not talk about it, just say, 'Mary, mind your own business,' but I can't help but notice that things are a bit, shall we say, tense around here of late. Are you okay? A simple yes or no is fine. No need to elaborate. I'm worried, that's all."

I chew on my chapped bottom lip while deciding how much to tell her. I don't feel like going too much into it, considering I told Jared about everything not long ago, and I'm rather sick of talking and thinking about it, but I don't want her to worry.

After watching her feed Max the same spoonful of beans no less than three times, I finally answer, "It's been rough." Then I don't know what else to say that doesn't sound like I'm tattling on her son, so I finish with a lame, "You shouldn't worry, though. It'll be fine. We're all adjusting."

"Hmmm," she murmurs, obviously skeptical of my assessment. After a minute's pause, she ventures, "Are you both adjusting, or is he asking you to do all the adjusting?"

When all I can do is stare at her and blink, she laughs. "I've known him his whole life. You think I don't know how he is? He's always had a very strong sense of right and wrong."

"Always?" I mutter, tracing the wood grain in the table.

She chuckles. "I didn't say he's never done anything wrong. But he's always had strong opinions about what's right. And he holds the people he loves to a much higher standard than people he knows more superficially. He gives acquaintances and strangers the benefit of the doubt much more easily than he does you or me. Or himself."

"I believe that."

Much to Max's frustration, she sets down his bowl of food, swivels, and grasps my hand in the middle of the table. "The stakes are pretty high here, don't you think, kid?"

Too choked up to talk, I merely nod.

She squeezes my hand tighter, ignoring Max's squeals.

"He's not playing fair." When I shrug, she smiles, returns her full attention to her grandson, and brightly asks, "What's for dinner tonight for us grown folks?"

Gladly accepting the change in subject, I glance at the clock on the microwave and frown. "Oh. Yeah. Um, I don't know."

"Well, don't you think you should start thinking about it, kid? Brice'll be home before you know it."

If there were any rebuke in her tone, I might bristle, but she seems simply to be making conversation and satisfying her curiosity, so I sigh and confess, "I'm a horrible cook. Sometimes it's best to let Brice cook dinner or order something in. Or go out somewhere. That's the one good thing about being invited so often to other people's houses for dinner: no cooking for me."

She smiles kindly at me. "Ah. Yes. I'd say it's definitely good to make Brice fend for himself sometimes. After all, you're not his personal chef or his maid. But…"

"I know!" I blush at what she has the good manners to leave unsaid. "I think it's more work for him to try to choke down the meals I make, though, than it is for him to make himself a sandwich."

She laughs at that description. "Oh, kid! Recipes are merely instructions. You can follow instructions, right?"

"Apparently not."

She stands and holds Max's bowl of food toward me. "All right then. You take over with this guy, and I'll root around in your cupboards and freezer."

Relieved, I gladly take the bowl and sit down in front of Max. "Thanks, Mary. Really, I—"

"Not so fast!" she interjects, her head in the freezer. "You'll be making it, but I'll be showing you some tricks. After all, who do you think taught Brice how to cook?

Augustus?" That thought brings out her deep chortle. "That man couldn't scramble an egg. So I was determined that Brice could."

"Well, thanks for that," I say sincerely.

She emerges from the freezer with two packages of pork chops and a bag of broccoli. Tossing the frozen goods onto the counter, she says, "There! Something simple."

While I give Max the last of his dinner, she tilts her head and asks, "Just out of curiosity, have you ever asked Brice to teach you how to cook?"

Sheepishly, I admit, "Well, he's shown me a few things. Which I then screw up with such regularity that he's started to tell me, 'Don't touch those steaks in the fridge; I'm going to grill them this weekend.' Or something like that. It bothers him to throw away food, which is what ends up happening about sixty percent of the time I cook."

She shakes her head. "Well, he never was a very good teacher. And he took to cooking naturally and likes to improvise, so I can see where learning from him would be confusing."

"Yes!" I'm relieved she understands. "He never makes anything the same way twice! And he doesn't measure!"

After laughing at that, she sticks her finger in the air as if she's just had an idea. "That reminds me. You're going to make dessert, too. And you're going to measure."

Brice looks up from his plate and pauses, mid-chew. I've seen him do that one other time, and it was right before he had to make a run for the bathroom after eating some turkey tetrazzini I made from a recipe I found online. And yes, it was that bad.

I haven't had a chance to take a bite yet. "What's wrong?" I immediately ask, my stomach dropping.

He finishes chewing and swallows. "This is excellent!" he answers. I wish he didn't sound so surprised, but the compliment makes me feel good, anyway.

"Thanks! Your mom—"

"Uh-uh!" Mary cuts me off. "You did everything. I merely oversaw."

"Yeah, but I never would have thought to add the—"

She widens her eyes at me. "You don't have to tell him your secrets!"

I grin at her. "All right." I glance over at Max when he squeals in his Exersaucer then cut into my own pork chop.

Brice watches me take my first bite and smiles when I nod. "See? I told you. Delicious, hon." He immediately goes back to eating, quickly emptying his first plate and loading up on seconds. "At the risk of asking you to give away your 'secrets,' is that balsamic vinegar you drizzled on the broccoli?" he asks.

"Yes," I reply succinctly, while he nods approvingly and devours his second plateful.

Mary, still working on her initial portion, implores, "Save room for dessert. Peyton made a cake."

After wiping his mouth, he smiles, but he looks decidedly wary, despite his best efforts to be encouraging. "Oh?"

"I know what you're thinking, and you don't need to worry. I followed your mom's recipe to the letter. It's not going to be a repeat of Jared's birthday cupcakes." I stand and offer to take his plate with mine and Mary's into the kitchen.

"I wasn't even thinking of that," he says unconvincingly.

"Yes, you were, and I don't blame you."

He grins. "Well, maybe a little. I can still remember that

texture. It wasn't so much a bad taste, but the texture was like sawdust."

Mary shoots him a glare. "Well, this cake is perfect. So, shush up, or you're not going to get a piece."

"Shushing," he promises, following me.

In the kitchen, I set the dirty dishes in the sink and walk over to the counter where the cake is. He steps up behind me and puts his hands on my waist.

"Hey. Thanks for making such a nice dinner. I know cooking's not your favorite thing."

I pause in my cake-cutting to lean back against him. "You're welcome. And I only dislike it because I'm so bad at it. It's fun when you know what you're doing." I serve up one big slice and two smaller slices on plates and hand the large slice to him, smiling up into his face. "Enjoy, monsieur."

Holding my eye contact and returning my smile, he takes the plate and fork I'm presenting and says, "I will, I think. Thanks."

Later, on the back porch, while we wait out Max's evening concert, Brice stares up at the twinkling stars while I work up the courage to say, "Hey."

He looks over at me. "Huh?"

"I'm sorry that I don't know—" I have to stop, clear my throat, and look away from his earnest face. Looking down at my shoes, I start again. "I'm sorry I don't know how to be happy here. I mean, *yet*. I'll figure it out, though. I prom—"

This time, he stops me by pulling me up against him and putting his mouth on mine.

After the kiss, he asks, "What can I do?"

"What?" I say, shaking my head, confused.

"What can I do to help you be happier? *I'm* sorry that I've messed this up so badly. I've led you around by the collar, like as long as you follow me, everything will be fine, but it's *not* fine. I'm being a heavy-handed jerk."

"I don't like being unhappy," I assert, deciding at the last second to leave off the words, "like my dad." Why dig up something that inflammatory after such a nice kiss?

"I know you don't! I was mad, and I said some stupid stuff because it was the easiest explanation for everything. And it got me off the hook. It was insensitive and—"

I attack his mouth and run my hands through his hair. Then I climb him like a scrummy totem pole and wrap my legs around his waist. He walks me to the (blessedly dark) back wall of the house, away from the light spilling onto the concrete patio through the glass back doors. The vinyl siding pops and gives slightly as he presses my back against it.

"I'm sorry."

"I'm sorry."

"I'm so sorry!"

"No, I am!"

It's probably the most un-erotic makeout dialogue in the history of the world, but we might as well be reciting poetry to each other, based on the physical response it's eliciting.

After a moan, I continue the un-sexy theme with, "I hope the neighbors can't see us."

He grunts, "Yeah, that would be embarrassing," but doesn't stop kissing my neck.

"I'm definitely not cold anymore," I announce breathlessly.

"Me neither. This is a perfect way to pass the time out here."

Fortunately, there's no more talking for several minutes, but then we both freeze in the shadows when we hear Mary call from the back door, "Hey, where'd you guys go?"

I snort against Brice's neck, but he shushes me and almost manages to say without laughing, "We're, uh, trying to decide where to plant a garden!" His voice breaks in the middle of the last word.

"In the dark?" she questions, stepping further onto the patio and trying to see in our direction.

Quickly, I hop down and stand on my own feet, straightening my clothes and rubbing my hand against what I know has to be visible beard burn on my neck. Brice turns more fully away from her and adjusts the front of his pants.

Wearily, he says, "No, Mom. If you must know, we were making out."

She waves a hand at us and turns to go back into the house. "Well, for crying out loud! Why didn't you say so to begin with?" she wonders irritably, closing the door and leaving us alone again.

We giggle like two kids, and he says to me, "Another example of honesty being the best policy. I don't want to mess with a garden this summer."

He looks down into my face in the dark. It's hard to make out his features, but I can see the sudden seriousness in his eyes when he says, "You and me: no more secrets, all right?"

Knowing right away it's going to be an extremely hard promise for me to keep, I nevertheless immediately nod my agreement. "No more secrets."

"That means nothing," he elucidates, in case it's not perfectly clear what the rules are. "Not even things you—or I—think are insignificant. There are no loopholes here."

"What about birthday, anniversary, or Christmas gifts?" I ask, more to be silly than sincere.

"Surprises are different," he allows. "But we have to be completely transparent about everything else."

"Starting now?" I check, hoping the rules aren't retroactive but needing to make sure.

He narrows his eyes at me, and I can tell he's wondering why I'd need to ask, but he merely answers, "Mmm, yes. Starting now."

To distract him from that detail, I ask, "Should we make a blood oath?" which makes him laugh.

"I'd rather seal it with a kiss."

Well, hell, when something is *that* official, there's no going back on it.

14

VOLUNTEERING

*I*t's a miracle! Okay, not quite. There are some definite causes for the improvement to my attitude and mood. It's amazing what a difference regular sleep, frequent sex (just sayin'), and good food can make. Add to that the feeling of accomplishment brought on by learning a new skill and the newfound ability to tell a parenting expert like Paul that he can save his baby-whispering techniques for some other poor saps who need it, because *we* don't need it anymore, and you have one contented mama. Bordering on euphoric.

I even think I've found a "cause," if I can summon the nerve to actually do it.

When I arrive at the church, Brice's office door is closed. I know from our conversation this morning at breakfast that he had a meeting with Pastor Long, Ben, and the Vacation Bible School Committee. Summer seems far off, but it will be here in what feels like the span of a week, so it's time to start planning this year's VBS theme and activities. I thought for sure the meeting would be over by now, considering it was scheduled to start two hours ago.

Brice must be having a more difficult time than he hoped. He's trying to convince everyone to move the week of VBS to earlier in the summer. He expected his biggest challenge to the change would stem from the favorite Lutheran excuse, "But we've always done it like this" (in August, in this case), with the status quo campaign spear-headed, I'm sure, by none other than Pastor Long.

Lucy smiles and explains what I already know is happening in there. Then she invites me to sit in one of the deep chairs next to Brice's door before going back to her work.

My butt cheeks have barely touched the faux-leather seat when the door beside me cracks open, and my husband's head pops out.

"Hey!" he whispers. "We're wrapping things up in here, I think. What's up?"

"Nothing special," I assure him. "I don't mind waiting. Just wanted to talk to you and take advantage of getting out of the house without Max." I wave him back inside his office and make myself comfortable.

After a few minutes of trying to puzzle it out for myself, I finally say to Lucy, "How'd you do that?"

She looks up at me with her usual vacant smile. "Sorry?"

I nod toward the closed door. "How did you let Brice know I was here without picking up the phone or going in there?"

Widening her eyes and shifting them toward her computer monitor, she says, "Uh, instant message?" in a way that makes it clear she's trying not to let on that she thinks I'm an idiot.

"Oh, right," I say with a nod. "Of course." I stick out my tongue and roll my eyes at myself. "Someone needs to get out of the house more often, I think."

She narrows her eyes. "Who?"

At first I don't understand her question, but when I finally do, I say, "Me. I was talking about me, since I didn't consider instant messaging as a means of communication between you and Brice."

Her shoulders relax. "Oh. Yeah! It was Pastor's idea. That way, if he's in there with someone, I don't have to interrupt them to tell him that someone else is out here. And he can give me instructions about what to say to someone if, you know."

"He doesn't want to be bothered?" I finish diplomatically.

"Yes!" She lowers her voice. "Between you and me, I don't know how he gets anything done most days. So many people in and out of here! It wasn't like that with Pastor Wiseman. But then again, Pastor Long did a lot more when Pastor Wiseman was around. So it makes sense that Pastor Northam is busier than Pastor Wiseman. Whew! That's a lot of pastors!"

I leave it at that and pretend to mess around on my phone so that she'll go back to whatever she was doing and leave me to my thoughts. Thoughts like, *I wonder why Pastor Long's workload is lighter with Brice around, as opposed to when Pastor Wiseman was the Senior Pastor?* Thoughts like, *No wonder Brice is up late so many nights, working in his office at the house.* Thoughts like, *What* does *Pastor Long do all day, then, besides get in Brice's way?*

Finally, the door opens, and a line of people parade from the other side. Each person who passes by me acts like it's been more than three days since the last time they saw me. As a matter of fact, they act like it's been three *years.*

"Oh, Peyton! How's that baby? Growing, I bet!"

"Peyton! I'm glad to see you're out and about. The baby keeps you busy, huh?"

"We'll be seeing you next week at the spaghetti supper, right? I saw you signed up for kitchen duty. What a blessing!"

"Where's little Max? Oh, that's right; Pastor's mom is visiting! It was so good to meet her last Sunday!"

And finally, "Peyton! How are things? You look positively glowing today! Doesn't she look wonderful, Lucy?" This from Vivian Long.

Lucy smiles politely, but Vivian won't let it go. "I mean it! You have roses in your cheeks and a twinkle in your eye!"

To her husband, she says, as if I'm not standing right there, "Wayne, I wouldn't be surprised if Max doesn't have a baby brother or sister by this time next year!"

With all the negatives strung together in her sentence, it takes me a while to figure out what she's saying, but when I do, I merely laugh and shake my head. "Oh, I don't know if that's in the plan," I say while edging toward the door, away from the giant couple.

"Your plan or God's plan?" Pastor Long quips.

"Both?" I try.

Vivian throws her head back and laughs with her mouth so far open that I can see her silver fillings. Impressive that she still has all of her own teeth. I can't believe Pastor Wiseman's wife didn't kick them out.

"Anyway, it was good seeing you two," I say, rushing into Brice's office and closing the door. Simultaneously spinning and speaking, I blurt, "Do I look pregnant?" to him—and Ben, whose presence I definitely didn't notice before this very second. "Oh!" I put my hands up to my burning cheeks.

Ben tilts his head and studies me from his chair across

the room. "Umm, I don't have much experience making that diagnosis," he admits. "I try not to guess at all. Got myself in trouble once when I guessed incorrectly."

"Ben, I'm so sorry! I didn't realize you were still in here. It seemed like a hundred people came out. What's the fire code capacity for this room?" I spew forth in a humiliated stream.

The two men merely stare at me. Finally, I collapse onto the couch against the far wall and finish, "I'm sorry; I'm interrupting. I thought you were finished, but I'll shut up so you can go on talking about what you were talking about."

Seriously, Brice says, "I believe that was our estimation of how many Chinese restaurants are in this town. To recap, I say more than a hundred, easily. Ben?"

"Not quite *that* many. Maybe upwards of thirty-five?"

"That's still incredible in a town this size," Brice declares, typing something into his computer. "And the winner is... Benjamin Eiffler! Thirty-nine is what the almighty Internet tells me. Thirty-nine!"

"What do I win, what do I win?" Ben asks excitedly, clapping his hands and almost dropping his legal pad and pen from his lap.

Brice's mouth is still hanging open, but he recovers enough to say through his laughter, "You were incredibly close with your figure! You deserve, at the very least, a fortune cookie. Hang on a minute!" He narrows his eyes. "Have you looked up this stat before? Did you hustle me, Benjamin?"

The ginger-haired youth minister's unable to keep a straight face when he replies mock-indignantly, "Never!"

After suffering through the Pastor Northam stare-down for a few seconds, however, he concedes, "Well, maybe. But it was several years ago, so there weren't that many restaurants back then. I had to pad my answer, accounting for the major population spike we've had since I last counted up the Chinese restaurants in the phone book. See? It was so long ago that I didn't even use the Internet back then to get my answer!"

"I'll allow it, then. And I'll take you out to lunch at your choice of one of those thirty-nine establishments next Monday."

"Oh, Pastor! I've been hoping you'd ask me on a date. God *does* answer prayers."

"Yes, he does, Benjamin." With barely a pause for a breath, he turns to me. "Now, what is this question you burst in here asking? Do you look pregnant? Stand up and let me get a look at you."

I shrink further into the couch cushions. "No. Never mind. It's stupid. Pastor Long and Vivian were freaking me out, but they're..." I glance at Ben, whose expression couldn't be more expectant if I were about to predict the date of the end of the world. "Silly," I finish weakly. He looks disappointed.

Brice's face assumes that goofy, faraway grin he gets whenever he talks about babies. "Wouldn't that be great, though, if you were? Max is getting so big and independent."

"No, it wouldn't be great," I say, before he gets too carried away. "It's been less than a week, but I'm already attached to sleeping again. I forgot how much I truly missed it."

"Yeah, yeah. Sleep is nice, but babies are nicer."

Ben slaps his notepad on his knee and rises. "Well, on that note, I'm out. I love babies as much as the next guy." He makes a contradictory face at me behind his hand as if he's trying to hide it from Brice. "But if we talk too much about them, I start to feel like I'm at my second job."

"What are you, an obstetrician by night?" I ask.

He stops at the door with his hand on the doorknob and turns around, blinking. "No. But I volunteer at the Pregnancy Crisis Center downtown."

"No, you don't!" I laugh at the idea, especially considering… "I came here to tell Brice that that's what I think I'm going to make my 'cause.'" I say the final word with the exact inflection and emphasis that Pastor Long has put on it every time he's talked to me for the past six months.

They immediately recognize my impersonation. One of them laughs loudly enough to distort my hearing. The other reproaches, "Peyton."

I turn to the more serious of the two. "Sorry. But that's how he always says it!"

Recovered, Ben says, "Well, it would be awesome if you decided to volunteer there. We need people badly. In all areas. You could be an intake counselor or make follow-up calls or assemble and distribute care packages. I do a little bit of everything, depending on what needs the most attention on any given day or what time I'm there. I like working behind the scenes, but it's all gratifying. I tend to do most of my work in the evenings, after I'm finished here. I'd be glad to take you anytime."

"This is a crazy coincidence," I say with a shake of my head. "I mean, of all the places I've considered! And I decide on this one, and *you* not only know all about it because you volunteer there, but you're here in Brice's office when I come by to discuss it with him!"

"Coincidence? I think not!" Brice scoffs. "Come on, Peyton."

I shoot him a dirty look. "Whatever it is"—I turn my

attention back to Ben—"it would be great if I could tag along with you some evening. Thanks!"

"No problem. I usually work there on Tuesdays and Thursdays."

"Then I'll meet you here next Tuesday at 5:00," I propose.

"Sounds like a plan."

"What about my dinner that night?" Brice half-kids. "Now that you're making human food, I'm getting used to having my meal waiting for me when I get home."

I lean across his desk and give him a peck on his forehead before crossing to the door. "Dial up one of those thirty-nine Chinese restaurants," I suggest with a sassy finger-wave over my shoulder on the way out.

"Do you hear that?" Brice mutters to Ben. "Martin Luther is spinning in his grave right now. Spinning."

15

BABY TALK

$\mathcal{C}$onfession time: I let Pastor and Vivian Long get into my head. At first, I told myself I wouldn't, because I was sure that the physical changes Vivian claimed to observe in me are merely the result of my being happier in general, not knocked up. Well, mostly sure. In a 99.9 percent way. So, to make that 0.1 percent of doubt a non-factor, I peed on a stick before Brice even got home from work tonight. Then I buried the test under the rest of the trash in our bathroom wastebasket. I just didn't want him to read anything into it. And I also didn't want him to know that I let anything Viv and Wayne said get to me. I'm aware that it's dumb and prideful. In other words, it's typically me.

But then all evening, the conversation and resulting promise Brice and I made after our ridiculous backyard makeout session had echoed through my head.

Like he said: total transparency, no loopholes.

Therefore, as I'm getting ready for bed, I unbury the test, letting it sit on top of the tissues and dental floss and Q-tips and other detritus of daily bathroom activity. I'm not happy about it, but I know it's the right thing to do. He has to be given the opportunity to know—and to ask his annoying questions about it. Because he will. It's inescapable. And I'll simply have to grit my teeth, swallow my pride, and be as honest as possible about it.

Damn, damn, damn.

This is a test, on so many levels, and I plan to pass it.

Sure enough, when he slides his legs under the covers after his turn in the bathroom, he stares at my reading profile until I finally say, "Can I help you?"

"Do you want to talk about what's in the bathroom trash?" he offers.

I turn the page on my book and reply bluntly, "You saw the result. What's there to talk about?"

"Well, are you relieved?"

"Immensely." I mark my place, set the book on my nightstand and grin at him. Then, more sincerely, I state, "I don't know what I'd do with another baby right now, Brice."

He looks like a child lobbying for a puppy (*"I'll feed it and clean up after it and take it for walks and…"*) when he says, "But it wouldn't be right now. It would be months from now. You'd be ready by then, right?"

I hold his eye contact and remain firm. "No."

"Aww, come on!"

"No! I still remember too vividly what it's like to be pregnant. It sucks. I have to forget a lot more about how much it sucks before I'll be glad to do it again."

He switches tracks. "Why'd you take the test, then? Because a small part of you wanted it to be true, right?"

I shake my head and laugh at him. "No. Stop trying to psychoanalyze me; it'll give you nightmares. I took it because… Well, I wanted to make sure Vivian and Wayne are as full of shit as I already think they are."

"Good gravy. That's not nice!"

His *Leave it to Beaver* response to my brutally honest answer makes me laugh harder. "I didn't say it was nice. But I haven't been able to get Vivian's flip-top head from my mind since she suggested the possibility. She's positively Muppet-like in her ability to open her mouth at such a wide angle."

"You're just being mean now."

"Yeah, well, I'm going to sleep just fine tonight. Because Max is sleeping through the night. And I'm not pregnant. The end. Best bedtime story ever."

After I turn off my light, he rubs up against me in the dark as I try to find a comfortable sleeping position—turned away from him.

Soothingly, he says near my ear while rubbing his hand up and down my leg, "It won't be that bad this time. Being pregnant, I mean."

"You, sir, are talking out of your ass and making promises you have no control over keeping."

His gentle chuckle moves my hair and raises goose-bumps on my neck. "It's not necessarily a promise. But this will be the third time your body's done it; it'll know what to do and won't be so resistant. And *you'll* know what to do and understand what's happening, so you'll be less anxious and stressed."

I sigh and decide to point out to him what he seems to be forgetting: "Well, it's not like I'm trying *not* to get pregnant. So, take up your pleas with your buddy, God. He's the One who's saying no right now."

That finally shuts him up. For a few minutes, anyway. Until, as I'm drifting to sleep, he says, "You have a point, you know. I'll have to remember to ask more specifically for what I want from now on."

Oh, great. In that case, I'd better get my spandex belly-panel jeans from storage and be prepared for the smug-fest when Vivian Long appears to be a modern-day prophet.

∽

Bottles, onesies, socks, receiving blanket, diapers, wipes, formula. Slide the box. Repeat twenty times. Move down the assembly line to sealing and labeling. Move further down the line to loading. And rest.

After more than an hour of putting together care packages and loading them in the PCC van in silence, I turn to Ben and say, "It's a tad late to deliver these, so now what?"

He takes a swig from his water bottle. "Someone else will deliver them in the morning. These layettes are for women coming home from the hospital tomorrow with their new babies. Most of them alone. We also have a shuttle service that stays busy helping single moms get home from the hospital or to their newborns' doctor's appointments. When you aren't allowed to drive, you have to get around somehow. And taxis are usually too expensive."

I stare at him for a few seconds before admitting, "I never even thought of that. So it's common for women who use this service to not even have family who can help?"

He nods. "Yep. More common than not. We like to pretend we've come a long way from the days when unwed mothers were shipped off to 'homes' to have their babies, but just because things are different now doesn't mean they're easier. What's easier is not to have the baby at all."

I squirm but hide it by putting myself in motion, picking up the scraps of trash that haven't made it to the can in the middle of the garage-like work area.

Since I don't want him to ask me why I chose to work with this charity, I steer clear of asking him the same question, even though I'm dying to know. Instead, I inquire, "What task do you enjoy doing most when you're here?"

After retrieving a push broom and swiping at the floor for a few seconds, he answers, "Intake counseling. I don't do it very often, though."

"That's the very beginning of the process, right? When expectant mothers fill out an application for services?" At his affirming nod, I ask, "Why is it your favorite?"

He keeps his eyes on the broom. "I don't know. A lot of times, I'm the first person they've talked to who is *happy* they've decided to keep their baby. I like being friendly and cheerful, and I enjoy telling them that their situation isn't hopeless, and that we're here to help. It feels good to brighten someone's day and make her feel good about herself."

"That's nice." I slide the boxes we didn't use back in their place between the wall and other collapsed boxes. Then I go about moving the bins of donated supplies up against another wall, out of the way but ready for the next time they're needed.

Tamping the broom against the floor to shake loose the dust and dirt clinging to the bristles, he says, "Yeah. It is. I wish I liked it for more selfless reasons, though."

"Just because it makes you feel good doesn't mean it's not a good thing to do."

"I guess. But…" He hangs up the broom on a nail by the rawhide string looped through its handle and faces me, his hands on his hips. "I don't know!" He laughs at his inability to articulate it. "I always feel wrong, getting so much satisfaction from helping them. I don't want anyone to think I have a Messiah complex, or something."

That cracks me up.

"What? I mean it!"

"Is that why you don't do intake counseling very much, even though you like it more than anything else? Do you hide yourself back here and do grunt work so that it feels more selfless?"

He blushes. "Maybe. I've never analyzed it that much."

"Don't be afraid of being a blessing to someone. That's just twisted."

Bordering on defensive, he says, "Well, there's another, more basic reason I don't interact with the clients more often."

"Which is…?"

Around a frown, he says, "A lot of them. Well, they don't necessarily want to see a guy when they walk through that door. And I completely understand that. I've even had women halfway through their entrance interview ask me to find someone else to help them. I don't think they *want* to feel that way, and it's not anything personal or based on anything *I've* said or done, but they can't help it. They're not comfortable around men."

"Oh. Wow. I never thought of that either."

"Yeah, well you're not thinking like a rape victim. Or someone whose boyfriend or husband knocks her around or deserted her when she told him he was going to be a dad. Or any other things that give all of us guys a bad name."

"There are some bad ones out there," I declare stupidly, thinking of one in particular who seems halfway decent (although self-absorbed and spiteful) next to some of the ones Ben's just described.

He doesn't make me feel dumb for stating the obvious, though. Instead, he merely nods contemplatively and says matter-of-factly, "Yep. My dad was one of 'em. Or so I hear. Fortunately, I've never met the guy."

Oh, shit. This is where I say something. Anything. This

is where I *don't* stand here blinking at him and staring, open-mouthed. Oh, gosh! Why can't I think of something, anything?

"Bummer," I unfortunately choose in my mental panic.

Bummer??? No. Tell me I didn't say that, like some vapid Hollywood starlet who's too cool to keep her mouth closed, for fear that it'll look like she cares enough to use the muscles that hold it shut.

He raises an eyebrow at me and smirks. "Uh, that's one way to put it, I guess."

I blush. "I'm sorry. I mean, that sounded so flippant, and that's not what I meant. I couldn't think of anything else to say! It slipped out. I'm an idiot. You don't know that about me yet—or maybe you do. You probably do. I'm sure word's gotten around. Anyway, this is just another example of me being an idiot."

Waving away my embarrassment, he walks to the door leading to the inside of the PCC and pulls it open, motioning for me to walk in front of him. "You're not an idiot, and you don't need to be sorry. I sort of sprang it on you. And you're right that it sucks. There's not much more to say about it."

"You're too nice."

He leads me to the office work area, where I'm assuming we'll be folding the flyers he told me about earlier. "Really, I just wanted you to know why I choose to volunteer *here*. I know it seems random or weird for a single guy my age to show an interest in this cause. Actually, I've had people—mostly women—come right out and tell me it's weird. I even had a date accuse me of trying to pick up women here. Here! Where they come for safety and support, at one of the most vulnerable times in their lives! I don't *think* I look like a total scumbag, but maybe I do." He sits at a table loaded down with multiple stacks of colored papers and invites me to sit across from him.

While he searches through the stacks to find the ones we're supposed to be folding, I laugh at the mental picture of him on the date he mentioned. "How did you go on with the rest of *that* date?" I wonder.

He shakes his head as he divides a stack of neon pink flyers in half, gives one of the portions to me, and starts tri-folding the ones in front of him.

"I didn't. I mean, I stared at her to make sure she wasn't joking, and when she insisted she was serious, I paid for her dinner and mine and said, 'It's been real.' Then I left. I met her at a mutual friend's wedding, and fortunately, I haven't run into her since our date. But ever since, I've been self-conscious about people thinking that's why I work here. It never occurred to me before she said something. Never! I mean, how would someone…?" He shakes his head and blushes. "Is it even possible for a man to *allow* himself to feel that way for someone in those circumstances?"

I pay close attention to making precise folds.

When I don't say anything, he assumes I simply don't have an answer and provides one for himself. "I don't think it's possible. I honestly can't imagine that, falling in love with someone who's carrying some other guy's baby. I wouldn't be open enough to the possibility for the feelings to develop!"

He thinks about it for a while as he folds, folds, folds. Then he says, "I dunno. Maybe it's because I haven't met the right person, so I don't know what it's like. Maybe it has nothing to do with the circumstances surrounding your meeting. Maybe the feelings develop, whether you're recep-tive to them or not. I mean, do you think you have a choice about who you fall in love with? Do you think you can choose *not* to fall in love?"

"I don't think so," I answer as flatly as possible.

Six more flyers fall into the box with other folded flyers. Then he says, "Maybe not. But you can choose not to act on it. You can choose, if it's not appropriate, to walk away."

Trying to lighten things up, I crack, "This coming from a guy who's admitted to never being in love."

He laughs. "You have a good point there. I don't think my opinion would change, though, even if I knew what it felt like."

"Well, your firm sense of right and wrong is admirable. You just have to make sure it's not under-informed." I'm amazed at my ability to keep my voice steady. Because this topic makes me shake on the inside.

HISTORICAL WORRIES

"It was awful!" I tell Brice later, pacing back and forth in the tiny bedroom he uses as a home office. He's sitting with the back of his chair against his desk, which is situated in front of a window that overlooks the backyard. Steepling his fingers under his chin, he watches me through his eyelashes, moving only his eyes to follow my pacing.

"You should have heard him," I continue. "I know I forgot some of the things he said, because I was so worried about moderating my reaction to what he was saying. But, really, I wanted to cry. And defend you."

"He wasn't talking about *me*."

"Yes, he was. Maybe not knowingly, but he was describing you. And he was absolutely disgusted with anyone who could 'allow himself' to fall in love with someone who's carrying someone else's baby." I stop and try to catch my breath.

He watches me for a few more seconds without saying anything before stating quietly, "Ben's a good guy. He doesn't have a lot of life experience to back up his strong opinions, but he's a good guy nonetheless."

"I *know* he is. That's what scares me so much! He's one of the nicest people I've ever met, yet even *he* wouldn't understand." I bite at my fingernail and examine the damage at close range.

Brice cups his knees with his hands and sighs. "Oh, Peyton. He's young. And ignorant. He was speaking for himself. It sounds like he was venting and that he felt comfortable enough around you to be completely honest and not censor himself. If he knew, he'd understand. And he'd probably be mortified that he stuck his foot in his mouth."

"I don't know."

"I do. He admitted he was relatively ignorant on the topic. If it comes to it, I'd be happy to share my experience with him and put things into perspective."

"No!"

"I said, 'If it comes to that.'" He rubs his face before quickly spinning in his chair to face his desk and type frantically.

"What are you doing?" I ask warily.

"Nothing," he mutters distractedly. "Making some quick notes."

"Please don't write a sermon about this."

"Not about *this*, necessarily."

"Brice, please!"

He continues typing, clicks "save," and turns back around to me.

"This is good, basic stuff. We, as Christians, are notorious for speaking out of turn. Or judging other people's reactions to experiences when we've had nothing similar happen to us, so we don't know how we'd act in that same situation. Obviously, I'm not going to reference your conversation with Ben, but I think the general theme it brings to mind is an important one. Right? We can *never* have all the information we need to judge someone else. That's why we should never do it."

I roll my eyes. "Lovely. Can we get back to the original conversation now?"

"I didn't think we ever left it," he replies innocently. Then he mumbles mostly to himself, "I'll have to look ahead and see where in the Lectionary this would best fit. I can always write it and hold it. It's a common, generic topic. *Too* common? *Too* generic?" He scratches at his neck and winces. "Maybe. I'd have to find a good, fresh twist on the message."

And he's gone. I spin on my heel and exit the room. He's too deep in thought to notice or stop me.

I'm finished talking about it, anyway. It's only upsetting me. This is the first time I've ever considered how "The Story of Brice and Peyton," from an outsider's perspective, reflects on Brice. It's always been a given to me that he acted honorably and was in the right, every step of the way. *I'm* the miserable sinner in the parable. I'm the one whose loose morals got her in a pickle. He was—and still is—the hero of the story. The risk that people might turn on *him* if they learn about Secret makes it suddenly clear how important it is that they never find out.

Still not confident enough about my cooking skills to exhibit them in a public forum, I've gladly volunteered for cleanup duty at the annual spaghetti dinner fundraiser for the Lutheran Women's Missionary League. "Gladly" is maybe an exaggeration. But when I asked, "Why don't we use paper plates and plastic cutlery?" and received the withering glare and "We always use *real* plates and cutlery for the LWML Spaghetti Dinner," I then willingly applied for the job of operating the industrial sprayer, garbage disposal, and dishwasher.

Marianne Pryce is supposed to be back here with me, but she's been doing more circulating and socializing than sanitizing. Which is fine. I like Marianne a lot, but she likes to talk. A lot. And I'm a bigger fan of companionable silence than polite conversation between acquaintances, especially when doing something as tedious as this. I just want to do my part as quickly as possible so I can go home. And never eat spaghetti again.

"You can hold him, but you can't take him home! We're sort of attached to him!" I hear Brice saying jovially, his voice coming closer with each word. The door to the kitchen whooshes open and whispers shut, and his rubber-soled shoes squeak on the waxed floor. "You about done back here, my little scullery maid?" he calls before emerging from between the professional-grade ovens and stopping behind my left shoulder.

I continue spraying sauce and noodles from the mountain of plates still in the sink in front of me, the disposal gurgling contentedly with each helping I give it. Without looking at him, I say, "Are people still eating out there?"

"A few."

"Then, no. I'm not almost done. Who's holding Max?"

"Vivian," he answers then pushes on my shoulder when I squeak sympathetically for my baby. "Be nice. She's not going to eat him."

"How do you know? She can unhinge her jaw, you know. I've seen it."

"Shhhh!" He looks over his shoulder to make sure no one's slipped into the kitchen without our realizing it. "I thought I'd come back here and keep you company, offer a hand if you needed it. Were we finished talking last night when I got sidetracked?"

In reply, I rotate my wrist so that the sprayer shoots water over my shoulder and hits him in the face.

"Hey!"

"Sorry."

"You did that on purpose!"

"Maybe. Payback for last night."

He laughs and pats my back. "Oh, hon. That's what I was afraid of. All of a sudden, you were gone, but I wasn't sure how long you'd been gone, and I couldn't even remember the last thing we said. Then it was late, so when I came to bed, you were out of it."

"You were in the zone," I excuse him. "We were basically finished talking. There's nothing more to say, really." I keep my eyes down on the plates.

"Well, I definitely don't want you worrying about what Ben said."

The old me would lie and say I wasn't worried. The sort-of-new me resists the urge to give him the answer he wants and says more candidly, "I'll try not to." I give him another quick mist for good measure.

He wipes his face without missing a beat in the conversation. "Worrying's not going to solve anything. And there's nothing to even worry about. What's the worst that can happen?"

"Hmmm. Let's see." I rattle off what's been going through my head since leaving the PCC last night: "Everyone could find out that I had a one-night stand with a gay man that resulted in a pregnancy and that you fell in love with me anyway, despite my immoral behavior and revulsive condition, and they most certainly will judge both of us harshly and might possibly defrock you."

"'Defrock' me? Wrong denomination."

"Whatever. You know what I mean."

"Not really. Anyway, how would any of this come to light—and in such harsh detail? Calm dow—"

A clink behind us makes both of us spin toward the sound. We're confronted with Marianne's back, her shoulders tense and bunched up toward her ears. She's frozen, as if she thinks we won't see her if only she stays still enough.

Brice clears his throat and rubs the back of his neck. His wet hair stands up in spikes over his forehead, and his collar is noticeably darker than the rest of his shirt, thanks to my assaults with the sprayer.

Motionless, I stare at her back until I realize I'm spraying water straight down onto my sneakers.

"Oh!" I quickly turn back to the sink and turn off the water and the disposal. The relative quiet is oppressive. Only the occasional clank of dishes glancing gently against each other in the faintly humming dishwasher competes with the sound of my heart pounding in my ears. Somehow I get the nerve to face the room—and the music.

When Marianne turns, she reveals her bright magenta face and an armload of stacked dishes and cutlery. She haltingly explains, "I wasn't trying to eavesdrop. I wasn't even trying to be quiet when I came in here, but I guess because of the water and the… the… thingy making all that noise, you didn't hear me, and so when I realized I was hearing a private conversation, I turned to leave and planned to make more noise when I came back in, so you'd know I was here, but… but…"

She rests the plates between her right arm and hip and

lifts her left hand, which is holding a utensil. "This damn fork—" She presses her fist against her mouth and blushes even further (which I didn't think was physically possible). "Oh, shit! Sorry. I didn't mean to cuss, Pastor!"

"I'm so used to it," he mutters, but then smiles and says more loudly, "Please, Marianne, don't worry about it. You didn't hear anything private."

She deposits her burden onto the metal counter with a clatter and wipes her arms and hands on her apron. "Yeah, I think I did, actually."

I'm way too focused on literally not shitting my pants or hyperventilating or fainting or all of the above to add to this conversation. What have I done? What was I thinking? Why did I have to say all that and at such a loud volume, to be heard over the racket of the disposal and the dishwasher? What in my history led me to believe that no one would hear me? Someone *always* hears me. I can't even mumble to myself in the grocery store about one brand of beans over the other without someone hearing and feeling the need to offer their two cents' worth.

But whether I'm willing to talk seems not to be important to the other two people in the room with me. Because they're both looking at me like nobody's going anywhere until I make some type of statement. All right, what are my options?

1. Cry. It's worked with nearly every impending traffic ticket I've faced. Except that one time, with that lady cop who didn't give a rat's ass that I was late to work on my first day back after maternity leave, because I didn't realize it was going to take two hours and a veritable miracle

to get from bed to desk when there was a
newborn in the equation. Heartless bitch.

2. Lie. Laugh and say, "You mean, what I just said?
Hahaha! That was an inside joke. We have a
contest going to make up stories about ourselves
that get more and more outrageous with each
telling. I'm winning!" Except there's no way
Brice will go along with lying. Damn him and his
principles.

3. Bribe. Plead and offer to pay her to never repeat
what she heard. No. I guess not. I don't have any
money (this stay-at-home-mom gig doesn't pay
worth a crap). Plus, I'm sure Brice wouldn't go
for that, either.

4. 'Fess up. And hope that she's merciful enough to
keep it to herself.

Who am I kidding? Number four's my only option.
Although, #1 might be happening whether I make a
conscious effort at it or not.

Before I can say anything, though, Marianne picks up
the plates and edges me away from the sink. "It's none of
my business," she says. I can feel the heat from her face,
which is still flaming. "I'll finish up in here. You and Pastor
and Max can go on home." She shoots me what seems to be
a genuinely kind smile.

When I don't move, she stops sorting plates from cutlery
and puts a damp hand on my forearm. "It's okay. I'm
embarrassed and would rather be alone. Please."

Brice pulls on my shoulder. "C'mon, Peyton. Marianne
has this under control. Thanks, Marianne."

"You're welcome," she quickly says. "See you tomorrow
morning at PoP."

The thought of having to face everyone tomorrow morning, after they've most likely heard what Marianne overheard, is almost too much to handle. Now I blush and tear up. "Oh," I breathe, no longer physically able to continue resisting Brice's efforts to lead me from the kitchen. I guess she doesn't need me to tell her right now that I won't be at PoP tomorrow; it'll make sense when I don't show up.

In the gymnasium, where all the tables are set up, the women sitting near Vivian and Max try to engage me in conversation when Brice and I appear, but I walk past them without even glancing in their direction. I make it to the gym doors at a near-run, leaving Brice to make whatever technically honest excuse he can make for me while he stops to get Max.

They'll find out the whole truth and nothing but the truth soon enough, I'm sure.

17

UNCOMFORTABLE KNOWLEDGE

I can't believe I'm here. I can't believe I allowed Brice to manipulate me into coming here today. I was weak after a sleepless night which I, unfortunately, couldn't blame on something as endearing as Max. Brice's arguments at breakfast, before my first full cup of coffee, seemed so reasonable at the time. Now, they seem like madness, the insane ramblings of a naïve—albeit cute —fool.

"Marianne's probably more embarrassed for herself than anything. I bet she won't tell anyone what happened or what she heard. Well, maybe she'll tell Clark, but he's a good guy, not one to gossip. Anyway, what you said could have been interpreted several ways. For all she knows, she misheard or misunderstood. She wouldn't pass along infor- mation if she didn't have all the facts. Plus she's ashamed that she used profanity in front of me—which, if she only knew."

I eventually tuned him out, so when he came to a stop and uttered an affirmation-seeking, "Okay?" I reflexively replied, "Yeah, okay," like a moron, so it wouldn't be obvious that I hadn't been listening to him as I fretted and stewed and tried to trick myself into believing that Marianne would come to any conclusion but the truth after overhearing our conversation last night.

He looked across the table at me with a mixture of affection and pride as a smile broke out across his face. "Good. That's the right thing to do." Then he went back to attacking his raisin bran.

It took some creative conversational skills to puzzle out what I'd agreed to do that was so "right," but I eventually came to the sick realization that I would be attending PoP, as if everything were business as usual.

So here I am. Max is hanging out with his dad for the hour, since Brice didn't have any appointments and will only be making final adjustments to Sunday's service. That's good, because I don't want my son to see the disapproving looks everyone will be sure to direct my way. He's the only person on the planet who still thinks I'm perfect. I'd like to keep it that way for a few more months.

Normally, I'm one of the last people to arrive at the classroom where PoP meets. That's because I tend to linger in Brice's office until the last possible minute before trudging through the hallways and into the Sunday school wing. Today, though, right after I set Max's carrier on the couch, Pastor Long rapped his knuckles against Brice's door and said, "Knock, knock!" in that annoying way that never fails to make me grit my teeth. I mean, isn't the sound of his knocking enough? We get it! The verbal knocks are superfluous and obnoxious, like him.

Before he could say or ask anything further to get my blood boiling, I mumbled a hello and goodbye in nearly one breath and made for the door. As I walked past him, I didn't even look up to see the expression on his face. Frankly, I was afraid of what I might see there, in addition to the usual disdain and disapproval. If he's already heard about my past through the rumor mill, then that would surely be a new reason for him to look down his nose at me.

But now I've gone from being in the company of one challenging person to another, as Paul's the only one in the classroom when I arrive. I take a seat with a clear view of the door. The knots in my stomach become tighter and tighter the longer I wait for the other moms to show up, but it doesn't seem as if Paul has any knowledge of what happened last night at the spaghetti dinner. That stands to reason, though; he and Marianne clash often in this group, so I can't imagine he'd be one of the first people she'd tell. It'll filter down to him eventually, but it won't come directly from Marianne.

While I breathe deeply and try to talk myself out of running from the room, Paul sets an array of what appears to be children's books, toys, and coloring books on a long table that makes up one side of the square in which the chairs are arranged today. I wonder if he'll still call it the Parents' *Circle*.

Even though I haven't asked, he explains, "I brought an example of some things to put in church-time activity bags to keep little ones occupied during the sermon. I've noticed that some children are having trouble being still and quiet lately. Not yours, though," he quickly qualifies. "Max is such an angel during church. How do you get him to be so good?"

I shrug and answer, "He likes church. Must be in his DN or something."

"It's not in my daughters' DNA," he says, producing the understatement of the decade (at least) as he straightens a plush toy and avoids my eye contact.

I wish I could muster a believable denial of what he's said, but his twin four-year-old girls, Dara and Sara, are the most disruptive of the bunch. They argue and cry during the sermon; they play tug of war with the offering plate; and they escape from Paul and his wife, Crystal, every chance they get, usually on the way back from Communion. Sara even punched Brice in the crotch once during a children's homily. Well, she tried. Fortunately, her aim was off, and his reflexes were fast enough that her fist glanced off his thigh. But still. The intent was clear.

"So today we're going to discuss some alternatives to being cooped up in that cluttered closet this church likes to call a cry room," Paul declares with a smug smile.

I'm about to defend the comfortable room, equipped with sofas and rockers, three cribs, changing tables, toys, and a closed-circuit TV so nobody has to miss a minute of the service due to a cranky child, but the other moms start to trickle in, so I decide to save the argument for later. I have to concentrate and analyze everyone's interactions with me, in order to try to determine how much they know. So far, nothing seems out of the ordinary. I get hellos, followed by each woman going back to their original conversations.

That's the pattern, that is, until Marianne arrives. She comes through the door, looks around the room, sees me, blushes, immediately looks away, and takes one of the available seats furthest away from me. I grab my purse from the floor and pretend to look for something in it in an effort to hide the tears of shame and frustration that I can feel building.

And why? Why am I so worried about what people—these people in particular—think? I wasn't concerned when Jason and Dustin came to visit, and I introduced them to everyone at Peace as, "my brother, Jason, and his partner,

Dustin," because that's what they are. I didn't even consider calling Dustin "Jason's friend" or some other truth-skirting euphemism. I know it raised some eyebrows, but I didn't give a damn what anyone else thought.

This is different, somehow.

Suddenly, the air next to me shifts as someone takes the seat to my left. I blink my eyes and look up to smile at the newcomer. It's Marianne. My smile involuntarily slides from my face.

"Uh, hi, Marianne," I mutter.

She shoots me her own shaky facsimile of a friendly greeting. "Hey. I, uh, I'm glad to see you this morning."

I can't help but laugh. "Are you sure about that?"

Chuckling, she says, "Well, maybe not at first, but, yes. Because I want to talk to you."

My stomach clenches. "Oh. I guess I know what you want to talk about, but…" I hope the look I give her conveys the appropriate level of regret when I state, "It's not something I talk about—to anyone but Brice."

"All right, ladies!" Paul booms from the middle of the square. "Let's get started. Lots to discuss today, including a very exciting announcement! In case you haven't already heard, the Board of Elders, the Board of Trustees, and the church as a whole decided at the last voters' meeting to go forward with construction of Peace's new daycare facility!"

He pauses while we clap our hands, some more enthusiastically than others.

"Now, I know this doesn't affect most of us," he continues, assuming his most condescending expression, "but this is a great option for those families who choose to lead a two-income lifestyle and need quality, Christian care for their little darlings. If they can't have Mommy or Daddy, then this is the next best option, and we praise God for that." Again, he leads the clapping.

During the applause, Marianne leans closer to me and whispers, "I understand. Totally. I don't necessarily mean that I want to talk about *that*. Just that I want to talk about what happened last night in the kitchen—"

"Ladies!" Paul looks pointedly at us. "I know this is exciting, especially for working moms like you, Marianne, but we really must focus and move on to our next topic."

She shoots him a dirty look, but he's already walked away, approaching the table and gesturing to the items on it.

"Sermon Sack!" He holds aloft a canvas tote bag with those two words embroidered on its front. "Isn't it cute? I came up with the idea myself. I thought we could each donate some gently used plush toys and books—and maybe even coloring books and crayons—to make up a few sets of these for parents with small children to pick up on their way into the sanctuary. That way, the kids will have something to keep them occupied during the service, especially during those *long* sermons, which—let's face it, ladies—are sometimes difficult for adults to sit through, much less little ones. Am I right?"

I'm still considering Marianne's whispered request when what Paul's said trickles through. I tense as it occurs to me that he may have made a tiny dig at my husband's sermons.

Before I can even decide how—or if—I'm going to react, Marianne pipes up confidently, "*Or* people could use the cry room when their children get restless. I seem to remember donating more than one of my Saturdays to converting that room from a storage area to what it is now, which is quite nice and comfortable. I wish more people would use it."

A woman named Karen, to whom I've only talked a

handful of times, chimes in. "I don't know. I kinda like the idea of a Sermon Sack." Paul beams at her. "I mean, sometimes it's not that Michael is being bad enough that I have to take him to the cry room, but he does get antsy. It's not disruptive to the people around us, because he's quiet, but it's distracting to me. Something to keep him entertained would be nice."

"Yeah. And it'd be nice for it to be something that stays here at the church, so I'm not lugging a bunch of our own stuff back and forth," Janie adds.

Olivia crosses her arms over her chest. "I think we're not teaching our children how to be still and *listen* if we're giving them things to play with in church. Church isn't playtime."

"Then you don't *have* to use them," Paul says with exaggerated patience. "But they should be available for parents who would like to try them out. Anyway, like I said before, it's unreasonable to expect anyone under the age of six to sit still for *that* long and listen. They don't have the attention span to do it, even if they wanted to."

"Maybe we expect too little sometimes," Olivia argues. "I hate to sound old, but when I was a kid, it was a given that I would sit still in church and listen—or else. So, I learned quickly how to do it. I wasn't allowed to play with toys in church, and the only 'cry room' I ever saw was the ladies' bathroom, where my mom would take me to spank me if I caused trouble during the service."

"Times have changed, sweetie," Paul replies patronizingly. "We don't spank our children for acting on impulses that are age-appropriate. We don't spank our children at all, I hope."

Marianne snorts. "Maybe 'we' should."

He rolls his eyes. "The point is, I think it would be nice to have this *option*."

"I think we're setting a poor example," Olivia maintains.

"I agree," says Marianne. "We already have a lot of options. There's a staffed nursery, where you can take your kids if you don't feel it's age-appropriate for them to sit through grown-up church; there's the cry room; and there's good old-fashioned, 'If you're not quiet, you'll spend the afternoon in your room when we get home.'"

Paul holds up the canvas bag in his hand. "And now there's another option: Sermon Sacks!"

"And if those don't work?"

All eyes swivel to me. My heart rate increases exponentially. It was my plan to keep a low profile today, like I usually do (or have, since my first, disastrous showing) but twice now Paul has implied a criticism that the church services are too long and boring, particularly the sermons. And I don't appreciate someone—anyone—hinting that not everything my husband does is wonderful (anyone but me, that is. I'm allowed; I wash his underwear).

Paul lifts his eyebrows in query. "Pardon? I guess I don't understand—"

"If your Sermon Satchels"—the screw-up is intentional —"fail to keep kids in line, then what? Maybe we should ask the pastors to perform song-and-dance numbers with catchy, kid-friendly lyrics. Or maybe our kids are getting their cues from us. You said it yourself, Paul, that sometimes it's even hard for adults to stay focused during the sermon. Maybe some of us view our children's antics as a welcome distraction from the droning going on behind the pulpit. Maybe we should provide Sermon Satchels for the adults, too. Purely an *option*, of course. I mean, some people simply have short attention spans. We can't expect everyone to be still and listen for twelve whole minutes once a week, right?"

"More like fifteen or twenty," he mumbles.

"Twelve, Paul! Twelve. Trust me. Time it out this Sunday, if you don't believe me." His contradiction and interruption make my temper burn hotter. "Of course, I suppose anything we provide in the adults' activity bags couldn't compete with the toys they already have at their fingertips, literally. Yeah, I've noticed people texting and tapping away at their phones and iPods—in silent mode, obviously—during church, sometimes pretending they're keeping a young child amused, other times being blatant about keeping themselves amused. What's next? Interactive video game sermons? Would that hold everyone's attention better? Because, apparently, God's word isn't cutting it. Is that what we're saying? Is that the message we want to give to our children? 'Don't worry about trying to listen to what Pastor's saying. Read this book instead. Color this picture. Play with this doll. Check the Sermon Satchel for better things to do.'"

"Sermon Sack," he finally corrects me. Then he claps his hands together once and says after a deep breath and with wide eyes, "Okay, then. We'll make a note of your opinion of the Sermon Sack, Peyton. I guess we can assume your husband will have the same opinion, when it's proposed to him."

The assumption that I'm merely Brice's mouthpiece infuriates me further. Although Paul's trying to move onto the next topic, I stop him. "I'm sorry, Paul, but I want to make sure everyone here—including you—knows that my husband's viewpoints are not necessarily mine, and vice versa."

"Okay. Moving on, then."

"No! Please. I'm not finished."

"But we have other things to discuss and not much more time," he insists, looking down at the list in his hands.

I pick up my purse from the floor and stand. "Oh, in that case, never mind," I spit, walking toward the door. "I just thought, since we often spend upwards of thirty minutes on topics like 'Soy versus Dairy: Which is the Bigger Evil?' it would be okay to spend a bit more time on something as important as methods for teaching our children how to feed their spiritual sides. My bad."

I storm from the room and don't look back to see what I'm sure are expressions of disbelief, mostly in regards to my sanity. Screw them.

It takes approximately thirty seconds for me to reconsider my rant and agree with those who may now have serious doubts about my mental wellbeing. By the time I get to Brice's office, barely pausing for Lucy's acknowledgement—since I can see through the open door that the most pressing thing on my husband's agenda at the moment is the dirty diaper he's changing on his desk (yuck!)—and I close the door behind me, it's painfully clear to me that…

"I've lost my mind. For real. I have officially, absolutely—"

"What'd you do this time?" he asks calmly without looking up from the task at hand.

Upon closer inspection, I'm relieved to see that he has a changing pad protecting his desk from Max's science project. I'm also relieved that I can still care about something as mundane as the risk of fecal contamination. Surely, that's a sign that I'm not too far gone, right? On the other hand, it's a horrible sign that Brice is using the same tone of voice with me right now that he often used with Jared.

There's no use breaking it to him gently. "I had a major

case of verbal diarrhea during PoP. As a matter of fact, I'm never going back there."

As if it's a choice! I've probably been blacklisted.

He sets Max's balled-up dirty diaper aside and, positioning a clean one under the baby's bottom, nods briefly toward the door. "You mind opening that?"

"Yes, I mind! I don't want anyone hearing us."

He coughs. "Please. I'm dying here."

I roll my eyes at his low tolerance for bad smells but honor his request. Then I walk closer to him so we can continue our conversation without Lucy overhearing. At a near-whisper, I say, "I blew up at Paul when he proposed providing activity bags for young kids to have during your boring sermons."

He raises an eyebrow and laughs. "Well!"

"I don't know what got into me! I was *furious* at him! And now that I think about it, the stupid activity bags—Sermon Sacks, he calls them—wouldn't be the worst things in the world, but—"

"Would they keep *his* kids quiet?" he asks, pulling Max's tiny jeans up and lifting the baby to his shoulder. "Because, quite frankly, I'm getting ready to have a talk with him and Crystal. Not only am I getting complaints from other members, but even *I've* been distracted a couple of times lately by the antics going on out there. That hasn't happened since I was still in Sem."

"Whatever. That's not the point! The point is that I shit all over his idea then got up on my soapbox about noisy kids and clueless parents and adults with microscopic attention spans, and everyone stared at me with their mouths hanging open. It was worse than the time I accused Paul of conspiring with you to trick me." I think about it for a second. "Well, maybe not. But it was still bad."

"Temper, temper," Brice scolds mildly, looking more amused than anything. Over my shoulder, he suddenly directs, "So, was it as bad as she's saying, Marianne?"

I whirl around to see that Marianne has, indeed, arrived.

"Oh, buh-rother." This nightmare just refuses to end.

She laughs at his question. "Well, it got everyone's attention. It's definitely the most any of us has ever heard Peyton say at one time."

I groan and eye my feet.

Marianne pulls on my elbow. "Come on. I think you need to go to lunch." She abruptly stills and sniffs. "Oh, my!"

Brice holds up the offensive diaper. "Yeah. Sorry about that. You guys can take this with you on your way out."

"I don't want to go to lunch," I blurt, looking back and forth between the two of them. "I mean, maybe some other time. I just want to go home."

She sighs. "Please? I need you to go to lunch with me. Think of it as a public service."

When I look to him for assistance, Brice stares blankly at me and merely says, "I don't care what you do, as long as you take that diaper with you."

18

A NEW ALLY

We go to the same place where Brice and I ate lunch with several families—including Marianne's—when we came to visit Peace for the first time. In many ways, that seems like a lifetime ago. In other ways, it feels like we'll always be "new" here. And being in this restaurant intensifies that feeling, because I remember exactly what I was thinking all those months ago: *I would* never *fit in here.*

At the time, it was a vague, nagging notion, since moving to Springfield seemed like such a remote possibility. To me, this town was like a pair of $600 orange stilettos: ridiculously impractical, horribly uncomfortable, and not my style. If only I'd known that I'd be wearing those shoes every single day for the foreseeable future.

In all fairness, life here has gotten more comfortable; I guess you could say I've broken in the shoes somewhat. There are benefits to being a member of a church family like Peace. Brice was right about never worrying about the church's budget. He's hardly talked about it at all. It's a non-issue. And that's incredibly refreshing and a huge relief, especially compared to the constant financial messes he had to deal with at Messiah.

Also refreshing are the people. Most of Peace's members are truly as happy and nice as they seemed during our first visit. Once I accepted that, the creepy vibe I experienced that weekend faded away. For every Pastor and Vivian Long there are three couples or families who are remarkably friendly and genuine; Brice hasn't had a whisper of trouble from the Board of Elders or any of the other church officers; Ben has been helpful and a joy to work with; and I'm even starting to warm to Lucy and her simple ways.

As a matter of fact, since Jared's pep talk last week, things have been looking up. But now, all the old issues are resurfacing. It feels like they're going to haunt me for the rest of my life, no matter what I do or where I go.

After we order our drinks, and I get Max settled in Marianne's arms with a bottle (she says she feels naked without a baby in her arms, so I gladly volunteer to "clothe" her with mine), she immediately says, "I know what I heard last night was none of my business—*is* none of my business—and I'd be lying if I said I wasn't curious to know more, but before we talk about anything, I want you to know that I won't ever tell anyone—even Clark—what I heard, without your permission. And I won't ask you to tell me more. Period."

I poke at my silverware wrapped in its paper napkin and study the veins in my hands. "Thanks," I reply quietly. "I appreciate that."

"And I hope you'll return the favor."

The smile in her voice makes me look up.

"Huh?" I tilt my head.

She chuckles and blushes. "You know. You won't tell anyone about the words I said when you and Pastor turned around and saw me."

I laugh. "You're kidding, right?"

"No! I'm still mortified! I can't believe that happened."

Shaking my head, I say, "Well, I'll gladly take that deal. I'll keep your big secret that you said some mild curse words, and you keep mine. Yeah. That's fair."

"I cuss all the time, though," she confesses in a silly mutter from the side of her mouth. "It's kind of my biggest weakness."

I never thought that such a simple admission could make me so happy. Suddenly feeling weightless and exuberant, like a kid on the last day of school, I say, "Me, too! Only, it's not really my *biggest* weakness. I wish!"

She waves a hand. "Oh, it's probably not mine, either. But it's a pretty unladylike habit. It's one of those things, though, that makes me *feel* better. If I'm mad or sad or frustrated, I always feel a little less of those things after I drop a dirty word. It's dumb."

"But effective."

"Yes!" She giggles. "Well, there you have it. I talk like a sailor. And then I kiss my daughter with that same mouth."

"I can keep a secret."

"Whew!" She sets Max's bottle on the table and sits him up to burp him. When he gratifies her with a juicy one right away, she says, "Oh, yeah! I feel so much better now, too!" She helps him continue with his lunch then tells me while still looking down at him, "Just so you know, I might have to kidnap this guy. He is unbelievably precious."

I grin over the table at them. "Thanks. I love how much he looks like Brice. It blows my mind."

Eyes wide, she glances up at me. "I know! No one would ever know he's not Pastor's son!"

"What?"

She holds up a hand. "I know, I know; you don't want to

talk about it, but I have to say—and then I'll shut up—I was shocked when I heard you say it last night."

"Say what?"

Looking slightly less certain, she nevertheless answers, "You know, that Max is the result of—I mean, Max's dad is… someone else."

Horrified she got that from what she overheard, I have to work hard to modulate my voice when I say, "That's *not* what I said! At all. There haven't been any other *partners* in my life since I've been married."

She blushes. "Oh, gosh. I'm sorry. I— I assumed—"

"You assumed wrong."

"Because this is the only baby you have, so…"

Our server arrives with our drinks, so I can't immediately set her straight. Not that I know exactly what to say. Do I want to tell her *everything*? I have to, don't I? Otherwise, who knows what other assumptions she'll wind up making?

The server asks us if we're ready to order. I'm not hungry, but I end up ordering the first thing I see on the menu that doesn't make me want to hurl (a bacon cheeseburger with fries) and sit back to recover while Marianne virtuously orders a salad.

By the time we're alone again, I'm calm enough to say, "I'm sorry I snapped at you."

"Let's change the subject," she suggests, looking like she's on the verge of tears. "I didn't invite you to lunch to insult you or pry into your personal life or—"

"I know you didn't." I take a deep breath. "I'm a skosh touchy when it comes to this topic, but I'd rather grit my teeth and fill in some blanks for you than have you incorrectly fill them in yourself."

"No. Please. I think I get it."

Remembering how Jared thought he understood, too,

and came to the incorrect conclusion that I'd undergone a procedure to avoid being a parent, I insist, "Really. I want to make sure."

I collect my thoughts while I sip my water, then say, "My first pregnancy—the one you overheard me talking about last night—ended in a stillbirth."

She nods sadly.

I know that doesn't explain everything she heard, so I continue, "And at the time, Brice and I weren't together, but we had feelings for each other that were more than platonic. A few months later, we started officially dating, I guess you can say, although it was a while before we told people we were seeing each other. *Not* sneaking around; just not broadcasting it. Because I was worried that people would make things difficult for him, since I was not the most virtuous person, and everyone at Messiah knew it, because they knew my whole story. Well, for the most part. They didn't know about my baby's father, but they knew enough. And when we moved here, I thought…"

"Nobody here knows. And there's no *reason* for us to know."

"Right. It's been nice. I didn't realize how much it bothered me that so many people at our other church knew. On the other hand, it's been hard, knowing there's such a big part of my past—a part of *me*—that's hidden, waiting to be uncovered."

She removes the empty bottle from Max's mouth. Draping a burp cloth over her shoulder, she smoothly lifts him to it and pats his back. "Wait a minute, though. What were you supposed to do, write an item about it in the weekly newsletter? This isn't something that comes up in conversation, any more than the fact that I took ballet in grade school. It's not that you're *hiding* it."

"Yes, I sort of am."

"No, you're not," she firmly defends me.

"Don't you think this is something you would have wanted to know before you called Brice to be your Senior Pastor?"

She thinks about it for a second, then says, "No. We called him, not you. And unless the two of you are doing something *illegal* in your private life, it should remain that: private."

"It's wrong to keep secrets," I mutter at my lap.

"It's *normal*. It would be weird if you disclosed all your personal business. And uncomfortable. It's not that you're keeping secrets; you're being discreet. There's a difference."

After another hefty burp from Max, she hands him back to me. I fish a teething ring from his diaper bag and hold it for him while he gums it.

As drool slides down my hand and into my sweater sleeve, I ask tentatively, "Would you rather not know what you know now?"

She laughs. "Uh, yeah! Because I feel like any chance we may have had at being friends is ruined."

"Why?" I feel the blood drain from my face.

She looks out the window, squinting at the bright sun bouncing off the cars in the parking lot. "Not because I think less of you or differently about you than I did before. Mostly because I feel it's unfair that I know something so personal about you, against your wishes. Even if I told you a bunch of private stuff about myself right now, it wouldn't be the same; we still wouldn't be even. Because I'd be telling you voluntarily."

I wipe my hand on my pants leg. "True. But why would that keep us from being friends?" Suddenly, I realize how desperately lonely I am for female companionship.

On a shrug, she declares while bringing her focus back to my face, "Well, it wouldn't stop me, but I have a feeling it would be an issue for you."

When I don't know what to say to that, she explains, "You're so closed-off! And now I guess I understand why you are. No offense, but your church in Chicago sounds like it was awful!"

"It wasn't!" I try to be as fair to Messiah as possible while also being accurate. "It was a much smaller church. I knew those people my whole life. We were a true church *family*. We fought like brothers and sisters. But they were also some of the most loyal people I've ever known. It's hard to explain."

"I think I know what you're saying," she says. "Peace isn't like that, though. We don't *know* each other on that level. We don't aim to know each other on that level, either. I feel like maybe you're expecting us—*me*—to be digging for dirt every time we have a conversation."

Max fusses, so I shift his position and rock him, hoping he'll fall asleep before our food arrives.

In response to her assessment, I say, "Well, when you have dirt to be dug up. Anyway, I'm a guarded person, in general. I can't help it. I didn't realize it was so obvious, though. I've made a conscious effort to be more open and friendly here." At her raised eyebrow, I groan. "I know! It's obviously not working, but you don't have any frame of reference."

"What? Did you refuse speak at your other church? Ever?" She nudges my foot under the table so I'll know she's joking.

For once, I don't immediately jump on the defensive. Instead, I answer, "Talking tends to get me into trouble, as you witnessed this morning. I'm not very diplomatic. But

I'm trying to be more gracious, like a proper pastor's wife. It's not working out very well, so far."

She sucks diet soda through her straw and looks at me through her lashes. After swallowing, she says, "Well, maybe Vivian Long can tutor you about how to be the perfect pastor's wife. She's an expert; just ask her."

I want so badly to take the bait and have a good, old-fashioned bitch-fest at Vivian's expense, but I know it wouldn't be right. Pretending Brice is sitting at the table with us helps me resist, and I take aim at myself, instead. "Someone needs to teach me, because I'm sure not gettin' it the way I'm going at it now. It'd be nice if there was a book. Maybe *Pastors' Wives for Dummies*?"

Marianne's laugh startles Max from his doze, but he quickly succumbs to his heavy lids once more after she covers her mouth to stifle it. "Sorry," she whispers.

I wave off her apology. "Come to think of it, maybe *I'll* write that book, based on the opposite of everything I've done so far."

Despite what she's found out about me in the past two days, she actually thinks I'm kidding.

19

GIRLS' WEEKEND

Being a stay-at-home mom is an important job that's often rewarding. I suppose I get personal satisfaction from a good day at it. And I take it seriously. But maybe I'm not doing it correctly. Because if I were, I'd be a lot busier, wouldn't I? I mean, I hear and read about these super-moms whose lives are way more hectic and jammed-packed than mine ever was when I had a full-time paying job outside the home. What are they doing that I'm not?

Granted, my child is currently still just past the "blob" stage. I recognize that. We're not driving back and forth across town to get to classes and activities. Our typical day generally consists of "hanging out." He takes two two-hour naps each day, during which I lazily plan what we're going to have for dinner, fold and put away laundry, sleep, or if I'm desperate, watch TV. I spend another two hours, total, feeding him, dressing him, and diapering him. And that's a conservative estimate. On Mondays, we go grocery shopping before his morning nap. Thursdays, we attend PoP meetings.

Lately, I've also jazzed up our weekly schedule with some

play dates with Marianne and Jessica, but because of her freelancing, Marianne's not a typical SAHM. When Jessica's napping, she doesn't watch *Ellen* or paint her toenails or sleep. She works at her other job. She goes to the trouble to find a babysitter for Jessica once a week and comes to PoP for one reason: to avoid going bat-shit stir crazy.

My life is so boring that I've started looking forward to PoP meetings (I wasn't blacklisted), even though I sit through them without contributing a single thing, especially since the Sermon Sack incident. Simply being out of the house and listening to adult people converse with each other—even about topics and issues that have me often resisting the urge to roll my eyes—is a welcome change from the tedium of the rest of the day.

So, when Max and I aren't doing the handful of things we do every day at the same time, we play "let's fill the hours until Dad gets home." Sometimes we go to the park. Other times, we play in the backyard. On rainy days, we read books and sing songs, and the hours drag by. He's usually fussy on those days. I think even he realizes our life is boring.

Brice's life, on the other hand, is far from boring.

"Are you going to miss me?" he casually asks, precisely folding four pairs of underwear and placing them in the open suitcase on our bed, where I'm seated, cross-legged, watching him pack for his three-day trip to Kansas City. He'll be attending a pastor's conference and guest preaching at a Lenten service at a church in Overland Park.

"Of course!" I answer. "Wait a minute. Why are you packing four pairs of underwear, when you only need two changes of clothes?"

"Just in case," he replies, as if it's obvious.

I laugh. "What do you mean, 'just in case'? Do you often

have accidents that require a change—or two—of underwear? Should I be worried?"

He tosses one black and one navy blue clerical shirt in the suitcase and says with a matter-of-fact sniff, "No, but the one time I don't prepare for such an event, it's bound to happen, so I always pack two extra pairs."

"You do? How have I never noticed this?"

"I don't know. Because it's not normal to count and analyze something like that, maybe?"

"You're calling *me* abnormal?"

"I know; it usually goes without saying."

"Uh!"

He grins and sticks out his tongue from the corner of his mouth while glancing up at me and tossing some socks on top of his underwear. "Oh, shitake mushrooms! You're distracting me. I forgot to pack white t-shirts."

Considering his suitcase is still open, I'm not sure how he considers the shirts "forgotten," which I point out.

"Well, they have to go under the socks and underwear, so now I have to take stuff out and repack," he explains.

After staring at him in disbelief for a few seconds, I say, "You're a dork. Just toss in some white shirts."

"No! They have to lie flat at the bottom! On the left side of the suitcase. Under the socks and underwear." He's grinning in acknowledgement of his peculiarity but taking out his skivvies to make room for the shirts, exactly as he's described.

My laughter has a nervous edge to it. "You're freaking me out a tad bit."

"This is how I always pack."

"I guess I've never had the pleasure of observing you before. It's a psychological study in crazy."

He finishes his rearranging, takes a deep, self-satisfied

breath, puts his hands on his hips, and looks down into the suitcase. "It's not crazy to be right." He nods once, pleased with the work he's done so far. Then he mutters, "Toiletries," and spins toward the bathroom. From there, he calls, "Are you sure you don't want my mom to come stay with you while I'm gone? She'd love it."

I rub my face while I answer this question for about the twentieth time. "I'm sure. Mitzi and Jen are coming, remember?"

He grunts while rooting around in the medicine cabinet.

"Other than that," I continue, "it's not going to be *that* different without you here."

When he pokes his head around the bathroom doorframe and shoots me an outraged look, I laugh and clarify, "I only mean that you're always gone during the day, so the evenings will be the only times that seem different. Plus, I can handle it. You think I can't handle it?"

"I didn't say that," he says, retreating, his voice echoing off the tile. "Did I say that?"

"No," I say sullenly. "It seems like maybe you're worried I can't, though."

He tosses some things in his overnight kit and zips it, placing it on the edge of the sink, where he can grab it in the morning right before heading out the door. "Well, nobody does bath time like I do," he concedes smugly, coming back into our room and carefully setting his open suitcase on the floor, up against the wall. He slinks toward the bed. "And I've heard Max likes the way I do *his* bath time, too."

I laugh as he slides across the mattress on his belly and nibbles playfully on my knee. "We'll both manage somehow until Thursday."

"Do you remember the bath time song that Mr. Bubbles sings? You have to sing the bath time song."

"I'll sing it," I promise.

"You have to do it exactly like I do, though, so that Max will give you his belly laugh. It's so cute!" He stares off into space for a second before adding, "Oh, and don't forget to squeal, 'Naked baby!' while you're drying him off. Or sing 'Stand up, Stand up for Jesus,' when you're putting his pajamas on. He loves that."

I pull on his hair. "Why don't you commute from Kansas City each night so you can make sure it's done right?"

He sighs. "I would if I could."

"What's your problem? You love these Nerdfests—I mean, Pastors' Conferences!"

"I don't want to go."

"Once you get there, you'll have a good time."

He shrugs his shoulders, flips onto his back, and rests his head in my lap. Looking up at me, he says, "I know. But I— I have a bad feeling. I'm all *uneasy* for some reason. I can't put my finger on it, though."

"Your suitcase is fine," I tease.

Swatting at my face, he claims, "It's not about my suit-case. I'm being serious!"

"Well, you're making me nervous, so cut it out." I rub at the wrinkle on his forehead. "We're going to be fine. It's only three days. Mitzi and Jen will keep me occupied and mostly out of trouble. probably." When he shoots me a mock-worried look, I go back to safer claims. "And I promise to do bath time exactly like you would."

His fingers flutter against my cheek. "I know you will."

"Plus, you're only going to be two-and-a-half hours away. And I have a congregation full of people I can call if I need *anything*. Marianne and Clark live five minutes away. What else can I say to ease your mind?"

"I don't know," he says morosely.

"Oh! You recently replaced the batteries in all the smoke and carbon monoxide detectors, right?"

"Yeah."

"See? There you go. Everything's in order."

"I guess."

His worrying is making me worry. A lot. Because he doesn't worry. Ever. He prays, I worry. That's the arrangement we have going. It's worked just fine for years. Why is he screwing with the system now?

"I'll call you every night." He makes it sound like a threat.

"Bring it."

Finally, he smiles again as he backtracks coolly, "I mean, I'll try to remember to call before Vince and I go out."

"Trolling for women?"

"Nuns, mostly."

"Maybe you should pack more underwear."

"Seven-thirty is bedtime," I inform Mitzi as Jen and I are heading out the door to go to the PCC. She's sportingly agreed to babysit Max, who—barring any off-schedule dirty diapers—will be in bed soon and won't be much work at all. That's a good thing, too, because Mitzi has a Skype date with Jared in a few minutes that she doesn't want to miss. I was originally going to skip my Tuesday night volunteering gig, but after just one day with my two best friends, it's obvious they need some time apart, and this will serve as a nice diversion.

"Eight hours, Peyton," Jen is saying now as she buckles her seatbelt. "Eight solid hours, trapped in a car, talking about wedding shit. Two weeks after I've broken up with someone I thought I'd be planning a wedding with. It. Was. Torture."

I pat her shoulder sympathetically while navigating the neighborhood streets and pulling out onto one of the busy main roads. It seems like it's always rush hour in this town! "I'm sorry, babe. What happened with you and Mitch, anyway? You never have told me."

She sighs. "I got sick of hanging around his place, naked," she says shortly but laughs so I know that's not at all the reason they broke up. I also know that's all she's going to say on the matter. "The point is," she continues, "I'm not in the mood to listen to sappy lovebird talk. So thanks for letting me tag along tonight."

"No problem. It shouldn't take long with three of us working. And Ben's a nice guy. He and Brice have become relatively close friends."

She smirks. "Oh, great. Is he a dork, like Brice? Do I need to watch my mouth around him?"

Laughing, I answer, "It would be nice if you kept your potty mouth under control, but he's not a prude, if that's what you're asking. And neither is Brice!"

"La-la-la! I don't want to hear— Actually, I do. What *is* Brice like between the sheets?"

"That's *not* what I meant!" I blush but try to figure out why. We used to talk about this stuff all the time. I never shied away from kissing and telling on guys I dated. But I've never shared those details about Brice with anyone. Not Jen, not Mitzi, and definitely not Nicole. And I'm sorely out of practice, which is evident when I stutter, "W-well, he's… I don't know! H-he's wonderful. Of course."

She can hardly respond through her laughter. "Ohmigosh, don't spontaneously combust over there! It was a simple question from one girl to another."

"I know!" I reply defensively, trying—and failing—to become un-flustered. "It's just... I mean, I don't talk about it."

"Yeah, and it's weird. I was starting to think he was crap in the sack, because you never talk about it. Sex used to be your all-time favorite topic."

Still is. But it's repressed. I think about it all the time. But to whom am I going to talk about it? My closest Spring-field friend, Marianne, isn't *that* close. Plus, she's a member at Peace. And nobody wants to hear about their pastor's sex life. Thank goodness!

Now that I think about it, though, I do miss talking about it. Maybe it's a sad commentary on our conversa-tional skills, but some of the best discussions I ever had with Mitzi and Jen were about sex. And Brice deserves to be bragged on. I mean, he's no slouch. First of all, he looks great naked. And he does this thing every time that drives me wild (he knows it, too), but not because it's necessarily erotic, or anything. On the contrary, it's very sweet and tender. He...

Suddenly, the brake lights of the SUV in front of us are dangerously close to my windshield.

When we come to a screeching halt, mere inches before my headlights kiss the other vehicle's back bumper, Jen stares at my profile, then asks, "Are you going to be okay? What the hell is wrong with you?"

I smile weakly over at her and admit, "You've got me all worked up over here!"

"What? For real? You haven't even said anything interesting."

"I said some interesting things in my head," I confess with a giggle while fanning myself with my free hand as we continue toward the PCC.

She returns an evil chuckle. "Well, well, well. I knew it!"

"What did you know? A second ago, you said you thought maybe he was a bad lover, because I never talk about it."

Tapping her temple, she says, "Ah, yes. But then the more I thought about it, the more I realized that you'd be more apt to talk about it if he was shit, because it's so important to you. You'd be complaining all the time if he wasn't 'meeting your needs,' so to speak. So you're quiet about it, because it's so good, you want to keep it to yourself. Hoarder! C'mon! Details!"

I pull into the PCC parking lot and say mock-regretfully, "Oh, darn. We're here. No time to continue this super-awkward conversation. And Ben's already here, too. So you're going to drop this topic, because—"

"Ding dong!" she interjects as she watches Ben alight from his car. She slides her sunglasses lower onto her nose and leers at him over the top of them. "Tell me that's him."

"That's Ben," I confirm, grinning.

She clutches her hands to her chest. "Oh, wow. You didn't tell me he was hot!"

"Uh…" *Probably because I don't think he is,* I almost say but choose instead, "I guess it never came up in conversation."

"Shhh." She waves her hand dismissively at me while opening her door and exiting the car. "Hurry up and introduce us."

Ben shields his eyes from the setting sun and beams at us as we cross the parking lot to meet him at the side door. "Hey! Pastor told me you had company in town. I wasn't sure if you'd be here tonight."

"I honor my commitments," I assure him. Jen nudges me painfully in the side. "Ow! Ben, this is one of my best friends, Jen. Jen, Ben."

We all laugh at the rhyme, then Jen flirts, "Nice to meet you, Ben. Peyton hasn't told me a single thing about you. You must be her latest secret."

His smile fades while I blink and try to convey an apology with my eyes. But he's not looking at me. He says tightly as he holds the door open for us, "No. That wouldn't be the explanation."

Jen tries again. "I just can't believe she's never mentioned you before tonight. It's like she's trying to keep you to herself."

"Jen," I warn.

"Oh, he knows I'm only kidding," she assures me, even though it's obvious he has no clue. She stands in the middle of the garage area and looks around. "So, what are we doing tonight? Put me to work, Ben!"

Rebound Jen has definitely come out to play.

Things got a lot less awkward once we did get to work. Ben and I introduced Jen to our favorite game, Layette Hoops, where we toss items into the boxes from a few feet away and get a varying number of points, depending on the item. Ben always beats me at this game, but it helps to pass the time and makes a sometimes boring job fun, so it's become our Tuesday night tradition when we've been relegated to care package assembly. The more Ben explains the game to Jen, the more relaxed—and flirtatious—he becomes. She's enjoying the encouragement and the game.

"How much did we say onesies were worth again?" Jen

asks, pencil poised above the index card we're using as a score sheet.

"Only five points. But every point counts," I answer, more as a consolation to myself, since—as usual—I'm getting shellacked.

"I don't know why," she mutters. "He's kicking our ass —butts."

"You have a nice, kickable ass—butt, though," he says suggestively to her before clearing his throat, as if the statement escaped without his permission. He makes a big show of taking aim with a brick of baby wipes, and they land with a thud into his box. "This game is getting too easy. Tell me more about your college escapades," he requests.

She readily complies, launching into a long story about the time she, Mitzi, and I travelled three hours on a whim to go to a rock concert for which we didn't have tickets, with the idea that we'd buy some from scalpers once we arrived. The show was sold out, but Jen managed to get us backstage, where we hung out with the band before and after the show. It was my one and only stint as a groupie.

The more comfortable the two of them seem to be with each other, the quieter and looser I become. I'm glad they're getting along, because I'm not feeling the best I've ever felt. Maybe it's the mini-orgasm I had in the car earlier, but I'm still feeling all hot and sweaty, and I'm suddenly exhausted. There's also a building, all-too-familiar nausea in the pit of my stomach. Oh, man! I hope I'm not coming down with something. A bunch of parents in PoP were complaining of a stomach bug going through their households. It would be just my luck to catch something from one of them. Lent has barely begun, and the lead-up to Easter is such a busy time of year. I don't have time to be sick!

I'm pondering this dreadful possibility when uproarious

laughter grabs my attention. I look up to see that I'm the subject of their hilarity. "What?" I ask innocently.

"You look simple over there, staring at that spot on the floor," Jen says. "Ben asked you a question."

I shake my head and smile. "Oh. Sorry. I was thinking about something."

"I'm sure you were," Jen mutters knowingly. Turning to Ben, she says, "I'm afraid I opened a big ole can of worms on the way here. Peyton may be distracted tonight. I think she misses Brice."

I clear my throat and widen my eyes at her, but I address Ben and apologize again for not hearing his question.

He shrugs and grins. "It's not a biggie. I was asking you if what Jen said was true."

"Probably not," I reply wryly, inwardly cringing at the possibilities.

"Were you a wild child? Because it's hard for me to imagine that," he says, taping closed a box.

Casually, I answer, "I suppose I had my moments."

Jen rolls her eyes. "Don't let her fool you, although it sounds like she's already done a decent job of that. Before Brice, she was the wildest of the three of us."

"Not true. You've always been the craziest one, Jen."

"Liar!"

Ben watches, amused, as we go back and forth, one-upping each other with stories of the other's exploits. It's all good-natured, and nothing scandalous emerges, until I start to run out of "safe" material and blurt, "At least I've never had to be bailed out of jail!"

She laughs and retorts, "Says the girl who got knocked up and ended up marrying a pastor, like some modern day Mary-and-Joseph story." She's still laughing as she straightens the contents of one of the care packages so Ben can tape it shut. When she realizes neither one of us is laughing with her, she looks up sharply, first at me, then at Ben.

He's pale and frozen, tape gun held limply at his side. I know I'm pale, too, because I can feel all the blood draining from my face into my feet. I think I might pass out. I need air.

"What?" she asks innocently. "You're not Catholic, so it's not like I'm saying something offensive or sacrilegious."

With narrowing vision, I rush to the heavy door and push it open, emerging onto the parking lot. I stumble into a patch of grass between the PCC and the business next door. The door bangs open and closed behind me, but I don't look over my shoulder to see who's followed me. Instead, I bend at the waist, brace my hands on my thighs, and retch at the ground. It seems like a week's worth of food gushes out.

Jen's perfectly pedicured toes and wedge sandals enter my field of vision as I'm coughing while my stomach makes sure it's truly empty.

After a particularly ferocious dry belch, I gasp, "You... are... such... an... idiot."

"I know!" she moans. "As soon as it was out, I regretted it, not because I thought it was a big secret but because I realized it may not be appropriate to laugh about something like that."

"How about all of the above?" I try to stand up straight, but it's immediately apparent that I've pulled a rib. "Ow!" I hiss at the twinge in my side.

"Are you okay?" She walks closer to me and puts her hand on my back.

Her physical contact brings on the tears. Through them, I say, "Let's see... I'm puking my guts out in a parking lot where anyone passing by can see me, and you just busted Brice and me out to one of the worst possible people from our church—"

"Ben? He's a sweetie. What do you mean, he's one of the worst possible people?"

"Not in general! But in this case, about *this* topic, he's the last person I ever wanted to know about it. And you come in, determined to be the comic and get a laugh at any cost, because you're on the rebound and horny. Damn it, Jen! I could punch you so hard in the ovaries right now!" Slowly, I ease myself into a standing position.

She backs away from me.

"Don't worry; I couldn't possibly hit you hard enough for it to hurt right now," I reassure her.

Over her shoulder, I see Ben exit the building and look toward us. I ignore him until he calls, "Are you okay?"

"Tell him yes," I command her. It hurts too much to yell it to him myself.

She does as I say. Then, when I walk toward my car, she goes over to him and says something. I'm assuming she's telling him we're leaving, although he's a smart guy and can probably figure that out for himself, considering I'm getting behind the wheel and starting the engine. I'm tempted to leave Jen here and make Ben bring her home, but I'm afraid what else she'll tell him if left alone with him, so I wait for her to trot over to the car and get in.

"Do you want me to drive?" she asks gently.

My answer is to back from the space and peel from the parking lot before she even has her seatbelt on.

20

BEANS SPILT

*W*hat I want her to do is go back in time and shut her yap. And possibly bring me some saltines and ginger ale. I feel wretched, both physically and emotionally. I thought I'd feel better, at least physically, after resting in bed, but that's not happening. My emotional state is severely impacting what's happening to me physically.

When Brice calls to check in, I instinctively try to pretend everything's fine, but when he senses something's wrong, he immediately jumps to the conclusion that it has something to do with Max.

"I knew it," he says. "I *knew* God was trying to tell me something when I didn't want to go out of town this week. Like you said, I usually enjoy these conferences, so there was no logical reason for me to be dreading this trip. As a matter of fact, I should have been welcoming the change of scenery, but no, I had a sick feeling in the pit of my stomach that I couldn't shake. And now this. What's wrong? Tell me, please. Do I need to come home? I'll leave right now, if I have to."

Shit. I've never heard him like this. He doesn't even

sound like himself. As a matter of fact, if he were talking about anything or anyone other than Max, I'd think he was goofing around for the purpose of amusing Vince, whose voice I heard in the background at the beginning of the call.

I snap, "Calm down before you have to use one of your spare pairs of undies!"

He's slightly more in control when he repeats, "Just tell me what's going on."

I lie back against my pillows and pinch the bridge of my nose in an effort to hold my emotions in check. Crying right now is only going to alarm him more. And what's the point in that? After a deep, shaky breath, I say, "There's no emergency. Not with Max, anyway." While I screw up the courage to tell him about the big thing, I give him the least important news. "I'm not feeling well, that's all. I barfed at the PCC tonight, while Jen and I were working there with Ben."

"Ew, really? Like, all over the place?"

"I made it outside," I say as succinctly as possible. Talking about it is making my tummy gurgle.

"Oh." He takes a deep breath. "I'm sorry. And that's all that's wrong?"

Damn. He would have to come right out and ask that, wouldn't he? So if I say no, I'm not only blatantly going against our stupid agreement (why did I *ever* make that agreement with him? I blame lust), but I'll be outright lying.

"No," I answer, my voice cracking when I picture the look on Ben's face after Jen spilled the beans. Not gonna get through this without crying. Double-damn!

On high alert again, he asks, "What is it? Oh, man. Don't cry. Whatever it is, it'll be okay."

"It's not okay," I insist.

He sucks in some air and says in a near-whisper, "Is it my mom? Just tell me."

Now I feel like a major jerk. First of all, that he'd think I lead with puking if something had happened to his mom is quite telling. Am I *that* self-centered? Second, that he'd think I'd wait for his nightly call instead of calling him right away says even more. And third, that he'd think I'd snap and razz him about his extra underwear if something was wrong with his mom.

"No!" I nearly shout. "No, no, no. Your mom's fine, as far as I know. Gosh!" I steel myself so that I can simply say it and end his suspense. "Ben knows."

There's a pause. "Ben knows what?"

"About… you know."

Apology in his tone, he says, "It's been a long day, and my heart is pounding right now, so I'm drawing a blank."

"Jen told him about Secret."

"What? Why? I mean, how did that even come up?" He doesn't sound at all as alarmed as I think he should sound at this news. He merely sounds befuddled.

My tears abate as anger takes hold. "Because she was flirting with Ben, and when she flirts with a guy, she always treats me like I'm her competition, so she was doing her usual level-best to make me look like an idiot in front of him, and I may have mentioned that I had to bail her out of jail once, which is hardly on par with what I went through with Secret, especially considering that her arrest was just a big misunderstanding, even if it was for solicitation, and she didn't even have to go to court over it, because it was all cleared up before they could file charges, and anyway, I didn't say what she'd been arrested for, so it's not like she had to bust me out to get back at me."

"Wha…? Jen was arrested for suspected prostitution?"

"Yes, but that's not the point. I told you, it was a mix-up. And we even laugh about it all the time now, so why'd she have to bring up something so hurtful about *me*? I wasn't trying to hurt her when I mentioned her thing. But she's so spiteful sometimes!"

He sighs. "Oh, boy. Listen. I doubt she said it to hurt you. Have you given her a chance to explain herself?"

"No! I've been too busy throwing up and crying. And now I'm talking to you. Anyway, I don't want to hear her stupid excuses. If you knew her like I do, you'd understand that this is what she does. She insults me and degrades me so she'll look better in comparison. But really, I blame Mitch. He broke up with her, or she broke up with him—she won't tell me what happened—so she's on the rebound, and she's all over Ben, and now he knows, and— and I could drive to Chicago and kick Mitch in the babymaker!"

He has the nerve to laugh.

"It's not funny!"

"Sorry," he replies, sounding anything but. "Don't be mad, but in a way, I'm relieved."

I'm speechless.

"You're mad, aren't you?" he asks in regards to my silence. "But when I think of everything that could have been wrong, and it's just this... I can't help but praise God for that."

When I can trust myself to speak without blowing up at him, I say, "I'm not in the mood for one of your sermons, all right?"

"I'm not going to preach a sermon to you," he says through clenched teeth. "I'm talking to you as a relieved husband, father, and son."

"I want you to take my side for once, without trying to get me to see it from another perspective. Is that too much to ask?" I start crying again and blubber, "This is a big deal to me! Ben knows. Marianne knows. Everyone's finding out, and I want to hide under the covers and never come out. I'm so ashamed of what happened, of who I used to be——"

"I'm not ashamed of it," he cuts me off. "Nor am I ashamed of you. Or Secret. Or myself. I'll get up in front of the whole congregation and tell them what happened——"

My stomach jumps. "Don't you dare!"

"To prove that I'm not ashamed. I'm not hiding it. I'm not keeping it a secret. It happened." Softly, he adds, "I wouldn't do that, though, because I know the topic makes you uncomfortable."

"Yeah, it makes me uncomfortable! Especially around church people!"

"They're just people."

"No, they're not."

He makes a frustrated noise. "So what? You'd be okay with someone you meet at the park with Max knowing everything, but you have to be a different person to the Denmans? Or the Longs?"

I squirm, finding it difficult to get comfortable in the bed. "No. Not different. Less transparent."

"That's duplicitous and wrong."

His cut-and-dried tone and attitude are pissing me off. "Okay, then, Reverend Honesty. Next time it comes up in conversation, I'll let *you* field the question. I'm sure you'll be able to put a wonderful spin on it that will have the ladies reaching for their hankies and the men slapping you on the back for being such an open-minded, stand-up guy!"

"There's no spin! We've often discussed how Secret's purpose in both of our lives was Heaven-sent. 'We know that in all things God works for the good of those who love Him and who have been called according to His purpose.'"

I squeeze my eyes shut. "Holy crap. Was that a Bible verse you just quoted?"

"Yeah. Romans—"

"I don't need to know its exact address, m'kay? My point is, you're going to quote Scripture at me during our argument? Seriously?"

Sanctimoniously, he replies, "This argument is, unfortunately, a part of my life, and I live my life according to Scripture."

"Unbelievable," I mutter.

"What? What did I do that was so wrong?"

Feeling deflated, I answer, "Nothing. You did nothing wrong. That's the whole point."

"Then why are you so mad at me?"

I flip from my side to my back and wince at the pain in my rib. "You are above reproach." When he snorts, I hurry on before he can object. "You always know what to do, what to say, and how to get people to understand even the most complicated issues. You rattle off Bible quotes during arguments with your wife. *That's* how good you are."

He starts to interrupt, but I talk louder. "Then there's me. I not only wouldn't think to quote the Bible during an argument, but I resent that you do and that it strengthens your point. And maybe you thought that transplanting me here would make me a different or better person, or at the very least, we could start over with a clean slate with all these nice, new people. But it doesn't work that way. I'm still me. Only now, I have to either choose to explain my past to a whole new set of people or pretend it didn't exist. Either way, I still do the wrong things, I still say the wrong things, and I still have no way of defending myself or my actions or my *past* to anyone."

After my mini-rant, he remains silent for quite a while.

When I think he's never going to say anything, he asks, "Where do you get such a twisted self-perception?"

"What?"

"I mean," he clarifies, "whose voice do you hear in your head when you're telling yourself that you do or say the wrong thing?"

I wrinkle my nose. "My voice. Who else's? Jiminy Cricket's? I'm a little off, but I'm not *that* crazy."

He chuckles. "Well, you're wrong about being wrong all the time. And I think you forget that nobody can hear your thoughts, so when you think you're saying the wrong thing, you may only be thinking it. And that doesn't count. As a matter of fact, I can't recall a single instance when you said something to someone else, and I thought, 'Wow. That was the wrong thing to say.'"

"That's because you don't attend PoP meetings. And you're nice. And diplomatic. And you always put the best construction on things. You always assume the best in people."

Laughing, he says, "Oh, Peyton. Nobody *always* does those things. You're right that I try, though. I choose to try. And it takes a lot of practice."

"Well, I don't want to practice, okay?" Absently, I rub at my sore rib. "People suck, for the most part. And as long as I remember that, there'll be less chance of one of them taking me by surprise with their suckiness. Like Jen did tonight."

"You need to make up with Jen," he says firmly. When I grunt obstinately, he insists, "At least give her a chance to apologize and tell you her side of it. Don't let this ruin your visit with your friends. You need this time with them."

I'm too tired to even ask what he means by that. I think I know, anyway, but hearing him say it will only force me to defend my crabby self, and I don't have the energy right now.

"I'm too sick to care," I lie instead.

"Do I need to come home and take care of you?"

"Yes," I answer, but he knows I'm kidding, since I have no patience with him when he hovers over me. "Just have fun with Vince and all the other nerds. What's the big discussion this time? Appropriate under-robe attire?" Unbidden, I get another flash of Brice naked and start sweating. What is wrong with me?

He jumps on the change in subject, seemingly glad I've stopped crying. "Close. Some of the guys here have stopped wearing their collars."

"Scandalous."

"I know, right? Vince and I are old-school, though. Plus, how else am I going to get special treatment when I'm out in public? Those upstart liberals are missing out on a lot of free cups of coffee in hospital cafeterias, not to mention great parking spaces."

"More for you, I guess," I say through my smile.

"Yep. Their loss."

We sit in companionable silence for a while, during which I catch myself dozing, feeling calm for the first time in hours. Eventually, he says, "Well, I guess I should let you get some rest. And honey?"

"Mmm?"

"Please, don't worry about Ben."

Oh. I'd almost forgotten.

Without waiting for me to reply, he continues, "Because it's going to be okay. You have nothing to be ashamed of. You have nothing to answer to him about. So just let it ride, all right?"

Tears gather behind my closed lids and leak onto my

cheeks, running into the creases next to my nose and pooling in the corners of my mouth. Even though he can't see me, I nod. A sob escapes.

He sighs and clicks his tongue. "C'mon, now. I need to know you're okay before I hang up and go with Vince in search of free beers in my clerical collar."

I laugh-sob at the mental image of them pub crawling in their "pastor shirts." "I'm fine," I manage unconvincingly.

"No, you're not."

"I am. I swear. I need to sleep and not think about things for a while, that's all."

"Then do that. I'll give Ben a call in the morning, to see if he wants to talk."

"Do you have to?"

"Yeah, I probably do." He doesn't sound happy at the prospect. "But don't worry about it, okay?"

"You keep saying that."

"Because I want you to hear it and heed it and not say, 'Yeah, yeah,' and go right back to worrying about it."

Ready to end this conversation, I tell him resolutely, "I love you. Give Vince a hug and a kiss from me."

"I don't think so. But I love you, too. And I'll call you tomorrow to see if you're feeling better."

"Yeah, yeah." I'm not counting on that being the case, but pact or no pact, I'll probably lie and tell him I am.

RECONCILING FACTS

I can tell by the timid knock that Mitzi's on the other side of the door. When I croak my permission for her to enter, she opens the door a tiny crack and slips through the opening as quickly as possible, as if she's trying to contain my germs in this one room.

"Hey," she says, smiling tentatively and offering me a plate of saltines and a glass of clear, bubbly pop.

I prop myself against the headboard and look down at the plate in my lap. Hmmm, not sure I can manage what looks like an entire sleeve of crackers, but a tiny nibble wouldn't hurt, right?

"Thanks," I say. I chisel at a corner of a cracker with my front tooth. My stomach responds with a scary noise.

She raises her eyebrows at me. "Maybe now's not a good time yet."

I sip my fizzy drink and set down the cracker. "Maybe not."

When it seems my stomach's not going to complain about the beverage, I sit back and relax. Mitzi perches at the foot of the bed.

"Thanks for keeping an eye on Max for me today," I tell her. "If I'd been home alone with him, this would have been a real challenge. I may have had to ask Brice to come home early." The thought makes me shudder. I'm no helpless girly-girl who needs her snuggy wuggums to take care of her, but since I haven't been able to stray more than ten feet from the toilet for nearly twenty-four hours now, taking care of a baby would have been all but impossible.

My bedspread is suddenly very interesting to my friend.

"What's wrong?"

She looks up at me and twists her mouth to the side as she appears to be considering whether to say what's on her mind.

"Is Max too much for you guys? Do you want me to call Brice to have him come home?"

"No!" she says quickly. "It's not that at all. He's such a good baby. We're having a lot of fun with him. Jen's doing most of the work." She looks pointedly at me while giving me this information.

I bite my bottom lip and grunt.

"She's really sorry, Peyton, about what happened with Ben."

"She should be. She should also be ashamed that you're the one in here giving her apology." I thought I was over my anger towards Jen, but talking about it to Mitzi is bringing it all back, full-force. "You should have seen her. She was in full-flirt mode." Unlike with Brice, I don't have to say much else for Mitzi to understand what I'm talking about. She's seen Jen's act a million times.

Now, she nods knowingly. "Right. And since I wasn't there, you were the foil?"

I gulp and defensively state, "You're not *always* the foil.

She's an equal-opportunity hater when she's trying to impress a guy."

"But I'm an easier target. She probably had to bring her A-game to look cool next to you, and she got carried away."

"She told you this?" I ask, narrowing my eyes.

My question receives a headshake. "Nope. But I know her. I know *you*. You were doing your quiet, aloof thing—"

"I felt like I was going to hurl up my toenails! There was nothing 'aloof' about me. I was hanging onto my stomach contents with sheer force of will!"

At least, that's how I seem to remember it now. I can't remember a time when I wasn't feeling on the verge of barf-dom. But thinking back more truthfully…

"I didn't want to get in the way of her flirting with Ben. He— Well, sometimes he flirts with me, but then he always seems to be embarrassed by it right away."

"That's kind of inappropriate," she remarks, somehow managing not to sound at all judgmental.

"Yeah. And he knows it. Hence, the immediate regret he always shows. And I'd be lying if I said it didn't make me uncomfortable, so I was trying to stay out of the way. Encouraging them, even."

She gives me a skeptical look.

"Honestly! At first, she wasn't saying anything too personal or embarrassing. And I like that you've found Jared." She blushes and grins. "So I got to thinking, maybe her breakup with Mitch happened at the perfect time. Ben's always talking about how hard it is for him to meet women and—"

"Whoa."

I relax against the headboard, winded and sweating.

"Since when are you a matchmaker?" she asks.

"I'm not," I say. "But the two of them together makes sense. And if Ben and Jen were dating—"

"Five hundred miles apart?"

I swipe aside that pesky detail. "Then maybe things would be less awkward between Ben and me. I want him to meet someone great. I want Jen to meet someone great. They're both great, even though she's sometimes mean. But maybe someone like Ben is what she needs! Someone mature and grounded and— and who wears clothes in his spare time."

Mitzi giggles.

"I never thought of trying to fix the two of them up. Distance was part of it, but mostly because I don't think of him that way. He's exactly her type, though. I forgot how much she likes gingers."

Now Mitzi grabs my foot. "Listen. This is all nice, but it's beside the point, isn't it? The point is that you and Jen aren't speaking, because she screwed up. And she knows she did. But she's afraid to bother you with her apology, because you don't feel well. I told her I'd come in here and feel you out, see if you're up to talking it out with her."

"I'm really not. I feel vomitous."

"You'll feel better once this is off your mind."

I know she's right. I know that this stomach bug isn't the only thing causing a knot in my gut. I know this can't continue. I know I'll regret it if I let the two of them leave tomorrow without clearing the air.

I sigh and flap my lips. "Fine. Send her in," I relent, feeling silly for saying it like that, as if I'm the President, or something.

She acts like it's perfectly normal as she grins at me and jumps from the bed. "Awesome. I'll go get her. She was feeding Max some dinner. She's been so good with him. I always thought she hated kids, but she's a babysitting rock star. Max loves her."

Good to know, in case I don't make it through this illness alive. Maybe she can marry Brice and pick up where I left off.

"And I thought for sure that Ben knew, because of where you guys volunteer together, and because you made it sound like he and Brice are good friends, and if I'd had any clue that he was in the dark, and you wanted to keep it that way, I wouldn't have said anything. You know that. I know it's a sensitive topic. I know it's not a joke."

"You sure treated it like one."

"I got carried away. And I've often thought about how Biblical the situation was, and it makes me giggle, so it just slipped out."

"You're kidding, right?"

She knows the answer should be yes, but it's obvious she's not kidding, so I explain, "Mary didn't have a one-night stand with the Holy Spirit to get pregnant with Jesus."

"I know that!"

"Well, your comparison implies that she did."

"Brice compared you to Mary in a sermon once."

"No, he didn't! Jen!"

"Well, he sorta did," she persists under her breath.

I let it drop, knowing I'm not going to be able to get her to understand and that we're getting off-track. Also, the two cracker crumbs in my stomach are wrestling in a puddle of Sprite and about to kick up some trouble.

"What's done is done," I eventually manage through a watering mouth, referring to her slip-of-the-tongue.

"He's so cute, though."

She must be talking about Ben. "If you say so."

"Do you truly think he'll stop being friends with you and Brice because of what happened with you and Stefan and Secret?"

The insides of my cheeks tingle, and my eyes water. "I don't know."

"I can't believe that. It was so long ago."

I open my mouth to tell her about the conversation I had with him my first night at the PCC, but that's when the stuff in my stomach hatches and executes its evacuation plan, and I have to run to the bathroom.

It goes on forever. I'm vaguely aware of Jen asking if I'm okay while I marvel at the body's ability to express its extreme displeasure with viral intruders, and I pray for God to make it end. I have nothing left to give. That doesn't seem to be a problem for my body, though; it doesn't care.

One second, I'm looking down into the toilet; the next, I'm blinking up at the dome light in my car.

Mitzi and Jen are arguing. "We should have called an ambulance."

"She's passed out, not dying. I'm sure she's just dehydrated. This is no worse than the time we had to take her to the hospital to have her stomach pumped after that frat house kegger. Shut up, get in the car, and drive."

"I don't know."

"Mitzi, I'm about to do something to you so that *you're* going to need an ambulance. Max is buckled in. Let's go."

"Are you going to call Brice?"

"As soon as I'm finished with this stupid fucking argument, yes."

The car starts. I groan from the reclined passenger seat.

Jen leans forward from the back seat. "Hey. You passed out in your bathroom, so—"

"I'm fine," I gasp. "Put me back in bed."

"You're not fine," Mitzi says. "We've been trying to wake you up for a long time. You're going to the hospital."

"No."

"Yes," Jen insists. "There's no debate. You're gonna get an IV, and your husband's gonna— Damn it; it's going to his voicemail."

She takes a breath. "Brice! Hey, it's Jen. Uh, don't freak out, but we're taking Peyton to the hospital. We can't get her to stop barfing. And then she passed out for about twenty minutes."

"Stay up there!" I say weakly toward Jen's phone, trying to communicate with the future Brice who will listen to her message.

"Don't listen to her," Jen tells him. "She's delirious. You should definitely come home when you get this. She's talking out of her gourd."

"He's guest-preaching right now. He can't hear you," I say incomprehensibly.

"Thanks, Einstein," she mutters. Returning to the message, she says in a rush, "Anyway, we're taking Max with us. Give me a call back at this number, and I'll give you an update. But you should probably get on the road first. We may not know anything for a while. Bye." She disconnects the call and pockets her phone while directing at Mitzi, "Yo, Grandma Moses, drive faster!"

~

What a relief to be alone! Well, sort of alone. At least I can pretend I'm alone, if I don't count the nurses that come in here every half hour to check on me. Yeah. Had to stay overnight for observation. Stupid, right? I tried to tell them that all they had to do was give me something to stop the vomiting and pump me full of fluids, and I could be on my way. But the results of one of the tests they ran on me made them decide otherwise.

I had no control over that, but I had a say about what I wanted for Max, and that was for Jen and Mitzi—both—to take him home. Brice had already called for three updates, so I was starting to get nervous that Loose Lips McGee was going to slip and tell him something I'd rather tell him in person. During their last call, I made sure Jen told him that she, Mitzi, and Max were going home to bed, so they wouldn't have any more information for him, and he should come straight to the hospital when he got into town. He'll probably be here any minute.

I'd rest my eyes while I wait, but I've been asleep or unconscious most of the day and evening, so my eyelids feel like they're stuck open. Plus, for the first time, possibly ever, I'm dreading seeing my husband.

I hear him arrive before I see him. My stomach flutters, but the drug they gave me to control the nausea is doing its job, so I don't have to reach for the puke pan on the rolling table straddling my bed.

A nurse at the station a few feet from my room says cheerfully, "Hey, Pastor! I wondered if our Northam patient was related to you."

He pauses right outside my door. "By marriage, yes."

The nurse giggles. "You're so funny! She's been quiet in there. Tell her not to hesitate to press the button if y'all need anything."

I roll my eyes but then smile and finger-wave as he enters the room and pokes his head around the privacy curtain.

"You're awake," he states the obvious.

"That I am. I've been eavesdropping on the nurses. Barb needs to dump her boyfriend. He's a tool."

He's too tense to laugh. Not a good beginning.

I try again. "You know Giggles out there?"

Taking a seat next to my bed, he pushes his hand through the side rail and squeezes my hand. "Yes. Her name is Gayle. I know her from my hospital visits. She's very nice."

"She has a crush on you."

He ignores that and asks, "How are you feeling?"

"Great. I wish they'd let me go home."

Nodding, he holds my eye contact and says, "Yeah. So, why won't they? I wouldn't think mild dehydration would require an overnight stay."

I pat his hand. "Now, I know you're worried about our insurance premiums, but—" The horrified look on his face stops me short. "Kidding! Wow. Tough crowd."

"I'm worried about you," he explains defensively. "And I drove like a maniac to get here."

"You shouldn't do either of those things. Everything's fine."

Maybe if I keep saying it, I'll believe it.

He takes a deep breath, sits back, and runs a hand through his hair. "The fact that they admitted you tells a different story."

My heart races, although I'm not sure why I'm suddenly nervous. He's going to love this news. I think. Probably. I smile shakily. "Well, they tend to be overly cautious with expectant mothers. Silly doctors."

His spine straightens, and the lines in his forehead flatten, but I don't see the overt joy I was expecting in his eyes.

"Are you still worried about insurance premiums and medical bills?" I quip, wishing those were my biggest worries right now.

After a quick shake of his head, he looks down at his hands in his lap. I give him some time to collect his thoughts (it's only fair, considering I've had a couple of hours to process the information). When he looks up after less than a minute, there are tears in his eyes, but he nods and smiles. "This is great news," he declares.

I'm not sure I agree with him, but the fact that he thinks it is a huge relief. I was starting to wonder for a second if he'd changed his mind.

He half-stands and leans over the bed to give me a kiss.

I turn my head at the last second so that his smooch lands on my cheek. "I may have puke breath," I explain, self-conscious of the possibility.

With a hand on my face, he pulls my lips toward him. "I don't care," he murmurs.

I've never been turned on in a hospital before now. Didn't think it was possible. But that shows how much I know, because as soon as his lips land on mine, I have an overwhelming urge to whip off my hospital gown, twirl it over my head, and fling it across the room. I'm actually calculating how long it's been since the last time a nurse has been in here and contemplating the logistics of having sex while attached to an IV when he pulls away from me, rests his forehead against mine, and says with a smile, "Your breath is fine."

In that case… So abruptly that he has to grab onto the bedrail for support, I pull him back in for another kiss.

"Mppph!" he muffles and laughs against my mouth. "What are you do—"

"I'm so happy you're happy," I say emotionally.

"Of course, I'm happy. Why wouldn't I be ha—"

"Because you didn't look happy when I first told you."

"It took me a second to figure out what you were telling me."

I break eye contact and look down at my lap. He takes the opportunity to escape from my grip and stand next to the bed, waiting for me to decide how to say what's on my mind. Or if I even want to say it. Or have the nerve to say it.

Finally, I whisper, "I couldn't come right out and tell you in the usual way. Those two words." I find the courage to look him in the eyes. "They're scary."

"Why?" he asks, stroking my hair when my eyes fill with tears.

I shake my head, shrug, and laugh at myself. "They just are. When I say them or think them, I get a vivid picture of how I'm going to feel and act and look for the better part of the next year, and it makes me panic a bit."

He makes soothing noises but knows better than to try to talk me down from the ledge. This gentle understanding makes me feel secure enough to add, "And I feel like I'm stepping into no-going-back territory with this stay-at-home mom stuff. That's even more terrifying. Max isn't even a year old yet!"

"He will be next week," Brice points out. "And he'll be much older by the time this baby's born, so—"

I moan at his use of that word. I'd been doing a bang-up job of not thinking about it as that.

He tilts his head. "What? Are you feeling sick?" At the possibility, he looks like he's going to bolt for the door.

"Not *that* kind of sick," I assure him.

Relaxing somewhat, he says, "Oh," but then he inquires, "What kind of sick, then?"

Instead of answering him, I demand, "Tell me everything's going to be okay."

He smiles and readily complies. "Everything's going to be more than okay. Everything's going to be fabulous. You'll see."

"Promise?"

"Absolutely."

Giggly Gayle enters the room at a brisk walk and with a cheery, "Hello! Time to check those vitals, make sure you're still alive." She glances at Brice and punctuates her statement with the type of laughter that's more befitting of a teenager.

He nods politely at her as he moves to the foot of the bed, where he'll be out of her way. As soon as her back's turned and she's pushing some buttons on the IV machine, Brice meets my gaze and gives me a wink and a private smile.

22

FRAUD

Things are okay. They are. I wouldn't go so far as to say they're fabulous, but that's not Brice's fault. It is his fault for making such a dumb promise; but then again, I'm the one who asked him to make it. And it's at least half his fault that I'm knocked up and spending way too much time with toilets, but placing blame isn't going to make things better.

What does make things better are generous doses of anti-nausea medication and staying busy, the former for obvious reasons and the latter because it keeps me from thinking about the next difficult conversation I need to have with Brice: the one about going back to work.

For now, though, there's plenty of work to be done at home, where I'm preparing for a visit from my family. We're celebrating Jason's and Max's birthdays together. During the weekend, Brice helped me clean up and get the house back in order after Mitzi and Jen's visit, but the rest of the preps are up to me. They mostly involve making sure I have what would be a year's supply of alcohol for Brice and me but may or may not last the four-day weekend with my family.

Apparently, Brice doesn't think purchasing booze should be a priority, nor should it be as time-consuming as it's turning out to be, so he's asked me to take a break from adult beverage acquisitions and enlisted me to help out in the church office while Lucy's out with a stomach bug (for real).

"Hey, Luce. Oh, hey. You're not Lucy," Ben states the obvious when he looks up from the hot pink sticky note in his hand and sees me sitting behind the church secretary's desk.

"Nope." I smile, but the awkwardness I've been dreading between us is definitely present. My strategy is to pretend like nothing's wrong until it's the truth.

After we nod at each other for a while, he asks hesitantly, "So, where *is* Lucy?"

"Oh!" I laugh nervously at myself. "She's sick. I'm filling in this morning."

He wrinkles his nose. "Do you think it's smart to be sitting there, touching all of Lucy's things, if she's sick? She was probably contagious the last time she was here. Germs can survive on surfaces for a long time, you know."

"What are you, a Lysol commercial?"

He manages a tight half-smile. "Sorry. I'm a bit of a germophobe."

"And yet you eat at all those less-than-sanitary Chinese restaurants in this town?" I say, suddenly paranoid about Lucy's germs. I won't let him know, though. Uh-uh.

Ignoring my observation, he holds up the sticky note. "Anyway, I was going to have Lucy type up a small handout for me to—"

BAM!

"I wanted this handout for—"

BAM! BANG! BAM! BAM!

He waits longer this time when there's a break in the noise from the new daycare construction, down the hall in the Sunday school wing. "Okay. Anyway, this handout is for—"

BANG! BBBBBBBBBBBAM!

"Oh, for crying out—"

BAM!

Brice walks through the door to the reception area, clapping Ben on his shoulder on the way past him into his office. "Hey, Bud! Construction crew's on site early this morning!" he announces cheerfully, raising his voice to be heard over the nail gun and hammering.

"YEAH, I CAN HEAR THAT!" Ben shouts back, right when the noise stops.

I put my hands over my ears and laugh.

From his office doorway, Brice raises an eyebrow at Ben. "Well, you don't have to yell about it." He receives a mock-glare as he continues, "The drywall is going up! Or is it sheetrock? Either way, it's exciting!"

"And loud," I add, reaching for and missing the note in Ben's hand.

The youth director laughs at my fail but drops the note in the middle of Lucy's desk. "I'd wait for her to get back, but I need this for tonight's Confirmation class. It snuck up on me, since classes have been moved to Tuesday nights for Lent. The handout is about the paintball trip this Saturday. Do you think you can print something out on orange paper? Half-sheets. About thirty copies? No, make that forty."

"What's the magic word?" I prompt in sing-song, as if I'm talking to Max.

"'Now'?" he guesses, the picture of innocence.

Brice whistles under his breath and goes into his office, closing the door behind him and drawing all the blinds.

As Ben watches this display, I keep my eyes on his face and explain casually, "He doesn't want to be subpoenaed for the trial."

Now that we're alone again, he reverts to being fidgety and stiff. "Oh. Ha. I get it. I was just kidding, anyway. So, do you think you can—"

BAM! BAM! BAM! BAM!

I tilt my head and pretend I need him to repeat the end of his request.

"Work something up—"

SQUEEEEE! SQUEEEE!

Poking my index finger against the back of my ear in the international signal for "Come again?" while laughing at his frustration, I cross my legs to keep from having an embarrassing bladder accident.

As soon as the band saw grinds to a halt, he takes a deep breath and finishes, "Please?"

I pull back my mirth to a benevolent smile and say, "Absolutely. I'd be glad to."

"Thanks. I'll, uh, come by later and pick them up." He walks backwards toward the door, running his hand through his hair and looking everywhere but at me. "You can just leave them in my mail slot."

As he's turning to leave, I say quietly, "Ben?"

When he spins to face me, his eyebrows lifted inquisitively, I take a steadying breath and lick my lips while I do a complete 180 on my previous plan to pretend nothing's wrong. "Can we, I don't know, clear the air? Maybe?"

He glances nervously at Brice's door and replies, "What do you mean? The air's clear. Isn't it?"

I give him a long-suffering look that must clearly communicate my plea for him to stop playing dumb, because his shoulders sag as he leans his body weight against the wall behind him.

Finding the courage that only results from being fed up with an untenable situation, I state, "I know from what little Brice has told me and from observing the two of you together that you guys, in typical guy-like fashion, have somehow gotten past what you found out last week. But it's just as clear—probably in contrast—that we haven't. You're like a totally different person around me. You treat me like a stranger. A stranger who's hideously disfigured and doesn't smell particularly good."

An involuntary laugh slips from his lips at that description, but he shakes his head and quickly sobers. "That's not true."

"It is! Ohmigosh, Ben! Yesterday after church, you held your breath around me for so long that you started to sweat. And the ceiling of this room is apparently super-duper fascinating."

SQUEEEEEEEEEEEE! CLANG!

He waits for silence, looking suddenly grateful for the racket, then says with his eyes on his shoes, "Listen. I'm sorry it seems that way. Pastor and I had a good talk about things, and—"

"You did?" Brice never told me that. With all the dehydration and pregnancy and hospitalization excitement, he never mentioned whether he'd called Ben like he planned, and if so, what they'd talked about or how it went. As far as I knew, they were doing the same pretending Ben and I were doing, only having a much more successful go of it.

He looks up. "Yeah. We did. I totally understand where he was coming from. And I get that it was God's will, so… How do you question that?"

I chew my bottom lip and nod. Then I say, "You try not to."

"Exactly."

I screw up more courage while a cacophony of sounds that seems never-ending prevents us from conversing. As soon as I have an opening, I blurt, "Then why are you being so weird around *me*?"

Again, he glances at Brice's door while shifting his weight from foot to foot. "Uh, I dunno. I guess when I'm around Pastor, I can forget about it. Maybe because we talked about it. But..." Now he looks directly at my face for the first time in the conversation. "I can't forget about it when I'm with you."

My hurt feelings ignite my temper. "You can't separate the person I am today from that messed-up person back then?"

"I guess. Maybe it's because Pastor seems to be the same guy now as he was then, but you— You're so different. I feel sort of tricked."

I widen my eyes at him and turn toward Lucy's computer, using his stupid paintball handout as a diversion while I blink back tears. He seems to get that I'm mad, but he must not see how upset I am, because he rushes on, "Anyway, it *stinks* to be one of the only ones who knows."

"Nobody's asking you to keep it a secret," I say snootily, typing up the details scrawled in Ben's messy handwriting on the sticky note. "An entire congregation in Chicago knows about it, so don't feel so special."

"I know, but I think about how you help out at youth group functions or interact with some of the teenagers. You've been a role model to them! Who am I to—" He breaks off and takes a deep breath. "It needs to come from you, okay? If people are going to find out, they need to find out from you, not secondhand, like some trashy gossip."

I look up sharply when I hear the emotion in his last sentence. He sniffs and blinks. By the time the next round of banging subsides, he's composed himself enough that I think I may have imagined his earlier discomposure.

Keeping his voice low, he says, "Anyway, I'll be darned if I'm going to give Vivian Long any more ammunition against you."

I tense. "What do you mean?" When he refuses to elaborate, I say hotly but equally quietly, so as not to draw Brice's attention to what's going on out here, "I'm forgiven, so Vivian Long—and anyone else for that matter—can suck it."

"You won't be as easily forgiven by them."

"Or you, apparently," I spat bitterly. Unable to look at him any longer, I go back to typing, furiously backspacing when I make mistake after mistake due to my shaking hands. "You know what? Never mind. I'm sorry I brought this up. I just thought— I don't know what I thought. I guess I figured that we could go back to being friends if we addressed the issue like adults. But apparently it's not that simple. So forget it."

When he simply stares at me, I glance at him and say, "I'm sorry you feel like you're in an awkward position, knowing what you know. Let me print these for you, and you can take them with you."

It takes him a second to figure out that I've abruptly changed the subject back to his flyers, but when he does, he says coldly, "I'll come back for them later," and pivots toward the door.

Before leaving, though, he pauses and says sadly, "I know it's not fair, because if he can forgive you, then who am I? Or who are they? But disillusionment sucks. I don't ever want to be the source of it."

I'm not sure if the "he" in his statement is Brice or God. It doesn't matter, anyway.

When I make contact with his arm on my way past him, he startles.

"Maybe you already are," I sob over my shoulder as I rush toward the ladies' room.

I'm standing at the kitchen sink, rinsing greens and paring vegetables for a salad (*blech*), when Brice gets home shortly before 8:00, after working late. I recently returned home from my Tuesday night volunteering at the PCC. I only went because I knew Ben wouldn't be there, due to his Confirmation class conflict.

After Brice and I share the usual catch-up information —"Max is in bed;" "I'm tired, but fine"—he invites me to sit down while he finishes putting dinner on the table. I gladly take him up on it and watch him from my perch on a barstool at the counter.

I catch the surreptitious glances he directs at me while he sets the kitchen table, so after the second time he asks, "Are you sure you're okay?" I answer with the question, "What do you know?"

He visibly relaxes, admitting, "Ben came to talk to me after you left. He told me about your conversation with him this morning. Why didn't you say something?"

After I returned from having a good cry in the ladies' room, the outer office was empty, and Brice's door was still closed. He'd told me first thing that morning that he was working on several assignments with some tight deadlines, so

I didn't take it personally that he wasn't sociable. I also didn't do anything to interrupt him. I printed and cut Ben's flyers, placed them in his mailbox, and surfed the Internet for the next three hours, occasionally answering the phone and getting up to walk around. Mostly, I tried (unsuccessfully) to avoid thinking too much about what Ben had said. It was an unusually quiet, long morning.

At noon, I IM'ed Brice and told him I was going to leave, since it was so quiet. He emerged from his office to kiss me goodbye, but I could tell I'd caught him mid-thought (or tweet, or blog, or sermon), because he was distracted and didn't notice that I was subdued. I also tried to inject more cheerfulness into my goodbye than I was feeling. It's not that I wanted to conceal from him what had happened between Ben and me, but it wasn't the time to go into it then.

I explain that to him now while he fills two glasses with ice and water from the fridge door.

"Ah," he answers understandingly. Then he reveals, "Well, I had to admit to Ben that I wasn't aware that things were still strained between the two of you. You guys seemed normal this morning. You were joking with each other when I went into my office a few minutes before he says this tiff took place."

"Did he call it a tiff?" I wrinkle my nose.

"No. I'm just saying, it wasn't really a fight."

"It got pretty heated."

He sets down our plates of food and, suddenly still, looks up at me. His jaw juts to the side, but he says calmly, "Huh. He didn't mention that." He pulls out my chair and gestures me forward. "Let's pray. Then you can tell me a more complete version of what happened."

~

"Uh, no. There was no mention of your running to the bathroom crying," he says while rinsing our plates and putting them in the dishwasher. It took our entire meal for me to tell him the story from my perspective.

I shrug. "Well, maybe he didn't want to upset you."

"I think that's exactly why he didn't tell me. Because I would have been plenty upset that he didn't come get me right away."

In response to the pinched way he's holding his mouth, I say lightly, "Why? I mean, I cry all the time. It wouldn't have been a news flash."

As a matter of fact, now that the confrontation is a few hours in the past, I don't know why I cried when Ben said what he did. Sure, my feelings were hurt that he admitted he thought less of me when he found out about Secret, but crying? I'm so sick of it. And I'm glad Brice was oblivious and that Ben didn't get him involved while it was happening.

He shuts the dishwasher and turns toward me with a long-suffering look. "You know what I mean."

"What would you have done?" I ask, rubbing my eyes.

I feel his arms around me and smile when he says, "I would have gone and given you a hug."

"Oh. Well, that probably *would* have helped," I fib. Taking my hands away from my eyes, I look up at him while I return his embrace. "Are you mad at Ben?" A part of me wants him to be, but for the most part, I don't want there to be hard feelings. Ben was merely being honest. Maybe too honest, but he can't help it that he's a dumb guy. Anyway, I was the one who forced the issue.

Brice replies, "No, I'm not mad at Ben. Puzzled by some of the things he said to you, but not mad. I thought the talk we had took care of this stuff."

I sigh and rest my cheek against his chest. "Yeah, well, there's definitely a double standard at work here. He's forgiven you, but he feels like I've been dishonest with him, like I had sinister motives for not telling him."

With a pat to my back, he lets me go but grabs my hand and pulls me toward the living room. "It'll be fine. The two of you need to forgive each other your shortcomings and move on. In the meantime, I'll rub your feet while you watch whatever you want to watch on TV."

I'm feeling better already!

THE FAMILY WAY

"Well, they were correct in the ER," Dr. Klein, my brand new obstetrician, announces, helping me to a sitting position. "You're pregnant. Only about four weeks along, probably, based on the date of your last period. But since there's no such thing as 'a little pregnant,' congratulations!"

I open my mouth to say something and close it again. It never occurred to me that they could have been mistaken in the ER. I've treated the diagnosis as gospel. I only came here today, on Max's first birthday and hours before my family is due to descend on my house, because I wanted to know my due date and get a refresher from Dr. Klein about everything I can and can't do for the better part of the next year of my life. Now, it hits me I could have gotten all of that information from the Internet. Pregnancy makes me stupid.

He consults a colorful slide wheel he produces from a drawer and says, "That makes your tentative due date November 27."

I nod at my lap and utter, "Wow. That seems like a long time from now."

"It will probably feel like a long time, too," Dr. Klein grants.

His statement makes me laugh for the first time all day. I don't know this guy very well, despite the fact that he's a member at Peace, but I already appreciate that he's not trying to drown me in the sort of optimism my personality doesn't have the capacity to process.

"It'll probably feel like a long time for your nurses, too," I apprise him. "Although I'll try hard to be a relaxed patient."

"Are you high-maintenance?" he inquires, narrowing his eyes at me.

"I can be," I admit. "The stillbirth I told you about made my second pregnancy scarier than it should have been."

"Understandable."

"But this time around will be easier, right?"

He pauses, looks me in the eyes, and says flatly, "Sure. If you think so."

"Reassuring," I mutter sarcastically.

Now he laughs. "I'm not in the business of lying to my patients. Every pregnancy is different. Some are easy; some aren't. You had one that ended tragically and another that ended early after complications. Those issues may have been biological; they may have been environmental. We don't know. But I don't want you to ever think you're being a nuisance. We need to be informed of everything, even if it's only to determine it's nothing."

"You say that now, but…"

Grabbing my chart from the counter by the sink, he taps my knee with it before tucking it under his arm. "You'll be fine. You strike me as the type who's harder on herself than she needs to be. Cut it out. It's not good for your blood pressure." He opens the door to the room a few inches. "I'll see you in a month. But if anything comes up before then, or if you have questions or concerns, just call."

I slide from the exam table while promising him I'll do exactly that.

His hand on the doorknob, he seems shy but determined when he says, "And Peyton, I wanted to say, too, thanks for choosing me from all the doctors out there. I mean, I'm new, and it's hard to build a patient base."

Holding my ginormous paper gown closed in the back, I say with an easy smile, "Oh. Yeah. Well, you know, Brice thought it would be nice to keep it in the family—the church family, that is."

He smiles back. "That's the thing, though. It means a lot to me. I don't get many patients from Peace. A lot of people wouldn't want someone they know or see every Sunday to see them like *that*." He nods at my half-nakedness. "Even though it's completely clinical and professional," he adds quickly.

My smile freezes, and I feel the blood drain from my face. Oh, shit. I hadn't even considered that! I was more worried that I'd have to tell him about Secret, but what with confidentiality and everything, I decided that wasn't much of a concern. The fact that he's seen my lady parts, though. Or what if I do something really embarrassing when I'm super-huge, like fart in his face? I'll never be able to go to church again. And that could be a problem, considering I'm the pastor's wife, and everything. I wonder if I could become a member at one of the other Lutheran churches in town. Would that raise some eyebrows? I don't care.

Pregnancy makes me so, so, so, so stupid!

He either doesn't notice my sudden horror or he's determined not to acknowledge it for fear I'll change my mind and start seeing a different doctor. He pulls on the door to crack it open once more. "See you next month," he says, sliding through the discreet gap and shutting it behind him.

Well, there's one more person at church that I'll never again be able to look in the eye.

～

Mom's hug is longer and stronger than any other I've received from her in recent memory. I don't mind. I realize with a jolt that I've missed her. Dad waits patiently for his turn, but when I step toward him, he, too, pulls me firmly against himself and holds me in place with a gentle hand to the back of my head.

"We've missed you, Princess P.," he murmurs, using a nickname I haven't heard since probably third grade, when I decided I was outgrowing such things and asked him to stop calling me silly names.

I gasp at the emotional response it triggers. Damn embryo makes me a blubbering idiot!

Quickly, I change the subject while leading my parents into our house. "Where are Jason and Nicole and all their people? I thought you were going to caravan and arrive together."

Mom answers, "Jason and Dustin needed a later start than we wanted, and you know your sister. Bladder the size of a pea. I'm sure she and Lonnie will be along soon, but they had to make more stops than we did. Oh!" She sets her purse down on the table by the front door and looks around herself in delight as the realtor in her takes over. "What a nice house! Your pictures on Facebook don't do it justice."

I lead them through to the living room, feeling pride swell in my chest when I say, "Thanks. It was fairly turnkey, considering it's brand new, but we've done a few things to make it ours."

"It's darling!" she declares. "And such a nice neighborhood, too, I noticed as we were driving in. This whole town, as a matter of fact, seems very nice and clean."

"It has its charms," I admit grudgingly.

I've lately come to see a lot more of Springfield's charms. Although I still miss Chicago a lot, I mostly miss the people I love who are still there. I'm getting used to the benefits of living in a smaller city, though. Arriving anywhere I need to be in ten to twenty minutes, no matter my destination, tops the list. I also love that I feel safe, even when Brice is out of town. Now, whether this is a foolish, false sense of security is another matter. The fact is, I never felt this safe in Chicago. It's not that I walked around in a state of constant fear or apprehension, but I was always somewhat on edge, always slightly suspicious of people and their motives. I'm getting out the habit of being that way, and it's nice.

After telling my parents to leave their luggage at the bottom of the stairs, I give them a tour of the ground floor, ending in the kitchen. There, I check the progress of the pot roast in the slow cooker and grab the celery, carrots, and potatoes, which I begin chopping. They'll be the perfect tenderness by dinnertime if I add them now.

Mom sniffs the air. "Mmmm. It was so nice of Brice to get dinner started before going to work this morning. What a sweetie!"

"Excuse me, but *I'm* the chef in this house. This is *my* pot roast."

She looks as if she's not going to believe me at first, but

then she says contritely, "Oh, I'm so sorry. Normally… It used to be that—"

"Yeah, I know." I grin over my shoulder at her while I chop the veggies. "But that's my job now. I'm still learning, but there are a few things I do well. Like anything in the slow cooker."

"Where's the birthday boy?" Dad asks, looking around the kitchen as if I may have Max stowed in a cupboard.

"Napping," I answer. "He should be up any minute, though."

That's especially true, since the other two carloads have arrived, and they aren't being quiet about it.

"You're such a drama queen! I was simply letting the biker in the passing lane know that in other states, that lane's only for passing, not hanging out there like you own it," Jason's explaining.

Dustin snorts. "Uh! You could have let him know without adding the obscene gesture. I thought we were gonna die!"

Lonnie interjects, "Well, you guys left town way after we did and still almost beat us here, if that's any indication of how many times we had to stop. I'd rather face death by biker than see every rest area between Chicago and here."

"I'd like to see how well you can control your bladder after pushing out three of your larger-than-average-sized babies, Lon. So, can it," Nicole says sweetly.

I poke my head around the doorway from the kitchen and announce, "The troublemakers have arrived!"

Sadie runs to me. "Auntie Peyton!" Looking up into my face after a breath-stealing hug, she accuses, "You painted the living room."

Solemnly, I reply, "Yes, I did. I used the green color we

both decided we liked, remember? What are you saying? You don't like it?"

She wrinkles her nose. "It looks different. But I guess I like it okay."

"Whew. It took a long time to paint. I don't want to redo it."

Nicole looks at the walls while making her way through the living room to greet me. "You did this? Or Brice did it, and you bossed him around?"

"I did it. I have a lot of talents now. And a lot of time to indulge them." I squeeze her and plant a playful, wet kiss on her cheek, ignoring her protests. While receiving hugs and kisses from the rest of the group, I say, "And just so everyone knows, I'm making dinner tonight."

"Is this a warning?" Jason asks. "Should we have the number of a pizza place on standby?"

"No. I know how to cook now, so I'm taking credit before you eat and assume—like Mom—that Brice made the food or that I had the meal catered."

"It smells great," Dustin declares.

I'm glad he thinks so, because it's making me want to barf. I forgot how much the smell of cooking beef nauseated me when I was pregnant with Secret.

All attention turns toward the baby sounds suddenly coming from the monitor on the coffee table. Jason perks up and makes a beeline for the stairs. "My birthday buddy's up!"

After he disappears upstairs, I ask Dustin, "So, how much longer until you guys have your own kids?"

He shakes his head and wrinkles his nose, "I think pets are more our speed. And being uncles is a sweet gig. All the fun without any of the responsibility."

I stare admiringly at him and say in a silly, awe-filled voice, "You are so smart."

Letting loose with one of his ear-piercing peals of laughter, he states, "Oh, Peyton. You're in your element. You just can't bring yourself to admit it."

"Amen," Nicole agrees. "Major denial."

For the sake of argument, I choose not to comment on that. Instead, I smile brightly and say, "Let me show you guys around, and we'll figure out where everyone's going to sleep."

Seven hours, one delicious dinner, lots of cake and ice cream, several presents, one impromptu kickball game in the backyard, and countless beers and glasses of wine (for everyone else) later, I lie face down on our bed, my feet dangling off the edge. Now that I've had the chance to relax, I've hit the brick wall. It would have been crazy enough, but I'm growing a life here, people! Not that I want to divulge that to the general public. Or even my parents and siblings. It's way too early for that attention-grabbing announcement.

Brice comes into the room after getting ready for bed and laughs at the sight of me. "You look pathetic."

"You sound drunk," I counter irritably.

"I mosht shertainly am not," he slurs in an exaggerated fashion that makes him sound like Harry Carey (God rest his soul). "I only had three—or was that four?—beers. What do you take me for, a lightweight?" He flops beside me on the bed and rests his chin on my shoulder. "Don't go to sleep yet," he requests in a whisper that raises goosebumps on my neck and arms.

It's my turn to slur, "I'm really tired, though." I suck in some drool that threatens to trickle onto the bedspread under my head.

He rolls onto his back and pulls me on top of him.

"Hey!" I protest half-heartedly. "Unhand me. I'm too tired for hanky panky."

"Hanky panky? Wow. Even I have never called it that."

I giggle with my eyes closed.

"And anyway," he continues, "I only want to know what the doctor said this morning. When's our landing date?"

My eyes fly open at the reminder of my doctor's appointment. It seems like such a long time ago. I'd almost forgotten about it, and that…

"Dave Klein has seen my cootchie."

"What?"

"That's what's going to go through my mind every time I see him at church. Did you think about that when you suggested I go to him for my prenatal care?"

He rolls his eyes. "It never occurred to me."

"Because it's not your cootchie."

"I like to think of it as mine," he retorts earnestly then says, "Ow!" when I flick him between the eyes. Rubbing the spot, he avows, "Just kidding! Anyway, what's the problem, again?"

"It's weird. And uncomfortable."

"He's a professional, though, right? He *is* professional, right?" Now he looks concerned.

"Yes! Of course, he's professional! Sheesh! That's *not* what I was getting at."

He appears to be confused again. "Oh. Then I'm not sure I follow."

"Never mind."

"No, I want to understand. Do you want to switch doctors?"

"I don't think I could ever make you understand, so never mind. You're right; he's a professional." I roll off him and stare at the ceiling fan above us. "Anyway, he seemed so grateful to have a new patient. I'd feel even more awkward around him if I started seeing someone else. I can't believe I didn't consider all this before making the appointment."

"If you're not comfortable, you should switch doctors. He'll understand. Dave's a good guy."

I turn my head and smile affectionately at him. "You do realize you say that about everyone, don't you?"

"Most people are good people," he defends himself.

"Yeah, well that's why it would be even worse to dump him. He's a good guy. And probably a good doctor. I liked him a lot until he brought up that he was glad I didn't feel weird about coming to see him. Then I had an 'Oh shit' moment of epic proportions."

We're both silent for a while. I'm pondering the hopeless ob-gyn situation, and Brice is no doubt thinking about at least three of the ten-thousand things currently on his plate.

Then he scoots closer to me and puts a warm hand on my belly. "You never answered my question."

"Probably because I forgot it," I admit, languidly running my finger up and down the back of his hand.

"When should we be expecting this house to get a little more fun?"

I smirk at him. "Well, I shouldn't be pregnant after November 27, so if that's what you mean."

He ignores my deliberate misinterpretation of his question and stares into space. "Late November, huh?"

"Yessir."

"Just in time for Advent."

"Uh, sure. That's true." Some people's husbands view everything in relation to sports seasons; mine follows the church calendar. I have to say, I prefer Brice's perspective.

"We like having babies at the busiest possible times of the church year, don't we?"

"Yeah. Bad timing, huh?"

Giving me a sharp look, he quickly replies, "No! It's perfect timing. No matter what."

I back down somewhat. "Keeps things interesting. For you."

Less intense, he nudges my nose with his. "I love it. I love you." While pressing his lips against mine, he runs his hand up my side and does that thing that almost killed Jen and me when I thought about it the other day while driving: he circles my waist with his hands and rubs his thumbs underneath the waistband of my jeans and my panties.

A full-blown makeout session ensues, but he comes up for air after a few minutes and says, "I thought you were too tired for 'hanky panky' tonight."

"I am, but I'm not too tired to 'express our love.'" If he's going to make fun of me, I have plenty of ammunition to give it right back to him.

He ignores my dig at his propensity for dorky euphemisms, pushes me onto my back, and says, "This feels more like hanky panky to me."

"It's going to feel like blue balls in a minute, if you don't stop turning everything into a linguistics lesson."

Ever the diplomat, he remarks with a grin, "I forgot how *persuasive* you can be when you're expecting."

My response to that is to pull at his clothes. Pregnancy makes me so horny!

POTLUCK SHOWDOWN

*a*s a group, Lutherans are obsessed with food. We've been foodies since way before it was cool. Of course, we don't go for anything trendy. Nope. We stick to the standard meat and potatoes and baked goods, plus any salad you can imagine (namely, the potato, Jell-O, and pasta varieties). In other words, if you ever have a desperate desire to throw up, simply think about a Lutheran potluck buffet table, and voila!

"You don't look so great," Nicole remarks bluntly after sitting across from me at the potluck fundraiser for the daycare renovation. "Did you catch whatever the church secretary had? If so, stay away! That's the last thing I need right now." Without waiting for my answer, she nods at the people around us in the church gymnasium. "Your church family is so cool, by the way."

It's not "by the way" of anything, but I'm in no condition or mood to point this out to her. I simply say, "Thanks."

"Yeah. I mean, you made it sound in all of our phone conversations like they were a bunch of whack jobs, but other than that Paul dude, everyone's nice. Of course, I can't wait to meet Pastor Long and the infamous Vivian," she mutters in a silly, pretentious accent.

I smile sickly. "I'm sure you'll get your chance any minute now."

My mom catches my eye and pantomimes about a sippy cup for Max, so I call down the table, "In the diaper bag. Side pocket."

Before I go back to my conversation with Nicole, my glance falls on Ben, who's sitting close to Dustin and Jason. The three of them are picking up where they left off after getting to know each another during the guys' first visit. Right now, they're laughing hard at something, or someone. Possibly feeling my stare, Ben looks sharply at me and quiets almost immediately. I quickly look away and back to Nicole, who's picking at her barbecue chicken. Ugggghh.

Brice joins us with his usual heaping plate of food. "Do you want some of this?" he asks me, pointing to it.

Without looking at the plate, I say as calmly and dully as possible, "No. Thanks."

He simply nods and tucks into his food. I avert my eyes.

While I'm searching for anything to focus on other than the food surrounding me, I catch Marianne's eye. She and Clark are sitting at a table with a bunch of PoP members. She covertly makes a gun shape with her forefinger and thumb and pretends to shoot herself under her chin. At that very second, Paul turns to her and asks her something. She guiltily sits on her "gun" hand and tunes back into the conversation while I bite my lip to keep from laughing.

Nicole looks over her shoulder, following my gaze, and asks, "What's so funny?"

I shake my head and reply, "Nothing. Just Marianne, being silly."

Ben, hearing the end of that, leans over and interjects,

more to Nicole and Brice than to me, "Oh, yeah. She's a trip. Did she ever tell you she tried to set me up with her little sister?"

I answer, "What? No!"

He laughs. "Yeah. She went to a lot of trouble and devised this elaborate scheme to get the two of us together. But I knew right away what she was up to when I showed up at her house, and there were all these thirty-something couples milling around, and her sister and I were the only single twenty-somethings at the cookout. It was so uncomfortable. And it *so* didn't work out."

Brice barely looks up from his plate. "Been there, about a hundred times."

Sympathetically, Ben says, "I'll bet," then after thinking about it some more he adds, "Yeah! What did *you* do in those situations? You know, before you met?" He nods at me, as if he can't bring himself to even say my name.

I pretend it doesn't bother me.

After wiping his mouth, Brice checks, "You mean when I was single, and it seemed like the members of the churches I served suddenly forgot their true mission and decided that finding me a wife—preferably someone related to *them*—was the new goal?"

"Yeah. Ugh. I bet that was miserable," Ben says, sounding a lot less sympathetic. I hide my smile behind my hand.

Brice seems to regret sounding critical and backpedals. "Well, I mean… They were all very nice about it, and their hearts were in the right place, but I got tired of smiling and nodding anytime someone told me, 'I know this really nice girl.'"

"Oh, come on!" I challenge. "Admit that it was mighty convenient that you never had to date like a normal person.

A constant parade of single ladies under your nose couldn't have been all that bad."

He sits forward and appeals to Ben, "How would you like it if every time you showed up to something associated with your job, there was at least one person in attendance who was specifically there to scope you out and/or turn in her application as your potential life mate?"

Ben winces. "That *would* get old," he tells me.

"It *does*," Brice insists to both of us. "It wasn't as bad at Messiah. Maybe because I was older by then and less eligible. But at the church in Kansas, it was ridiculous. It got to the point that I dreaded potlucks."

"Now, that's just wrong," Ben cracks.

"I know!"

I say, to nobody in particular, "This complaint is coming from the man who claimed not to notice that ninety percent of the women at Messiah flirted shamelessly with him on a weekly basis."

Brice blushes but claims, "By then, I had learned how to ignore it or tune it out. I *had* to, in order to get anything accomplished!"

"Poor you," I say with a pout and a pat to his knee.

Laughing, he continues, "My point is... What is my point?"

"I have no clue. If I didn't know you better, I'd say your point is to brag about how irresistible you are to the fairer sex."

Ben's laughter is highly gratifying, as is the sheepish look on Brice's face at my accusation.

"No! That's not what I meant at all!" he protests. "Oh, I remember now. My point is, being the constant target of matchmakers isn't fun." He swats at my shoulder. "There. Stop putting words in my mouth."

I say sternly, "Well, you're married now, so if anyone here tries to set you up with someone…" I make a motion with my hand like an umpire calling out a batter on strikes. "Excommunicated!"

With similar earnestness, he remarks, "We rarely do that in the Lutheran church, hon."

"Well, that would be just cause, I'd think."

"This is an animated table," Pastor Long says, sidling up to us and smiling tightly. "And who do we have here?" He turns his attention to Nicole. "Oh, you must be Peyton's sister. The family resemblance is unmistakable."

It is? Nobody's ever said that before. Nicole is cute and perky, and I'm, well, not. She also weighs about a hundred pounds, and that's when she's wearing all of her favorite jewelry. I, on the other hand, try to avoid getting on a scale wearing anything more than my birthday suit.

While I puzzle through Wayne's awkward, incorrect observation, Brice recovers, wiping his mouth and saying, "Pastor Long, this is Peyton's sister, Nicole." She waves and smiles. Then he goes down the rest of the table, pointing out the other family members who are new to the associate pastor.

"Quite the crowd," Pastor comments when all the introductions have been made. "What's the occasion?"

"It was Max's first birthday yesterday," I supply, having rediscovered my equilibrium. Jason shoots me an outraged look, so I laugh and add, "Oh, and Jason's birthday the day before that."

"Well, it's a busy time of year for a pastor to have houseguests. Kudos to you, Pastor Northam, for being able to juggle it all," Wayne simpers. "Although, you *did* seem rushed before Lenten services yesterday. Maybe your mind was going in too many directions?" He says it teasingly, eliciting a good-natured smile from my mom and a smirk from my dad, but I know he's serious, and it immediately raises my hackles.

Before thinking better of it, I turn sideways in my metal folding chair so that I can look up at him. My heart pounding, I say sweetly, "I had everything taken care of at home, but when one pastor is doing the work of two for a church this size, there are bound to be a few glitches now and then."

Now I focus on my husband, whose plate must be whispering the secret to life, based on his rapt attention to it. "I didn't notice anything amiss during the service last night, though, so it must not have been that big of a deal." I place a finger on my chin contemplatively and say, "Come to think of it, though, there *was* something missing." I face Pastor Long once more and ask innocently, "Where were *you?*"

He begins to stammer out the answer I already know (he was at one of his grandsons' basketball games) when Brice stands up and pokes at my elbow. "Can I have a word with you a second?" he asks in a way that sounds more like a demand than a request.

Pleasantly, I reply, "Sure," careful to keep my expression neutral, as if I have no idea why he wants to talk to me privately.

At first, he leads me to the hallway outside the gymnasium, but there are some kids from the youth group loitering out there, away from their parents' supervision, so he motions with his head toward a Sunday school classroom. I bravely enter the classroom ahead of him. He follows, closing the door behind us.

As soon as the door's closed, he whirls on me. "Are you kidding me?"

"He's an asshat, calling you out in front of my whole family!"

He clamps his teeth together. "Keep your voice down," he growls.

"No! If you're not going to stand up for yourself, then I will."

"I don't need you to stand up for me, all right?"

"Yeah, you do. Otherwise, he just keeps poke-poke-poking at you, until he gets a reaction. Well, I'll give him a reaction."

"You just did."

"And he deserved it. Criticizing you for being unprepared for the service last night—which isn't even true!—while he has his priorities so far out of whack that it's comical."

"Lower your voice. I'm not going to tell you again."

"Good. Save your breath. I'm done standing around while he bullies you."

"I can handle myself, thanks. And I'd rather handle things *my* way."

"You mean, not handling them at all? Or handling them in such a way that he doesn't even know you have a problem with him?" I roll my eyes. "Real effective."

"You have no concept—" He quickly adjusts his posture into something more casual as the door swings open right next to him. His spine straightens, his arms drop limply to his sides, and his mouth snaps closed.

Nicole pokes her head into the classroom. The rest of her body soon follows. She closes the door and rests her back against it. She smiles sheepishly. "So, I think I sort of did something wrong just now."

Neither Brice nor I say anything, so she continues. "You see, uh, after you guys left, Mrs. Jerkwad came over—I knew it was her, because you're so right, Peyton; she *does* look like a Muppet."

"Nicole!" Brice snaps. "What the…?"

She blinks at him. "Oh. Sorry. Anyway, she came over and asked what was wrong—I mean, it was totally obvious that you were pissed off at Peyton, Brice. Your face! And I was trying to brush her off, when Sadie interrupted me to ask me something about when she was a baby—you know it's her favorite topic when she's around Max."

Brice rolls his hand at her in a "get on with it" motion, so she continues in a rush, "And, anyway, that old biddy corrected Sadie and told her it wasn't polite to interrupt, so I — I—" She blushes. "Well, that pissed me off, so I may have told her off."

Brice buries his hand in his face and muffles, "What did you say?"

Nicole laughs nervously. "It's not *that* big a deal. I took her aside, so it's not like everyone heard me."

"Nicole," I prod.

She sighs. "I only said that maybe my little sister had given her the impression that we're the type of people who welcome unsolicited advice, but we don't. And…"

"*And?*" Brice uncovers his face and says incredulously at the fact there's more.

Defiantly, she finishes, "And that it's time someone clued her in, because she and her husband seem to have forgotten their place."

Brice groans.

She adds quietly with a wince, "I also may have used the word 'pompous' to describe her husband."

For several tense seconds, he says nothing but simply looks back and forth between the two of us. Finally, he asks, "What is *wrong* with you two?"

I look down at my feet and mutter, "Well, I didn't call anyone any names."

Nicole snorts back a laugh but quickly apologizes when she gets the death look from her brother-in-law.

He takes a deep breath to calm himself and stares into a corner of the room. "This is positively super," he mumbles sarcastically while rubbing the side of his face.

"It's not *that* horrible," I attempt, receiving a nearly identical look to the one Nicole received.

This time, though, he backs up the look with words. "Not only have you two said offensive things to two people in a very public setting—"

"Nobody else heard. And I don't know how the truth can be so offensive. You *do* do the work of two pastors here!"

"But you basically did it in such a way that makes it seem like I sit around trash-talking my associate pastor and his wife in my spare time."

"You don't have any spare time; that's the point."

He stares at me while chewing the inside of his cheek. That is *not* a good look to have leveled at me, but I stand my ground. I will not squirm. I will not blink. I will hold firm. When it's clear he's not intimidating me, he pivots on his heel and exits the room without another word.

Nicole shoots me a commiserative guilty look. "We're in trouble now."

I'm as angry with myself as I am with her, but it's easier to be mad at someone else, so I snap on my way past her as I follow Brice, "Way to go, dillhole."

"PRIVATE" CONFESSION

*P*ancake batter sizzles on the griddle. Loudly. I didn't realize it could ever sound that loud in a kitchen full of people. Brice is manning the ladle. The other seven adults are positioned in various locations around the kitchen—Dustin and Jason at the breakfast bar; Lonnie leaning up against the wall; and Mom, Dad, Nicole, and me at the kitchen table—staring at Brice, none of us sure what to say. I wish the kids were here. At least they'd be a diversion. They're wound up, because we're going to the zoo as soon as Max wakes up. But Nicole, wanting to keep the house quiet for Max during his morning nap, insisted they play in the backyard while they waited for brunch to be ready.

I've never been a great conversationalist, so if everyone's waiting for me to get things rolling, we're going to be sitting mute for a long time. Anyway, I'm still miffed at Nicole and feeling self-conscious after last night's events. When we got home, Brice made some mumbled excuse about needing to do some work in his office and disappeared upstairs. I attempted to play the part of the good hostess after putting

Max to bed, but I felt rotten, so I begged off the game of Scrabble that was forming and went to bed. I heard the rest of them carry on without me just fine. When Brice came to bed, I looked at the clock to see that it was well after midnight.

This morning, the tension is palpable.

Finally, Jason sighs and says, "This is miserable. What the hell's going on?"

Dustin laughs loudly. "I didn't want to say anything, but yeah. Brice isn't *that* interesting to watch."

"All right you three," Mom says to Nicole, Brice, and me. "What's the deal? Everything was fine, until Peyton got lippy with Pastor Long. The three of you disappeared for a few minutes, and it hasn't been the same since."

None of us says a word at first.

Since everyone already knows about my part in this fiasco, I'd love to throw Nicole under the church bus, but just like when we were kids, I have this irrational impulse to protect her. It's unfair and backwards, too, since she's the older sister. She should be the protector, but that's never how it's worked. I've always covered for her, whether she was sneaking out to meet Lonnie when we were teenagers or begging me to keep any of her other ten thousand secrets as we've journeyed into adulthood.

So, yet again, when the silence drags on and approaches "unbearable" status, I decide to change the subject. I take a deep breath and reveal, "I'm pregnant again."

At nearly the same time, Nicole blurts, "I mouthed off to Pastor Long's wife, so Brice is mad at me, too."

"I'm not mad at anyone," Brice pipes up unconvincingly before going back to his stony silence and pancake flipping.

I glare across the table at her. "A quicker confession

would have been nice, so I could have saved myself the trouble."

"I can't do anything right, can I?" she says in my direction.

"No, not really."

Mom grasps my hand and breathes, "Oh, Peyton, that's wonderful!" I'm assuming she's referring to my news, not Nicole's declaration of guilt.

I smile wanly. "Yeah. We very recently found out, and it's not the most ideal timing, but—"

A snort from Brice's side of the kitchen draws everyone's attention back to him.

Mom turns around in her chair to address her son-in-law. "Congratulations, Brice! I'm so happy for you, too, hon!"

He raises his metal spatula in a halfhearted acknowledgement before continuing to monitor and flip his flapjacks.

She blinks at his lukewarm reaction to her good wishes.

Lonnie mutters with a grin, "Your elation is overwhelming, dude."

Brice pretends not to hear him, but his jaw muscle twitches, and he drops a pancake onto the floor while trying to transfer it from the griddle to the waiting platter, already stacked with several cakes. He sighs loudly as he bends over to pick up the victim and tosses it at the trashcan. It misses.

"Son of a nuthole!" he hisses, stomping over to it. He peels it off the floor tiles and flings it with authority into the wastebasket.

"Did I miss something?" Dad asks, seeking an explanation from the rest of us. Finally, he appeals to Brice. "Is something wrong? I'm lost."

"I'm confused, too," Mom admits. "Are you two not happy about this? I'd think you'd be happy about this."

Brice smiles tightly. "Overjoyed," he assures everyone. "At least, *I* am."

"You don't seem like it," Nicole ventures. "You seem pissed off, as a matter of fact."

"It's taken us by surprise," I explain. "And I shouldn't have mentioned anything about the timing. Brice gets annoyed when I say that."

"I don't need you to make excuses for me," Brice says in a hard tone of voice.

"I'm not ma—"

"You are."

"What's wrong with you?" I snap, hurt that he'd rebuke me in front of everyone for something I wasn't even aware I was doing. If pressed, I'd probably say I was offering an apology more for my own behavior than his.

He merely shakes his head, places the last pancake on the platter, sets down his spatula, and heads for the back door, which he yanks open, exits through, and slams.

Dad doesn't hesitate to jump from his spot at the table to follow him.

Everyone else stares at me. Nicole finally asks, "What the heck?"

I'm as perplexed as they are, although if I thought long enough about it, I suppose I could come up with some possible reasons for his anger, but they'd still just be guesses, so I'd rather reserve comment.

Instead, I say lightly, "Brunch is ready. Let's eat. I'll get the kids."

~

My shoulders tense as I open the back door. They relax when the yard reveals only my two nephews and niece, who look expectantly at me.

For a second, I forget why I came out here. When it occurs to me, I smile at them and announce, "It's time to eat."

They cheer and run toward me to get to the door. On Sadie's way past, I put a gentle hand on her shoulder, lean down, and ask, "Where'd Grandpa and Uncle Brice go?"

Wordlessly, she points to the small gardening shed against the back fence.

"Thanks," I mutter, staying on the back step and staring at the structure as I struggle with myself and try to figure out what to do. Part of me thinks it would be best to go back inside and eat a few pancakes so I'll have something to throw up later. Another part of me wonders if I should be protecting Brice from my father. They've never been the best of friends. What if Dad's giving him a major ass-chewing right now? And still another part of me simply wants to know what they're saying.

Curiosity wins out.

I cross to the shed, telling myself that I'm not trying to be sneaky—I'm fetching them for brunch—but proving myself a liar by creeping to a near tiptoe the closer I get to my destination. I stay to the right of the double-door opening, peering through the crack near the hinges. Brice's back is to the doors. His shoulders are slumped while he fiddles with something on the small woodworking bench on the far wall of the structure. Dad's leaning against the end of the tool bench, looking remarkably sympathetic.

"And you know, complaining's not my style," Brice is saying now, "but it's times like this that I miss my dad even more than usual."

"I'm sure."

"He always knew what to say, and it wasn't necessarily what I wanted to hear, either. He had a way of…" He trails off emotionally before letting loose with a frustrated grunt. "Never mind. Whatever. What I'm trying to say is, maybe he'd see something here that I'm not. He'd probably tell me I'm overreacting. And maybe he'd tell me to stop worrying so much about how Peyton reacts to everything and everyone and more about what she's feeling to bring on those reactions."

Dad chuckles. "I've found it's pointless to dwell on any of that. Not just with Peyton, mind you. Women in general. Especially when they're in *that* condition. They're irrational and hopeless."

My mouth drops open, but I somehow manage to contain any indignant noises that want to escape.

"I just want her to be happy!" Brice insists. "That's it. Period. It's not complicated." He abruptly stops speaking to hand over the thing he's been holding. It's a large wooden car. "I've been making that for Max. Or I was. Haven't had time to work on it in a while. But I found the instructions online and thought I'd give it a try."

"Jesus was a carpenter," Dad points out.

The observation makes Brice laugh sadly. "That he was. So was my dad. As a hobby, not as a profession."

Dad follows the lines of the car with his finger and holds it up to the light, inspecting it with one eye closed. I change my angle so I can better see the toy through my peephole. Brice hasn't shown it to me yet. It looks exactly like the picture in the online instructions he showed me when he decided to make it, although it still doesn't have wheels.

Suddenly, Dad opens his other eye and looks straight at

me. Shit. He quickly turns his attention back to the car, then to Brice, and returns the toy to his son-in-law.

"Very nice," he remarks. "Max is going to be old enough to enjoy that before you know it. Seems like yesterday he was born."

"I know. He'll be off to college next week. At least, it'll probably feel like that."

"It will, in hindsight. But sometimes, in the midst of chil-drearing, it can drag and seem like it's never going to end."

Scratching at the car with a scrap of sandpaper, Brice says, "Well, I don't think of it as a sentence. I like being a dad."

"Yeah, but you're out of the house upwards of sixty hours a week, aren't you?"

"Something like that. But I wish I got to spend more time with him."

"And I'm sure Peyton wishes she got to spend a little *less* time with him. Or at least more time outside of the house. Being a stay-at-home mom has probably been a big adjust-ment for her, don't you think?" Dad moves closer to him and glances knowingly at me through the crack in the door.

"And I'm completely sensitive to that!" Brice claims.

"Are you?"

"Yes!" He sets down the toy and turns more sideways to face my dad.

I shrink away from the gap, pressing my body against the rough side of the structure, content with simply listening for now.

Brice continues, "I recognize the challenges she faces as a wife—*my* wife—and a mother, and I try to do whatever I can to help make things easier. But I thought marriage was a reciprocal agreement. When is she going to try to make things simpler for me?" He laughs bitterly. "Oh, galoshes.

That sounds so pathetic when I say it out loud. Never mind." His voice gets closer to me as he says, "I guess I needed to say it out loud, though, to realize how ridiculous I sound."

"Brice, wait!" Dad calls toward him while I dash toward the back of the building to hide.

Evidently, Brice stops, because Dad continues, "It's not ridiculous. It's human. You're right; marriage is about give and take. You can't have one person giving everything and the other person taking everything. It won't work for long that way."

"She doesn't 'take everything.'"

I'm touched to hear him defend me, even though I'm still rocked by the other things he's said. What does he mean? I *am* happy! And while I may not be thrilled to be a stay-at-home mom, I don't *hate* my life. I certainly don't gripe about it to him enough that he would think I hate it, either.

"Obviously," Dad says, acknowledging Brice's generous claim that I'm not the worst wife in the world, "but it sounds like she could be slightly more giving."

Brice says nothing, and I can't see him, so I'm not sure what his response to that is.

"Son, nobody ever benefits from being a martyr."

"I'm not being a martyr," he mumbles in response.

"Yeah, you kind of are."

"I'm not! I'm simply trying to figure out how to let her be who she is. I don't want to force a certain lifestyle on her—"

"She signed up for this lifestyle when she said, 'I do'!"

"Well, maybe I didn't make that clear enough. Maybe it's *my* fault she's not giving me the support I need. Maybe I was so intent on being with her that I deliberately didn't let her know what would be expected of her as my wife, because I knew deep down that it would scare her away."

I look down at my bare feet while my heart breaks as he emotionally tells Dad, "She told me she wasn't cut out for this. More than once. But I ignored her. Or I told her it didn't matter. And sometimes it doesn't. She doesn't need to know how to cook—although she's improving at that, thank goodness—or knit or a bunch of the other things she thought pastors' wives needed to know how to do. But…"

"It's more about social things, right?"

"Yes!" He sounds relieved that Dad understands. "And I know she can do it! I *know* she can. She got along with people—very difficult people, sometimes—for a living, before we moved here. But it's as if, when it comes to our church family and the different personalities that inevitably make up the congregation, she's deliberately trying *not* to get along with people. She finds fault with everyone; she picks fights with people, as you witnessed yourself last night; she seems to go out of her way to be contrary! I don't understand."

Doesn't he see that I'm *trying* to help him out? I'm *trying* to make things easier for him when I speak up in his defense at PoP meetings. I'm looking out for his best interests when I stand up to Wayne for him. I don't know what else to do!

I hear a sound like a hand being clapped onto a shoulder, and Dad, his voice closer, commiserates, "She probably doesn't understand, either. I doubt she realizes she's doing all that. The Peyton I know doesn't like confrontation, so I can't imagine she'd be doing anything in a conscious effort to bring it about."

"She just needs to—I don't know—grow up!" Brice explodes.

A tear plops onto my painted big toenail. Snot's making

its way through my sinus cavities and will be dripping from my nose at any second if I don't do something about it. I don't dare sniffle and give up my position, especially since Dad's prying some good stuff from Brice now.

"So, this isn't really about the new baby, is it?" he asks.

There's a pause, then Brice answers, "Yes and no. I mean, it's yet another thing that she's determined to be a pessimist about. Instead of seeing it for what it is—a blessing and a gift—she has to focus on the *timing*." He snorts.

My head snaps up. What? What the hell is he talking about? I *do* want this baby. I *do* see it as a blessing and a gift. Is it a crime to be practical and acknowledge that a couple more months from now would have been better? He's usually all about practicality.

As if he can read my mind, he informs Dad, "She's hiding behind that. What she means but doesn't want to come out and say to everyone is that she doesn't want to have another baby right now. It's not what *she* wants. She says the timing's not right. But what it boils down to is that it's not what *she* wants. Well, that's not a valid reason to question God's will. She's selfish!"

Despite my Herculean efforts, a painful sob breaks loose from my chest, followed by an equally agonizing hiccup. The volume of both is easily loud enough to betray my presence.

Sure enough, mere seconds pass before Brice's head pokes around the side of the shed. His eyes widen as all the color drains from his face. "Peyton, I—"

Before he can say anything else, though, I'm running across the backyard, crashing into the house, and taking the stairs two at a time to our bedroom, where I close and lock the door before collapsing onto our bed.

I can't believe he thinks those things about me! I'm

selfish and willful and determined not to fit in or get along with anyone here? What about Marianne? What about Ben (until recently)? I have friends here! Sort of.

And excuse me for not being a selfless saint! *I* have to be the one to carry this kid for forty weeks; *I* have to be the one to hurl up everything for at least three months—possibly more; *I* have to be the one to give up all my favorite foods because they're not healthy or they're too spicy or salty or whatever; *I* have to be the one to give birth or at least recover from major surgery, after they cut me open—again —to get him or her out of me; *I* have to be the one home with an endless cycle of diapers and bottles and naps—or lack thereof. So screw him!

Oh, I did, didn't I? And look where it got me. Well, how about this: never again! And how about this, too: I'm finished trying to fit my round self into this square hole of a life.

MAKING AMENDS

a faint tap on the locked door startles me awake but receives absolutely no response from me. I don't want to talk to anyone. They all take Brice's side on everything, anyway, so what's the point? Whoever is out there only wants to convince me that Brice is right—as usual—and that I need to put on my big girl panties and stop ruining everyone's day. Well, screw them, too. They can go to the zoo without me, if they haven't already.

I look over at the clock and see that it's a distinct possibility they've been and are back. It's nearly noon. My temper tantrum (however justified) wiped me out.

Another rap followed by Brice's voice. "Peyton. C'mon. Let me in."

I refuse to answer. I don't care if it's infantile. He already has a severely low opinion of me, obviously, so why waste precious energy trying to change it?

When I sit up in bed, I immediately feel that familiar mouth-tingling, tummy-turning urge to run to the nearest toilet, so I do. Afterwards, I brush my teeth, and I'm emerging from the bathroom, wiping my mouth, debating the feasibility of staying in bed all day, when the sight before me stops me short. Brice is waiting for me, sitting on my side of the bed, his hands hanging between his knees.

"How the...? The door was locked!"

"Picked the lock." He holds up a tiny metal pin pinched between his thumb and forefinger. "There's one of these resting on top of each door jamb."

Not after today, I promise myself.

I poke at his shoulder then press harder in an effort to let him know he's in my way and that I want to get back in bed.

"I want to talk to you."

"No, you don't."

"Yes, I do!"

"You don't. You think you do, because you think you're going to apologize for what you said, and I'm going to tell you it's okay, so we can get on with the day. But it's not going to happen that way, so you'd be better off going to the zoo with everyone else."

"They're already gone. I said I'd stay here with you."

"How nice of you. But you should have gone with them."

He sighs. "Why? So you could lie in bed all day, feeling sorry for yourself?"

Instead of answering him, I go on the attack. "You know, I never realized it was your style to talk shit about people behind their backs. You always act like you're above that."

"I wasn't talking sh—mack about you. I was frustrated, and I was trying to explain my frustration to your father."

"Yeah, your new buddy. He knew I was there the whole time."

The look on his face tells me that piece of information is definitely news to him. While he's processing that, I take advantage of his limp state and edge past him to get in bed. As I'm settling on my side, showing him my back, he turns at the waist and drapes himself over me.

"Get off me. Please," I mumble.

He ignores my request. "I'm sorry what I said hurt you."

I blink and swallow against the tears rapidly building in my head. "I feel so stupid," I choke.

"Why? I'm the one who was overheard whining about things."

"You were telling my dad how horrible and selfish I am. How socially retarded I am. How nobody here likes me." I break down now, my body shaking so much that it makes Brice shake, too.

"*Shhh*. I didn't say any of that."

"Yes, you did! You said I'm selfish, and I need to grow up! And that it seems like I go out of my way to *not* get along with people." I gulp in a breath. "But you know what? That's not true! I've been trying very hard to get along with people—a lot harder than I ever did in Chicago. Up there, I didn't care what people thought, but here, I care. A lot. The fact that I'm not getting along with people doesn't mean I'm not trying. I'm trying! Really hard! And failing."

He waits while I wallow in that realization and wail at my social ineptitude. But before I've calmed down after that thought, I'm onto the next one.

"And I love this baby, okay? I would have twenty of your babies if it wasn't for the barfing and the bland foods and the ugly maternity clothes and the insomnia and— and C-sections and breastfeeding—I *hate* breastfeeding. But I suck at being a mom, too. I love Max more than I ever thought I could love another person, but that's not enough, is it? I'm bored to death with this stay-at-home-mom shit. And leaving the house only to go to a weekly meeting with a bunch of parenting fanatics or to volunteer for a couple of hours a week at the PCC isn't cutting it. I have to get out of the house more regularly. To do something I *want* to do. Not something I think I *should* want to do. If that makes me self-ish, then you're right; I'm selfish. Of course, you're always right."

I'm not sure how much of what I've said is actually understood by Brice, since what's coming from my mouth bears little resemblance to anything in the English language.

He sits up and pulls on my shoulder so that I'm lying on my back, looking up at him. Placing a hand on either side of my face, he says, "Hey," appearing more concerned than I've seen him in a long time. He must think I've lost it this time, for real. All the other times were mere practice runs.

"I'm... okay.... Just... l-leave... me... alone!"

"I'm not going anywhere."

"I th-think I'm g-gonna puke."

He jumps from the bed and clears the way for me to get to the bathroom. While I vomit, I continue messily crying. It's an amazing feat of multitasking, if I do say so myself. It takes several minutes to clean myself up. Upon re-entering the bedroom, I'm relieved—and hardly surprised—that Brice is no longer there. He either ran for a different toilet when he heard my performance, or he left before it was a necessity.

I sniffle and hiccup my way back to the bed, where I slide under the covers and pull the bedspread all the way over my head. The resulting claustrophobia is an improve-ment over the other forms of misery I'm experiencing.

Unfortunately, my solitude doesn't last long. My cotton tent peels back to reveal my husband, who's holding a glass of water. I take dainty sips from it while he pours a dose of anti-nausea medication into a tiny plastic cup. "Let's settle that stomach."

I accept his makeshift peace offering, taking the medicine into my mouth a little bit at a time and swallowing it as slowly as possible. When it's gone, I give him a puffy-eyed half-smile as he takes the cup from me and sets it on the nightstand next to the bottle of medicine.

He clutches my hand. "I'm not always right."

"I know!"

"Do you?" he checks with a tilt of his head. "Because sometimes I think— Well, I mean— Sometimes it seems like you put way too much stock in what I say."

"I know you don't know everything, okay?"

He nods. "Yeah. Logically, I'm sure you do. But when it comes to things I say about you, you remember everything. And you treat things I say that may have no basis in fact, that are based on my *feelings*, and often said in the heat of the moment, as if they're the final word. I can't read your mind, you know? That would be a handy trick sometimes, but I'm just a stupid guy, like any other stupid guy, when you get right down to it."

"But you counsel people. You understand what motivates them. You know human nature. You see things that other 'stupid guys' don't see. So when *you* perceive me to be selfish or willfully anti-social, it means more than someone like, say, Lonnie accusing me of being those things. He'd be making a wild guess in most cases, but you... You know what makes people tick." My runaway emotions threaten again, but I breathe them away and swallow them down.

Pressing his forehead against mine, he says, "Oh, Peyton. It's not the same with you. I can't be objective with you like I can be when I'm counseling other people. My emotions are tied up in yours, and they color my perceptions. So when you push my buttons, like last night? And this morning? I might make the mistake of intentionally misinterpreting your motives. Because in that moment, I'm angry. I want to think the worst of you. It makes me feel better. And it justifies my own childish behavior. It makes it okay for me to vent to your dad, instead of sharing with you how it makes me feel when you nit-pick everything and everyone in an effort to hide the fact that you're scared."

My eyes overflow at the knowledge that he understands that much. Because I couldn't have explained it to him, myself, if I'd been given a million years and a degree in psychology.

He smiles. "Oh. I got that one right, huh? Because *that* was a wild guess."

I nod.

"And I don't know about other guys, but this guy…" He sits up straighter and points to his chest. "Nothing gets this guy angrier than fear. I don't like to be afraid. And when I think of—" He clears his throat, looks down at our linked hands, and starts again. "When I think that you may never be truly happy with me, with the only life I have to offer you, I— Well, that's the stuff of sleepless nights."

When it's obvious he's not going to look me in the eye, but I don't have a voice to answer him, I sit up and curl against him, sliding my arms between his arms and his body and pressing them against his shoulder blades. He buries his face in my neck, his eyelashes tickling my skin. I shudder at the sensation, so he pulls away and checks, "Are you okay?"

I nod while tightening my hold on him. "Just don't let me go."

∾

My family left immediately following church on Sunday, which left Brice and me to get back to our "normal" routine, whatever that is in the two weeks before Easter. Holy Week is next week, which means I won't see Brice much at all (although he's been keeping a lot more regular hours since I called out Pastor Long on his lackadaisical schedule. I'm totally taking credit for that).

However, despite our little heart-to-heart on Saturday when everyone else was at the zoo, it's been tense between the two of us, so I'm not necessarily dreading the time apart. I have made a major decision, though, and I don't want to wait until after Easter to talk to him about it.

As we were saying goodbye in the church parking lot, my dad held me hostage with his hug and murmured near my ear, "I know you're hurt by what you heard, but you needed to hear it."

When I relaxed into his embrace, and it was obvious I wasn't going to try to get away from him, he added, "You have him so far up on a pedestal that you don't realize he's human, and he has feelings, too, feelings that you tend to ignore when you're too busy dealing with your own. And that's not fair."

"I know," I acknowledged with an emotional sniff.

He pulled back and kissed my cheek. At a volume more appropriate for a larger audience, he instructed, "Be good to each other."

Brice joined us and puts his arm around my waist. "We will," he promised Dad. "Don't worry."

Dad smirked. "Practice what you preach," he suggested wryly.

Don't worry. That's what Brice tells everyone. *"Why worry when you can pray?"* And I always thought he spoke from experience. But I'm beginning to see that he *doesn't* practice what he preaches when it comes to worrying. He *does* worry. A lot. Until recently, he's hid it well, too. But either he's not hiding it well anymore, or I'm getting better at reading him. Regardless, I can tell he's worried. About many, many things.

And I want to stop being one of those things. I need to get happy and stay happy.

Tonight, during our dinner of cashew chicken (I'm craving the stuff like crazy, because pregnancy makes me disgusting!), when I tell him I want to end my career as a full-time domestic engineer, he stares at me until I clear my throat to prompt a more verbal response from him.

"Oh? Hmmm. But I thought… That is… Of course, if that's what you want to do," he stutters and stumbles, dropping his fork against his plate.

Max, thinking his dad's being silly, giggles in his high chair and throws the plastic baby fork he'd been clutching while shoveling food into his mouth with his free hand.

"I do want to," I insist.

"I thought…"

"What?" I encourage when he trails off and seems hesitant to finish.

He leans over to pick up Max's fork, seemingly more to avoid eye contact with me than to retrieve the utensil. Handing the cutlery to Max and resuming his own eating, he chews and swallows one more bite before saying carefully, "I know you've talked about getting out more, but I thought, maybe, that you were just venting. You know, like we all do after a bad day. An 'I-hate-my-job' kinda thing."

When I again gape at him, he laughs nervously. "Okay, that would be a no, I guess. Sorry I'm so clueless." He says this last part irritably, a touch of defensiveness in his tone, but he looks down at his plate while stabbing at his last chunk of gravy-soaked breaded chicken and asks neutrally, "Where are you going to apply?"

I shrug, trying to sound casual as I address the part of this that gives me the most pause. It's been a long time since I've looked for a job. "I dunno. I guess I'll see if any of the places downtown are hiring. Or I can inquire at the art museum."

He nods but doesn't indicate whether he thinks those ideas are brilliant or shit-tastic. I refuse to pull his opinion from him like an over-eager theology student, so we sit across from each other in tense silence until he finally realizes that's all I have so far and offers lamely, "Okay. Good start."

The last thing I want to do is fight about this. I have a feeling this is a conversation he's been dreading for some time, despite his claims of ignorance. Instead of calling him on it, though, or making him feel bad for wanting a more traditional home life, I simply say cheerfully, "It's worth a shot. I think it would be a lot of fun, even if it's only part-time. I want to get out there again."

"I get it," he says with almost no feeling or inflection. He wipes his mouth and stands to carry his plate into the other room to rinse it and put it in the dishwasher.

I stare after him through the dining room doorway. He disappears from view as he moves down the counter and starts putting away the leftovers. I see glimpses of his long legs through the two-sided fireplace.

Not surprisingly, his lukewarm reaction to my announcement brings on the all-too-familiar sting of tears. I *want to* want to be a stay-at-home mom (that's right; two "want to's."), but just because I want to want something doesn't mean I do want it. Or that I'm even capable of doing it. There are a lot of things I *want* to do that I can't do for various reasons. Wanting to be a stay-at-home mom is one of those things. It sure would make my life easier, for one thing. There's something in me, though, that makes it impossible. I can't make myself want it.

I know I'm not alone in this. My mom, a realtor, often told me that she *needed* her job away from us, so I'm not surprised that I'm the same way. And I've read articles in parenting magazines by women who say they couldn't be an SAHM if someone paid them double what they make at their paid careers. Too much of their identity is tied to what they do outside the home and what they'd been doing for years before their children came along.

We can't all be like Nicole, born to be mommies.

The bottom line is, I can't do this anymore. I can't have PoP be the highlight of my week. It makes me want to do bad things to myself. I need something else. I need to leave the house every single day. I hate that I need it. I hate that taking care of Max and being a "domestic engineer" isn't enough. But it's not.

And boredom isn't the only factor in my decision. In the beginning, I didn't want to leave Max with a stranger—or a bunch of strangers at a daycare. If Nicole couldn't watch him, then I didn't want to be away from him. Now, I'm not as picky.

That sounds horrible.

What I really mean is… Okay, that *is* what I mean. I'm not as picky. I've discovered—sometimes through personal experience (unfortunately)—that he's not as fragile or delicate as I originally thought. He's a tough little guy. But he's not incredibly adventurous so far, either, so I don't constantly worry about what he's going to do the minute his caregiver's back is turned. He's as laidback as his father, if not more so, and remarkably low-maintenance for a baby.

Plus, the church daycare would be an ideal solution for us, because Max—and any of our future children—would be only a few hallways from Brice. It won't be too long before the construction is complete. Until then, I'm sure we can figure out something. We have to.

Brice returns to the dining room with a wet washcloth and begins the task of squeegeeing the food from his son's face and hands. His brusqueness makes him scarily efficient. I watch for a few minutes but eventually rise from the table. As I'm leaning over to get my plate, he says, "Leave it."

I clear from my throat the pesky tears that have taken up residency there so that I can grunt, "Huh?"

"Leave it," he repeats, lifting Max from his high chair. "I'll get it later. Let's go for a walk. Get some fresh air."

"Do you need fresh air?"

"Yeah. I think you do, too."

"I do?"

He nods. "Let's go."

I follow him as he leads the way into the garage, where he pulls the stroller from the trunk of my car and shakes it open, popping the various hinges effortlessly into their locked positions. He does everything one-handed while I stand idly by, half-cognizant that I should be stepping forward and offering to help, considering he's holding the baby, but unable to break from this trance I suddenly find myself under as I observe him.

He's so capable. This man before me isn't the clueless, inept, bumbling father we see portrayed in TV shows and movies and commercials. He knows exactly what he's doing, and he could—literally—do everything with one hand tied behind his back, as long as the other arm wasn't occupied by a child. That's more than I can say for myself. I've never attempted opening that stroller one-handed. As a matter of fact, I'm sure I've never opened it without uttering at least one curse word and breaking into a sweat.

It's not just the baby gear, either. From temper tantrums to teething to fevers to bath time, he takes everything in stride. Even as much as bad smells bother him, he's never shied away from changing a dirty diaper. As a matter of fact, it's like he magically knew how to change the first one he was presented with. When I'd marveled at that, he laughed and said, "It's not rocket surgery, hon." And I thought, *Maybe I've been brainwashed by Hollywood to think all guys are hopeless when it comes to babies.* And maybe I have. But I think Brice is a cut above the rest. He's definitely been blessed with the daddy gene. It puts my maternal instinct to shame.

As we set out on the sidewalk away from our house, I blurt, "If I could handle a stroller like you do, I don't think I'd need to find a job."

"Okay," he says uncertainly. "But you *do* have a job."

"You know what I mean."

He sighs. "As usual, no."

My belief that he's being obtuse causes me to snap, "If I were good at being a mom, I'd like it more, okay? That's what I mean."

Looking around the sunshade and down at Max, he says, "It appears he's still alive. And he's a happy guy. I never notice any strange bruises on him during bath time. So I think you're doing fine. Don't use your stroller-unfolding technique as supposed proof of your remedial parenting skills."

"You just made that thing your bitch," I point out, gesturing with my thumb toward our driveway, which is receding over our shoulders as we walk at a brisk pace toward the end of our street.

He rolls his eyes. "I'd hope that I have a tad more upper body strength than you do. And I've used this thing a hundred times for jogs and—"

"That's another thing! You take him with you everywhere on your days off. Whereas I devise all sorts of excuses on the weekends to go places without him."

"You're with him all week; I'm not." He turns more toward me and says, "Listen. I'm not going to have this conversation. If there's something missing from your life, then I'm not going to stand in the way of your filling that void with a job outside the house. But please, don't list 'bad mother' as one of the reasons you want to go job hunting."

"I'm *not* fishing for compliments, if that's what you're irritated about."

A mirthless laugh falls from his lips. "French's mustard!!" he lets go in a strangled cry.

"What?"

He doesn't explain what I surmise is another one of his unconventional curses, but he does say, "Peyton, you're completely missing the point."

"I am?" I don't want to be as stupid as I apparently am, but I have no idea what his point is, if not to try to make me feel like I'm not as bad a mother as I think I am. "Maybe *you're* missing the point," I say, going on the attack.

"I'm not," he assures me. "I promise."

"Then I guess you're going to have to be more explicit, because I don't get it, okay?" My voice cracks on the last word, but I walk faster to discourage any cry breaks. We will *not* stop for tears, especially the irrational, hormonal ones that are currently in control of my life the majority of the time. I rush on, "I want you to understand that I *need* to work. It's not just a matter of boredom. I need to have something in my life again that I'm good at."

"And I'm telling you that you don't need a reason at all! Slow down!"

That's when I notice he's practically jogging to keep up with me, which means I'm merely a tick away from my running speed, and I'm gasping for air.

I come to a complete stop and bend at the waist, bracing my hands right above my knees.

"Why were you running?" he asks.

"I don't know!" I answer honestly. "I didn't realize I was."

He lightly pounds the stroller handle with his fist while he waits for me to catch my breath. When I stand at my full height, he repeats, "You don't need a reason. I'd rather you didn't manufacture a bunch of them, because you think you need to lobby for what you want."

I open my mouth to object, but nothing comes out.

"I mean, is that the husband I've been so far? One who makes you feel like you have to justify everything or ask permission or receive approval?"

I shake my head, and not just because he looks so hurt at the prospect of the answer being "yes." He *isn't* like that. After thinking about it for a few seconds, I say, "Maybe I need to justify it to myself."

"Why?"

My effing face effing crumples as soon as the effing thought crosses my effing mind, but I manage to say it anyway, as angry as I am at the fact that I'm effing crying, *again*. "I don't want to be selfish. I don't want to admit that I want something that's in *my* best interests, not our child's—our *children's*."

"Well, it's not *not* in their best interests."

"No, it's not about them at all!" I blot under my eyes with my fingertips.

"So?"

"Shouldn't it be?"

He shrugs. "It's not my first thought when *I'm* making career decisions. Does that make me a bad father?"

"No!" I immediately answer. "But that's different."

"Why? Because I'm the less important parent?"

"No!"

"Then enough with the guilt trip. You want to earn a paycheck doing something that's intellectually stimulating, something that requires you to shower and dress and leave the house more days than not. You want to use knowledge and skills that you paid good money to learn in a university setting. You want to socialize and fraternize with other people who have similar knowledge and skills."

"Yes!"

He continues walking, looking toward the horizon as he hangs a right turn. I hurry to catch up to him.

"Well." He squints down at me and smiles. "Good for you. I'm proud of you."

"You are?"

He nods.

I know that shouldn't matter as much as it does, but it does. He's not the type of guy to demand a say in matters like this, but I still care what his say is. Would it change my mind? Probably not. As a matter of fact, if he was a jerk about it, it'd probably make me more determined. The fact that he's being supportive doesn't make the prospect less attractive, though.

While I'm thinking all this, he explains, "I like that you like to be challenged intellectually. That's a good trait to model for our children."

"I've never thought of that."

"Because that would mean you're cutting yourself some slack."

"You don't think I'm selfish? This time?"

He scratches the side of his nose with his thumb and chuckles. "Oh, boy. That's going to haunt me for the rest of my life, isn't it?"

"Maybe," I say with a smile.

"You're not being selfish," he says, giving a more direct answer to my question. Then he adds, "You're also not off the hook."

"What do you mean?"

Grinning, he replies, "In addition to whatever you wind up doing for a paycheck, you're still going to be a mom." He places a sympathetic hand on my shoulder. "Sorry to be the one to break the news to you."

"Aw, man!"

"Aw, man!" Max parrots.

When we've finished laughing so hard that we have to stop and support each other, I say, "See? I wasn't kidding earlier about being an inferior mommy. Even someone as sweet as Max can't deny it."

Brice's mouth is still smiling, but his eyes are serious when he says, "If you don't stop trash-talking my wife, we're going to have a problem."

I duck my head and continue walking. "Fine. You don't have to get all Jason Statham about it."

"Oooh! Is that the b.a. bald guy who does all the cool driving stunts? Do you think I'd look cool with a shaved head?"

Oh, Lord.

TWISTER

*T*he bald truth: I don't sleep worth shit when Brice and his extra pairs of underpants aren't at home. He's my human body pillow. When he's not in bed with me, I can't seem to get comfortable. Or warm. Never mind that the high temps have been in the low 80's for two weeks already, and it's only May. My internal thermometer doesn't subscribe to norms (shocking, I know). I've considered bringing Max into bed with me, but I don't want to reintroduce bad habits. No, I'm a grown woman. I can handle two nights of little to no sleep. I've done it lots of times before. I'm getting older, though. It's not as easy as it used to be.

Tonight, I'm lying in bed, staring at the ceiling, rubbing my baby bump, and thinking back to my phone call with Brice a few hours ago. I felt the first flutters earlier today, and when I told Brice about it, he got all choked up. The memory of it is choking me up. But that's nothing new for me. I'm a little more emotionally stable now than I was a few weeks ago, but not much. I've resigned myself to being a basket case for the next twenty-five weeks, at least.

Brice is at Concordia Seminary in St. Louis. Now that

the rush of the Lenten and Easter seasons is over, he's meeting with a few future pastors in the seminary's graduating class, feeling out the possibility of Peace's calling an assistant pastor to offset some of the duties that he and Pastor Long (ahem!) are too busy (or lazy, in someone's case) to do well and consistently.

Despite some of the difficulties Brice had with Jared, he told me that having a vicar around led to some fresh thinking, and that's what Peace needs now. In other words, he wants another person on his side of things, so they can gang up on Pastor Long. He'd never say that, of course, but I know that's his strategy. Smart guy I married.

The plan was for Max and me to go with Reverend Smarty and combine his business trip with a visit to his mom's. Then I got a job. Which is awesome, by the way.

I'm still home with Max in the mornings, but I work afternoons at a tiny boutique gallery downtown that sells funky craft items and art that some may describe as "kitschy," but that I think is whimsical and fun.

My co-workers are fabulous, too. Nobody takes themselves too seriously, so we have a good time, oftentimes at the expense of some of the shop's flakier contributors (and contributions). And I've already been told that I can bring the new baby to work with me after my maternity leave, until he or she is old enough that I feel comfortable taking the baby to daycare with Max. It feels very much like family. I come home nearly every day feeling content and ready to be an engaged, happy wife and mother, even when I'm bone tired.

And I still volunteer at the PCC on Tuesday nights. I wouldn't say things are back to "normal" between Ben and me, but we've silently agreed to forgive each other—or pretend our disagreement never happened (the latter is probably more likely). We don't play Layette Hoops anymore, because Ben seems determined to do our assigned tasks each week as quickly and with as little conversation as possible. He's never rude, but he also isn't overly pleasant. I've learned, however, to stop taking personally the pregnant pauses in our polite conversations. Well, at least I'm practicing that. I'll get more practice tomorrow.

Now, if I can only get some sleep, I'll be much better equipped—both emotionally and physically—to do just that.

We're folding flyers. Great. I was half-hoping it would be a busy day at the center, so they'd still be working on intake counseling when I arrived after dropping off Max at Marianne and Clark's house. That's a crappy thing to hope for, I admit, considering a busy day means more women in *crisis* are needing our services. But when you're selfish like me, it's hard to control wishes for things that are in your best interest. And tonight, it would be in my best interest if Ben and I were working on different things, surrounded by other people. My heart literally sank when I saw we were the only two people here, and we were going to be sitting across a table from each other for two hours.

After suffering through fifteen minutes of tense silence, I finally say, "You know, my friend, Jen, really liked you." Although it's dangerously close to the most uncomfortable of topics, there's a strange comfort in pretending like it's no big deal.

He thwarts me with, "Weather's supposed to get nasty tonight."

Stung, I nevertheless go with the safer topic. "Now, when you say 'nasty,' what are we talking about here? Storms?

Wind? Hail?" Finished with my first stack, I grab another stack of leaflets and begin tri-folding them.

"I mean, like, tornadoes," he answers matter-of-factly.

I laugh. "Oh. Yes. Auntie Em!"

"They're not funny. You saw what happened to Joplin. I volunteered with the cleanup effort, and it was unbelievable. I've never seen anything like it. And we've had our share here in Springfield, too, and other nearby towns, like Branson."

"I'm aware of that; I've caught a newscast or two over the past ten years." Abruptly, I stand up and say, "Be right back." After my impromptu trip to the ladies' room to drain my low-capacity bladder, I return to the table and resume folding.

Ben, aware of my condition for a while now and used to my abrupt exits from rooms for one reason or another, doesn't miss a beat in our conversation. "Do you and Max have a safe place to go if the storm sirens go off? Is your house one of the handful in this town with a basement?"

I wrinkle my nose. "No. And what's up with that, anyway? Isn't this Tornado Alley? Shouldn't basements be, I don't know, *mandatory*?"

On a shrug, he explains, "The ground's too hard or something. Too much limestone. It's not cost-effective to dig basements."

"Oh. Well, I guess we could go to Marianne and Clark's house. They have a walkout basement."

Laughing, he says, "You can't get in your car and drive somewhere in the middle of a tornado warning."

"Why not? They live, like, five minutes from us. I think I'll have plenty of warning to make it that far."

"Unless you live in a trailer, you're not supposed to leave

your house once the sirens sound. Flying debris can be as dangerous as the storm itself."

"Thank you, Bill Nye the Science Guy."

"I'm only trying to help! I don't want Max to get hurt because his mom's an ignoramus."

"Thanks!" I pick up the pace on my folding. I notice he does, too. Oh, is this a game? I fold even faster, until I give myself a paper cut. "Sonofabling-bling," I hiss, reaching for one of Brice's favorite anti-curses.

Ben smirks. "Anyway!" he continues with his severe weather safety sermon, "Do you have a ground floor bathroom with no windows and no exterior walls?"

I suck on my bleeding finger and look toward the ceiling while I picture the layout of our house. "Um, no. Wait! No."

"How about closets?"

"Yeah, but they have stuff in them," I answer after removing my finger from my mouth and examining it at close range.

"Are they on the ground floor?"

"One of them is, yes."

"Then empty it out when you get home, so you and Max can crawl in there if the weather takes a turn for the worse, like they're predicting."

We return to working in silence for a while. A long while. Then Ben surveys the seemingly endless stacks of flyers still waiting and sighs. "Maybe we should leave some of this for the volunteers to finish tomorrow and get going so you can pick up Max and get home. Isn't he at the Pryces' right now? You might consider staying there tonight, if they have a basement."

I pause to study his profile. "You're being serious, aren't you?"

"Yes! Why wouldn't I be?" he asks, looking over at me.

"Because the chances of this weather happening, much less a tornado hitting *my* house, are incredibly slim."

"Tell that to someone who's lost *everything*. And I'm not just talking about material possessions."

Despite my squirming, he follows my shifting eyes until it's less awkward for me to simply give in and make eye contact. When I do, he says, "Promise me you'll at least clear out that closet tonight."

"Fine! If you'll stop being so intense and weird, I'll promise."

He laughs. "Good. I mean, I'm just trying to save you from getting into trouble. Pastor would be so pissed at you if something happened to Max."

"Ha. Ha. Ha."

"Two more stacks, then let's call it good. I'm starting to get nervous," he says, reaching for a lilac-colored pamphlet, which he folds in double-time.

I'm not as worried as he is, but I'm tired from working all afternoon on very little sleep, and I'd like to get home, get Max settled, and put on my pajamas so I can call Brice and catch up with him. I try to match Ben's pace, careful not to bleed on the papers. He finishes before me and wiggles his fingers impatiently at my stack. I give him the majority of what's left, and when we're through, he says brusquely, "All righty then. Let's lock up and go. I'm gonna do a final sweep of the building to make sure we're the last ones here."

While he's doing that, I step outside. We've been in a windowless room nearly the whole time, so what I observe upon exiting the building makes the hair stand up on my arms, and it's not only because the temperature has dropped a good twenty degrees. Something's definitely not right.

The most disturbing thing is the color of the atmosphere. The dusk is a sickly yellowish green, and the sky is green-gray, reminiscent of the color of the outside of a hardboiled egg yolk. More subtle is the eerie stillness. The ever-present breeze that's been kicking up all sorts of allergens for the past week is suddenly gone, and the street that runs in front of the PCC, usually busy, looks like the setting for a gun fight in a modern-day Western. Plastic shopping bags serve as tumbleweeds.

I'm shivering at all of this when the emergency siren blares less than a block away.

I clamp my hands over my ears.

Ben comes rushing through the door next to me. "Oh, shi—oot!" he hisses. "We should have stopped sooner. Dang it."

Despite the growing sense of unease I'm feeling, I try to play it cool. "Calm down," I implore him as I lower my hands to my sides. "Has anyone ever suggested that you may have PTSD from your experiences in Joplin?"

"This isn't funny."

I wasn't joking. Somehow I think he'd be more offended by that than if I were joking, though, so I keep it to myself.

He bites his lower lip and looks from the PCC building to the other places—mostly offices that are closed for the night—up and down the street. "We need to find the safest place possible to find shelter."

"Yeah, it's called 'home.'" I start to walk away from him. "Good night! I'll see you later! Be safe!"

He sprints after me and grabs my arm. "Where are you going?"

"I'm going to pick up Max." I shake my elbow loose from his grip.

Grabbing my other hand, he tries to pull me back toward the PCC. "No, you're not. He's safe with Marianne and Clark. We need to go back inside."

"You're crazy!" I snap, the first twinge of full-blown fear tickling my tummy. "I'm not hiding out in that building! If something does happen—which I highly doubt—I want to be with my son. Now, let me go!" Fear has always triggered my short temper. If Ben doesn't stop pushing my panic button, he's going to see a side of me that's not very attractive. In a hurry.

Shouting to be heard over the siren—and now the wind, which is picking up—he says, "I was kidding earlier. Pastor would be plenty upset if something happened to you. Or the baby." He nods down at my bump but quickly looks up at my face again. "And if he found out that I let you drive away in the middle of a tornado warning, he'd have every right to strangle me."

"Brice isn't going to strangle anyone!" Again, I try to break free from his grip, but he's holding on to the point of giving me bruises. "Ow! You're hurting me!"

He seems sorry, but he doesn't loosen his clutch. "Please, Peyton. Don't do anything stupid." The wind whips his gingery hair forward onto his forehead and straight back again as it changes direction in a matter of seconds.

Suddenly, it's like someone's pulled a shade on the sun. Over Ben's head, I see debris floating through the air. Large pieces of insulation and trash appear weightless as they lazily submit to the wind's whims.

"It's a simple storm," I insist, although a lot less confidently than before. "I need to be with Max."

His jaw squares as we participate in our parking lot showdown. Finally, as a plastic bag slaps against his back before being carried off toward a neighboring building's rooftop, his shoulders sag, and he releases my hand. "Okay, but we're staying together!" he shouts while hurrying to the PCC to lock the door.

I don't waste time answering him. I turn and run toward my car. Deep down, I don't believe anything horrible is going to happen, but it's hard to be optimistic with those sirens shrieking. It's possibly the most psychologically discomfiting noise I've ever heard, right up there with Paul's daughters arguing loudly during a sermon.

In my car, I fumble to get the key in the ignition, but by the time Ben opens the passenger door and hops in, the car is on, and I'm pulling through the parking space before either of us has our seatbelts on. Ben immediately scans through the radio stations to try to find up-to-the-minute storm coverage. It's on nearly every station, so he doesn't have to search very hard. I can already tell that the voices of the excited storm chasers aren't going to do anything to soothe my nerves.

As I whip out of the parking lot, he says, "I'm going to be keeping an eye on the sky, and if I tell you to stop the car, you need to do it right away without asking questions. Got it?"

"No!"

"What do you mean, 'no'?"

"I mean, I'm not stopping this car unless I see a tornado coming straight toward us."

"Well, that's why I'd be telling you to stop, for Pete's sake!"

"Oh. Right. Okay. But then what? We get out of a perfectly good metal car?" I swerve to avoid a door in the middle of the road. A door! Like, an *interior* door to a house. Ben doesn't seem to have seen it, so I don't bring his attention to it.

Leaning forward, braced against the dashboard as he looks up through the windshield to the west, he answers, "Yes. A car is not a safe place to be in a tornado. And we're not going to just stop the car in the middle of the road and get out; we're going to pull into a place of business and run inside as fast as our legs can carry us."

"That's not going to be necessary."

"It may be, and if it is, you need to trust me and listen."

"You're freaking me out, and there's no need to pan—"

"PULL OVER!"

"What? Where?"

"The first place you can find!"

"No, I mean, where is the tornado?"

"I-it's right over there! It just dropped from the cloud. Due west! No, don't look at it! Just keep your eyes on the road and find a place for us to take shelter. Oh, fuck, fuck, fuck!"

"Ben!"

"I'm sorry! I'm freaking out."

"I don't care about the f-word! Just—Oh, fuck me! There it is. Shit! I've never seen one in real life before!"

"Pull over right now! At that gas station!"

"Okay, okay! Stop yelling at me!"

"I'm staring down a tornado! Yelling is the only mode I have right now!"

"Me, too!"

I take the turn into the gas station on nearly two wheels, almost simultaneously jamming the car in park and pulling the keys from the ignition. We both jump from the car, ducking our heads to avoid being pelted by the golf ball-sized hail that's begun to fall around us. As I turn to see where Ben is in relation to me, I spot a huge sheet of plywood sailing straight toward his head. The wind sucks it away before it can make contact with his temple.

"Oh, shit! You almost died!"

Oblivious to his close call with death, he snaps, "What?

Get inside!" He pushes against my back to propel me toward the gas station door. Through the glass door, I can see several terrified people huddling near the back of the store, by the dairy cases.

Before walking in, I turn and look deliberately at the funnel. It's not as close as it seemed when we were so vulnerable in the car, driving toward it. It's wider than it first was, though, so I know it's building strength. Debris hovers on its periphery like flies around a dirty, rabid animal. I stare at it, wondering what it's currently chewing up.

My house is over there. Are any of my interior doors landing on city streets? Marianne and Clark's neighborhood is also in that general area. Did they make it to their basement with my baby (and theirs)? And the church. Surely, though, a tornado wouldn't have the stones to touch a house of God, right?

"Go!" Ben shouts through gritted teeth. He reaches around me and pushes on the door. As he edges past me, he grabs my arm and pulls me inside.

TOTAL KNOCK OUT

*E*veryone says a tornado sounds like a train. *"I heard a roar, like a train."* They're wrong, though. They have the "roar" part right, but it's nothing like a train. A train doesn't make things personal. A train is controllable. It has brakes. It has gears. It—for the most part—runs on a track and has a predictable path. I know other survivors are referring to the sound, not the behavior, but I still disagree with the comparison. On behalf of trains everywhere, I take offense to their being likened to something so callously catastrophic, so monstrous, so random. And what I heard when the gas station roof peeled off like a yogurt lid and blew away like it was no heavier than a flimsy flap of foil was the roar of a thousand devils.

I barely paused in my intense praying to squint up through the rain and hail. I wanted to look the demon in the eye while I prayed for God to kill it and spare those of us in its path. Okay, so it's dramatic as hell, but that's what I was feeling, until I abruptly didn't feel anything else.

I wake up on a stretcher behind an ambulance in the gas

station parking lot. I have a blooming goose egg and a whole lot of questions.

"What happened? Where's Max? Where's my car? How long have I been knocked out? What time is it?"

The EMT tells me a flying quart bottle of motor oil knocked me out. Hit me right between the eyes. Gives a whole new meaning to "T-zone oiliness." I don't get any more answers than that, though, since the paramedic thinks *his* questions are more important.

"Do you know your name? What day is it? What's the date? Who's the President? Do you know where you are? Are you experiencing blurry vision? Ringing in your ears? Nausea? Vertigo or dizziness? How many weeks along are you in your pregnancy?"

After every answer I give him, I say, "My son was in a tornado!" It makes me sound simple, but my head hurts too much to think of a better, more succinct way of letting them know that I urgently need to get to him.

Finally, the EMT says while shining a tiny penlight into my eyes, "Lady, a lot of people have been in one tonight. For your safety, you need to answer my questions. Then you and your husband can get home to your son."

I nearly come off the stretcher. "Brice? He's here? Where?"

The guy points to Ben, who's a few yards away, talking to a police officer and a firefighter. When he sees me sitting up, he nods and says one more thing to the officials and trots over. I'm glad to see he's okay, but I'm disappointed to the point of tears that he's not Brice.

I bury my face in my hands but quickly pull my fingers away from the tender lump on my forehead.

"Hey, what's wrong?" Ben asks gently, looking to the paramedic for answers when I'm not capable of stringing words together into a sentence. "Is she going to be okay? Is the baby okay?"

The EMT nods tersely. He's obviously rushed; there are lots of other people waiting for medical attention. "I'm not seeing any signs of concussion, but wake her up every hour when she sleeps tonight, to check on her."

He lists a bunch of symptoms for which "my husband" should be on the lookout throughout the night and tells us to report to the hospital if we notice any of them. Then he turns his attention to the next member of the Walking Wounded Club, a guy with glass particles embedded in his upper arm.

I hop down from the stretcher and look toward where I left my car. It's still in the same place, amazingly enough. The metal overhang that used to keep the gas pumps and customers shielded from rain is now twisted, one edge of it resting a few feet from my back bumper. The back window of my car is busted, but the tornado must have sucked the safety glass up with it, because there's no sign that the back window ever existed. Not one piece of glass is lying around the car or on the ledge behind the back seats. Other than the missing back window, the only damage appears to be the pockmarks left by the storm's giant hail.

I'd marvel at this phenomenon, but walking in a straight line is taking most of my concentration. It's as if the parking lot is tilted at a thirty-degree angle. And I feel like I do after I've had one too many—okay, *one* Long Island iced tea.

Ben grabs my upper arm and pulls me up against his side. "Whoa, whoa! Steady there."

"I'm fine," I snarl at him. "Don't you dare do anything to draw the attention of that— that ambulance-driver-dude!" Words aren't coming easily.

"The *paramedic*, you mean?"

"Yes, him.

"But your equilibrium is definitely not right," he points out unnecessarily. "And he said—"

"Forget what he said! I need to get to Marianne and Clark's. Now!"

He sighs. "I had no idea before tonight how stubborn you are."

"You have no idea about a lot of things, okay? Now, help me get in the car; you're driving."

"I don't know."

I stop next to the passenger door and turn to face him, my nose nearly touching his. To everyone else milling around, it probably looks like we're having a tender moment, thankful to have survived our ordeal. At least, that's what I'm counting on when I smile sweetly and murmur, "Ben, so help me God, if you don't take me to my son, I'm going to— to hurt you so that no woman will ever need the services of the PCC because of you."

He cocks an eyebrow at me. "Well, I'd like to think no woman ever will, regardless."

"You know what I mean. And after I shove your balls so far up into your body that you look like you have a goiter, I'm going to leave you in the fetal position in this parking lot and try to drive *myself* home. I'll probably end up dead in a ditch. But I'll make sure I live long enough to write a note to Brice that it was all your fault. Get. Behind. The. Wheel. Now."

He opens the door for me and guides me down to the seat by my elbow.

"Thank you," I chirp up at him.

"No problem. I'll just, uh…" He closes the door before finishing his thought and jogs around the back of the car to the driver's side, where he quickly gets in.

Getting to Marianne and Clark's house is an exercise in patience, forbearance, and perseverance, none of which come easily to me on a good day, much less on a day when I've stared down death, I've been bonked on the head with Pennzoil 10W-30, and I'm worried to the point of throwing up (twice, on the side of the road while we've waited in traffic) about my baby boy (not to mention the one currently hitching a ride with me). I've also had the urge to poop my pants, but I have a strong enough sphincter that I've staved off that embarrassment (I know it's a weird thing to be proud of, but when you're me, you have to brag on the rare occasions you get the chance, even if it's about something as indelicate as sphincter control).

It would help my anxiety if I could use my cell phone, but I have no service. Neither does Ben, whose provider apparently has the same problem as mine: area cell towers are either overloaded or destroyed. That's my theory, anyway. I don't know enough about technology to be sure that's what's going on. The bottom line is, I can't get in touch with my husband or the people who are with my son —hopefully. Oh, crap. I can't think about the alternative.

The radio's no help, either. The coverage of the storm's aftermath sounds like a *War of the Worlds* remake. I finally reach over and switch it off with a shaky hand.

After three more detours, two more puke pit stops, numerous traffic jams due to idiot gawkers, and a complete emotional breakdown on my side of the car when I try— and fail—for the one billionth time to reach Brice or Marianne or Clark on my cell phone, we arrive at the Pryces' neighborhood right before 10:00. It appears to be blessedly untouched. In the dark, it doesn't even look as if there's any trash or debris in the yards or stuck in the trees. The light of day may tell a different story, but for now, it seems like a normal night on a typical American street. You'd never know that mere blocks away, all Hell has broken loose.

I want to jump from the car before Ben has the chance to put it in park in Marianne and Clark's driveway, but I already know from previous attempts at walking unassisted that I'm not very adept at it tonight. As in, I can't do it. I realize this may be a serious problem, but it's so low on my priority list right now that it's barely registering as a blip on my psychological radar. I have two goals: hold Max and talk to Brice. That's it. Everything else can wait.

The former has to wait until I'm seated on the couch in the Pryces' living room. I can't hold myself while standing, much less a baby, so as soon as Ben helps me get settled on the cushions, Marianne deposits Max into my lap. Then she starts crying, full-force.

"We thought—I mean, we didn't *want* to think it, but— we couldn't help wondering… Because we couldn't get in touch with you. And— and we've tried calling Pastor, but we couldn't get him, either, which was just as well, I guess, since we had no idea what we were going to tell him."

Clark puts an arm around his wife's shoulders and kisses her hair. "*Shhh*. Honey, it's okay. Everyone's fine."

"Everyone's not fine!" she insists. "Look at her!" She gestures to me with an open palm. "She almost died! And she looks like something from *Star Trek* with that bump between her eyes!"

Marianne's outburst is upsetting Max, who squirms against me. He has no idea why I'm holding him so tightly. Or why he's up during the middle of the night (for him). I loosen my grip on him, but the usual things I'd do to soothe him, like rocking or bouncing, will bring back the dizzies, and I'd probably fall over on the couch, so I try to savor the sound of his crying, despite what it's doing to my pounding head. A couple of hours ago, I wasn't sure I'd ever hear that cry again.

Ben collapses next to me and says with a sigh, "C'mon, everyone. Let's all take a few deep breaths. It's been a long, harrowing night, and it's far from over, especially for Peyton." He explains to the other two adults that I need to be taken to the ER to see a doctor, since he's now convinced I have a concussion.

"I'm not going to a doctor until I talk to Brice, though," I say obstinately.

Ben pinches the bridge of his nose. "Now, that's ridiculous, and you know it."

"It is not!"

"It could be a long time before phone service is restored. You need medical attention—and soon!" he says.

"He might be on his way home right now," I posit. "In that case, he'll be here in a couple of hours."

"You have no way of knowing that, though!" he explodes, jumping from the sofa and taking Max away. He whispers something in the baby's ear and hands him off to Marianne. "Put this poor kid to bed." Before I can object, he turns his attention back to me. "And you! I'm finished arguing with you tonight. You've seen Max; now you're going to see a doctor. Who knows how long it's going to take to get to the hospital from here. I should have driven you straight there the second time you barfed up your guts."

Marianne flinches at his blunt description and takes it as her cue to leave the room, carrying Max upstairs, where he'll probably sleep in a portable crib in Jessica's room.

"We'll be back here before Pastor can make it into town," he says more quietly, switching tactics.

"You don't know *that*!"

"Help me out here," he appeals to Clark.

Clark steps forward, kneels in front of me and looks into my eyes. "Ben's right." I snort, but he explains, "Really. You're not well. I can't believe they released you. Let Ben take you to the ER. You need to think about yourself and your other baby now. Max is safe here. Marianne and I will keep trying to get in touch with Pastor. We'll tell him everything, and have him meet you at the hospital or here, wherever you happen to be when he arrives in town."

"I want to go home. I'm so tired."

"You will go home, eventually," Ben cuts in. "With Pastor. After we make sure your brain's not bleeding."

What I know he's deliberately not mentioning is that I may not have a home to go home to.

DOUBLE TROUBLE

T have a terrible headache. Oh, yeah, and a Grade 3 concussion. The head injury's not as bad as it sounds, though. I mean, how much damage can a quart of motor oil do, right? Turns out, a fair bit, when it's traveling at a high rate of speed. But it didn't do as much damage as it could have done in my case. And everything else is fine. I suppose.

Sleep is now permissible, but I'm not sure it'll be possible for a while. I definitely won't be sleeping until Brice gets back to Springfield and takes me home, which Clark has seen with his own eyes and has assured me is still standing. Probably missing a few shingles, if the ones in the yard are any indication, but a few well-placed tarps will make do until we can get a roofer out to inspect and fix the damage. All in all, we're one of the fortunate families.

The same can't be said for our church family. The church is gone, for all intents and purposes. And what's left of it will have to be knocked down in order for us to rebuild. While Ben, Marianne, and I slump in various locations around the Pryce living room, Clark tries to describe the devastation to us.

Again, until sunrise in a couple more hours, the full extent won't be clear, but he says it's obvious even at a glance that the building—including the nearly finished daycare addition—is a total loss. I'm half-listening to his account of the initial site walk he attended with Pastor Long and some of the other elders, all of whom walked as close to the rubble as the emergency officials would allow, when I hear a car door in the driveway.

Still unsteady on my feet, I nevertheless hurry to the door, ignoring both Marianne and Ben, who call after me to "take it easy" and "be careful." Barefoot, I pick my way across the cold, damp grass to meet Brice in the middle of the lawn. I'm vaguely aware of the chilly, humid air on my exposed arms, but seeing him makes me feel all warm inside.

"Hey," he greets me quietly, giving the raised bruise on my forehead a cursory inspection before folding me in the best hug I've ever felt. After several silent seconds, he says, "You should be inside, lying down."

I know he's right, but there was no way I was going to lie on the couch and wait for him to come to me. I'm too emotional to say even that much, though. I simply hold onto his neck like he's the only thing keeping me from being sucked into another vortex. He kind of is, anyway.

When I think I can manage it, I pull away just enough so I can see his face. Dragging my fingers under my eyes, I sniff and give him a watery smile. "What about your meetings tomorrow?"

"What about them?" he counters. "I've already called them to tell them what happened and that I was going home to be with my family."

"I know. But—"

"Of all the silly things you've ever worried about, I think that one takes the cake."

"You have commitments!"

He chuckles. "Yeah. Here. With you. Now, let's go inside. You need to rest, and I need to talk to Clark about what's going on at the church. And I need to get a report from Ben about what happened to *you*. You know, in case you decide to leave something out when you tell me later." He winks and squeezes me up against him as we walk to the front door, but I know he's not kidding.

I also know he's justified in suspecting I'd do such a thing, so I don't get defensive. I merely say, "We have a deal, though, right? I have to tell you everything now."

"That's true. You do."

"No lying."

"Nooo. Definitely not." He opens the front door and holds it for me.

I motion for him to close it again. When he does, I look him in the eyes and say, "So, I'll have to tell you exactly how scared I was that I'd never see you or Max again."

He wraps his hands around my upper arms and gives an encouraging squeeze to each one. "It's okay to be afraid. I was afraid, too."

"Oh, then I don't feel so bad."

"Yeah. I told you those extra pairs of underwear would come in handy."

Instead of laughing as hard as I normally would at his saying something like that, I take a deep breath, swallow hard with a clicking sound, and ask, "Do you have a clean pair left?" He raises his eyebrow inquisitively, but before he can wonder aloud why I want to know, I reveal with a sheepish wince, "We're gonna have twins."

It probably seemed cruel, but I couldn't stand to stare at his drawn, pale face and wait for his reaction for another second, so I pushed open the front door and led the way into the house before he could respond to my revelation. I wasn't being malicious, though. I didn't have anything else to say on the topic. I wanted him to know right away (I'd been bursting to tell someone since they gave me the news at the hospital), but I didn't necessarily want to discuss it that second. We had so many other issues to confront that were of a more immediate nature. Looking back, though, it wasn't very nice to leave him gape-mouthed on Marianne and Clark's front porch after he'd driven half the night through severe weather to get home. Would it be too flimsy to blame the concussion?

Now, after a torturous morning of entertaining Max, who is, for the most part, still on his normal schedule, in spite of all the excitement from last night, my mouth is practically watering at the sight of my bed. In my house. Which remains standing, miraculously enough. The only thing standing between me and that beautiful bed is Brice.

He's been on the phone in his office most of the day, trying to coordinate a recovery plan with members and elders and staff, but I distinctly hear him say as I close Max's bedroom door after putting him down for a nap, "Hey, guys. I'm going to have to jump off this call and take care of some stuff here at home. Pastor Long, I'll call you later this afternoon—does 4:00 work for you?—to get caught up.. Great…. Thanks. You guys have been awesome. Bye."

He practically bursts through the door, bumping into me in the hallway.

"Oh. Hey. I, uh, Is Max down for his nap?"

"He is." I can't help but smile at his deliberately casual manner. "And I'm headed that way. I haven't slept in a couple of days, so…"

"What? Why not?" He follows me into our bedroom and pulls back the covers on the bed, motioning for me to get in.

I giggle at the chivalrous act. "Thank you, m'lord," I say in an English accent, giving him a tiny curtsy before sliding between the covers. In my normal voice, I say matter-of-factly, "Well, besides the obvious—a tornado almost killed me, so I've been busy with that—I don't sleep well when you're gone. Or when I'm pregnant. You know that."

He sits on the side of the bed and brushes my hair away from my forehead. Then he stares at my goose egg and says, "I won't keep you awake."

"It's okay," I reassure him. "I don't think there's going to be any stopping the sleep in a few minutes, anyway. You might as well keep me company until it hits me like a jug of motor oil."

With a slight smile, he says, "I hope it's less violent than that."

"Me, too."

He opens his mouth to say something else but stops.

"What?" I prod.

"Nothing," he answers with a short shake of his head. "Nothing. It can wait." He kisses my forehead, just to the left of my boo-boo. "Sleep."

"You don't want to rest while Max is sleeping?" I check. I wouldn't mind having my human body pillow during my nap.

He stands. "Nah. If I go to sleep now, I won't sleep tonight. I'd better keep moving. There's a lot to do and think about." Rubbing his face, he says from behind his hand, "It's overwhelming." His hand falls to his side, and he blinks down at me. "Actually, you know what? I might step out for a few minutes while you two are resting. I need to go for a run, or something, to clear my head. Will that be okay? Do I need to stay here with you? Wait. I might need to stay here with you. What did the doctor say?"

"He said I'm going to feel weird for a couple of days, but I'm not in any danger. Go." My eyes droop, and my vision blurs, but not because of any injury to my brain. The exhaustion is taking over. "I'll see you when I wake up."

"Yes. You will. Okay. I'll be back in a few."

He bends down for one more kiss on my cheek and leaves the room with a soft click of the door.

When I wake up, I'm completely disoriented. My head still feels like it's underwater. It's dark in the room, so I'm not sure if the 5:43 time showing on the clock radio is a.m. or p.m. And I'm covered in sweat from the dream that shocked me awake, a dream that a newborn baby was being torn from my arms by a tornado with a face. Vivian Long's face.

All right, now that I'm awake, it's a funny dream. I'm not laughing, because it hits a bit too close to several nerves, but if I'd had this dream six months ago or if I were anyone else being told this dream, I'd probably laugh. Vivian's face is the scariest part. That yawning mouth.

Whether it's morning or evening (I'm assuming it's the latter), I slept past the end of Max's nap—and then some. Brice must have gotten Max up. It's sweet that he didn't want to wake me, but I know he's busy, and his 4:00 phone call with Pastor Long couldn't have been easy with a baby crawling around and making noise.

Noise. There's a definite lack of it here, now that I think

about it. As a matter of fact, it's as silent as a tomb. Wait. Different comparison, please.

I sit up, stretch, and groan at the headache still lurking in the background. Time for a re-dose of the wimpy pain killer I'm allowed to take in my delicate state. After swallowing two pills with a handful of water from the bathroom, I shuffle downstairs and find a note stuck to the fridge with a magnet.

"Took Max with me to the church. Site cleared. No danger. See you later. −B"

Oh. Evening it is, then. I've never heard of a pre-dawn site walk.

I'm trying to decide if I'm hungry enough to go to the trouble to eat (yes, everything is a chore right now; I'm still so tired!) when the garage door buzzes open. I hear one car door slam, then a pause, then the other door slamming, followed shortly by the door to the kitchen opening.

Max squeals with delight when he sees me. Brice flinches.

"That scary-looking, huh?"

He manages half a smile. "No. Just surprising. The house is dark; I thought you'd still be in bed."

"Just got up," I admit. "Thinking about dinner. You hungry?" Grunting incomplete sentences is going to be my new thing, I think. It's much more verbally economical. I cross the kitchen to stand in front of him and give Max a raspberry on his cheek. "Hey, Stink."

But Brice shakes his head. "No. I fed Max before we went, and I'm feeling pretty sick, actually. I— I need to sit down.." He sets Max on the kitchen floor and drops into one of the chairs at the table, resting his forehead on his folded arms.

Keeping the baby in my peripheral vision, I stand behind my husband and put my hands on his shoulders, rubbing his smooth neck with my thumbs. "Are you okay?"

"No," he muffles pathetically. "I'm not."

"Clark said it was bad."

He rubs his forehead against his wrist. "Yeah, well, it's something you have to see to believe."

"I wish you would have woken me up, so I could have gone with you."

Lifting his head, he says, "You needed to sleep. And I don't want you to see anything to upset you more than you already are about everything."

"I'll have to see it eventually," I argue.

"But not today. You've been through enough."

I try not to let his protectiveness annoy me. He's allowed to look out for me. It's nice. Mostly. "I'll be okay until the next time those sirens go off. Then you'll see 'upset,' I'm sure."

He spins and sits backwards in his seat, gripping the chair back so tightly that his knuckles turn white. "I'm not talking about that."

"My head's fine. Or will be."

"That either."

I know what he's getting at, but I'm too tired to have this conversation.

While I continue to play dumb, he reaches around the chair back and puts a palm on my bulging belly. "You haven't told me how you feel about this. Them."

Max is my savior, deciding he's sick of crawling around on the (admittedly dirty) kitchen floor and crying at my feet. My dizziness seems to have disappeared for the time being, so I chance picking him up and carrying him around the kitchen while I prepare a bottle for him. My silence on the topic stretches, until I change the subject altogether.

"Where are we going to have church on Sunday? And how are you getting the word out to everyone?"

He looks for a minute like he's not going to answer me, but then he sighs and says, "Phone calls and emails. Facebook. Twitter. The elders and Lucy have that taken care of. And a nearby high school is letting us use their auditorium. All four of the Peters' kids go there right now. They're honor roll students. One is the student body president. We're golden on that front." Standing, he adds, "Everything else, on the other hand…" He remains exactly where he is, looking down at his feet.

Suddenly, it hits me that *everything* is gone. *Everything* everything. Not just the structure. Everything *in* the structure. His vestments. The altar. Communion stuff. Christ's body and blood are scattered all over creation, thanks to that damn tornado! I hand Max his bottle and stuff my free fist against my mouth as it all sinks in, finally.

When a whimper breaks loose, Brice looks up from his shoes, tilts his head at me, and bites his lip. "Yeah," he says on a breath. Then he takes Max and sets him down on a blanket on the floor in the living room. Returning to me, he wraps his arms around me and rubs my back. "I know," he acknowledges. "It's difficult to process."

I nod against his chest and cry, "What are we going to do? *How* are we going to do it all?"

Sounding more like the man I know, he replies confidently, "With God's help. And the Synod's. They know what we're going through and what we need. We're not alone. It's intimidating right now, because we're struggling to come to terms with things and figuring out what needs to be done, looking at the big picture. But once we have a plan, we'll take it one step at a time, and— and before you know it, this will all be a horrible memory. And we'll be stronger—as a congregation, as a couple, as a *family*—because of it. Good things will come of this. Trust me."

"I do."

"I know you do. I'm sort of talking to myself, too, though," he admits.

"This is such a nightmare!" I lament.

He doesn't realize I'm no longer only talking about the storm that knocked down the church but the one that's about to descend on our family when he replies, "There, there. This is just a temporary setback..."

I look up at him. "No, I mean, *this*." I point at my baby bump. (Or is it called a "*babies* bump," in this case?)

His face freezes, then morphs from placid to stern. "That's enough of that!" His harsh tone makes me flinch. My insides suddenly feel frozen. When I try to pull away from him, he holds me in place. He jabs a finger toward my midriff. "*This* is a dream come true, not a nightmare. And if it weren't for everything else vying for my immediate atten- tion, I'd be doing a much better job of making that clear." He scoots a few inches back so he can place both hands on my belly. Speaking down at it, he says more softly, "This is a reminder that life continues, no matter what else is going on, no matter how dismal everything else seems. This is *hope*. This is—is wonderful."

My eyes fill, and I nod. In regard to this particular issue, I don't care about our agreement; I'm *never* going to tell him that I almost told the ER doctor I'd rather have a brain bleed than what he discovered. I didn't say it out loud, so it doesn't count. And I don't honestly feel that way; it was merely a gut reaction to some news that I wasn't prepared to hear after such an awful night.

Therefore, I say something I've only said a handful of times to anyone else. "You're right."

"I know I am."

"Well, you don't have to be obnoxious about it," I say with a sniffle.

He grudgingly replies in a sullen tone, "Sorry. I got cocky."

I laugh through my pent-up tears. "Yeah, well. Don't let it happen again."

MITZI'S WEDDING

*O*h, man. I look like a giant eggplant. And, my friends and family are all liars! I refused to look at myself in the mirror at the final fitting yesterday, but everyone told me I looked wonderful in the bridesmaid's dress for Mitzi's wedding. A small part of me knew they were just being nice, but I had no idea how far they were stretching the truth. They were stretching it even further than the waistband on the pantyhose I'm currently stuffed into. Silver lining: standing next to me will accentuate what a beautiful bride Mitzi is.

I groan in the hotel room bathroom, bringing Brice running, his eyes wide. "What's the matter? What's wrong? Are you having contractions again? I knew we shouldn't have traveled this far from home. I mean, Dave said it was okay, but you forgot to tell him you've been having contractions off and on, so he didn't have all the information. Oh, gosh. I can't perform this wedding tonight if you go into labor."

I wait for him to run out of steam. Then, looking at him in the mirror, I say, "Are you finished freaking out?"

He sighs. "Maybe. You're not having contractions, are you?"

"Not yet," I say. "But they may not be far behind. Look at me!"

He looks me up and down, his brow furrowed, his eyes still full of worry. "What's wrong?"

"I'm gi-normous, Brice."

His face slackens, head tilts, and mouth curves upwards. "Awww, no, you're not. Well, yeah, you are, but——" When I laugh, mock-outraged at his acknowledgment, he rushes ahead, "——it's for a good reason! And— and you're gorgeous!" I shoot him a skeptical look before double-checking the mirror to make sure he's crazy, so he says, "I swear!" He ventures further into the bathroom and hugs me from the side, resting his chin on my shoulder and rubbing my enormous belly. "Those guys in there are God's little miracles. And every time I look at you, it takes my breath away."

"Because I suck all the oxygen from whatever room I'm in," I grumble, unable to stifle my smile at his complimentary words.

He laughs loudly at that mental image. Straightening, he lets me go and kisses me on the cheek. With a swift pat to my butt, he says, "All right now. If you're not going into labor—or pretending like you are to get out of being in this wedding—" My face lights up at the heretofore unexplored possibility but quickly dims again when I think of how disappointed Mitzi would be if I couldn't be part of her big day. "Then we need to get moving. I told Jared we'd meet him at the vineyard an hour early. I'm sure Mitzi and Jen will be glad to see you early, too."

I don't know why. I'll only be sitting somewhere with my feet elevated, and I won't be much help. That's why Jen's the official maid of honor; I couldn't perform all the responsibilities in my current, bloated state.

Eight weeks from my due date, I already feel like I did right before I had Max. I'm beyond miserable. The two boys in there seem to be constantly duking it out, and my internal organs are the casualties of their non-stop hand-to-hand combat. In particular, my kidneys and my bladder are suffering, but the twins like to play soccer with my ovaries from time to time, too.

After sliding my swollen feet into the ballet slippers that will stay hidden under my long dress, I rest on the side of the bed for a few minutes, mopping my sweaty brow. When we can't wait another second without being late, Brice hoists me up by both hands and ushers me to the car in the hotel parking lot.

Mitzi and Jared are now officially husband and wife. I experienced a few minutes of panic toward the end of Brice's blessedly short wedding message, when Harris and Brooks were doing their gladiator impressions, and I was unsure if I was going to be able to remain standing for the rest of the service, but some deep-breathing exercises calmed them down, and I persevered. I'm so glad, too. I knew if I sat down that everyone's attention would turn to me, and the last thing I wanted was to distract anyone from the beautiful service that Mitzi and her mother worked so hard to plan.

Plus, I'm so happy for the new couple that I don't want to be distracted by the two nearly full-term babies under my dress. It's always about them lately. Today is about Mitzi and Jared.

Right now, I'm watching the bride and groom as they

slow dance under the grapevine-covered pergola in the vine-yard's courtyard. Jen is nearby, dancing with Max, his chubby cheek pressed against hers. Based on her expression, you'd think she was dancing with Prince Charming. Sadie has her ear against my belly. I absentmindedly stroke her hair while smiling vacantly at the scene before me. I haven't felt this content in a long time. It doesn't get much better than this.

"Food or foot rub?" Brice asks, holding a plate out to me as he finally joins me at our table, standing over Sadie and me.

I was wrong. It *does* get better.

I smile up at him and reach for the plate. "Who says I have to choose?"

"You don't," he concedes, relinquishing the food into my possession. It's only cheese, raw veggies, and crackers, but I'm starving and don't even care what it is. He pokes Sadie on the shoulder. "Hey, Sades. They're not going anywhere."

She sits up and grins at him. "I like feeling them moving around."

He takes the seat on the other side of me. "Why don't you go see if Jen needs help with Max?" he gently suggests.

She immediately and cheerfully follows his recommendation, skipping off across the makeshift dance floor.

"You didn't have to shoo her away," I tell him as I rest my plate on my belly and my feet in his lap.

"I think it's crowded enough in and around your lap. It was making me claustrophobic just watching the four of you." He digs his thumb into my heel.

My eyes flutter closed and my mouth falls open. "Oh, that's nice," I say on a moan. "Will you do that to my lower back later?"

"Of course. Is your back hurting?"

I crack an eye at him. "It's always hurting. But especially when I have to do a lot of standing. Thanks for keeping your message short, though."

He winks at me. "I'm not as clueless as I sometimes may seem."

"Hmmm," I murmur wryly.

"Hey," He stops rubbing and gives my foot an affectionate squeeze. I open my eyes to see what could possibly interrupt my pampering. He smiles shakily. "I had a message waiting on my phone after the wedding. It was from Pastor Long."

I immediately tense, and he chuckles. "Hey, now. Don't get like that."

It's involuntary. Even though Pastor Long has been a lot more productive and cooperative since the tornado (I mean, who wouldn't be? It's kind of ridiculous to continue to be an ass under such difficult circumstances), there's no pretending anymore that he and his wife are my favorite people, and the feeling is mutual. We co-exist, because we have a similar goal in the reconstruction, but we don't go out of our ways to talk to each other.

When communication is absolutely necessary, we're polite to the point of using something that resembles the Queen's English. It's awkward and uncomfortable, but I like it better this way. It's more honest and takes a lot less energy. Brice is frustrated by my propensity for grudge-holding, but I can only change so much about myself at once, and getting along with Wayne and Viv ain't at the top of my priorities list right now. Or anytime in the near future.

I make a conscious effort to relax and smile at my husband. "Sorry. What's so important that he had to call you while you were away on personal business?" I can't resist the temptation to point that out.

He saves his breath on scolding me for my observation and answers, "They'll be done with the church reconstruction on October twenty-first."

At his mention of Secret's birthdate and our wedding anniversary, I flinch then mumble, "Huh. Of course. What other date could it be?"

He shoots me a lopsided grin. "Right? I thought the same thing."

"It would be a nice anniversary present," I quip. "I didn't realize the third anniversary was the sanctuary anniversary, but I'll take it."

"Seriously, though, there's something about that date, huh?" he asks softly.

"It tends to transform the tragical into the magical," I say, trying to keep things light so I don't start crying. I put my feet on the ground and set my plate on the table.

He sits back and puts his hands on top of his head. "There's no such thing as magic. Or the word 'tragical.'"

"Poetic license," I explain before taking a long drink of water.

"So, it's going to be a busy couple of months," he says.

That's an understatement. "Yes, it will be."

"We'll have the church dedication at the end of this month and two new babies at the end of next month—or sooner. Then it will be Advent and Christmas."

I nod. "Do you think you can handle it?"

"I think I'm glad the new assistant pastor starts next week."

After receiving a quick kick to the ribs, followed by another to the kidneys, I grunt and say, "The boys agree. You're definitely gonna need some reliable backup at Peace. Something tells me we're in for sleep deprivation on a scale that we never thought possible."

"Bring it," he challenges with an adorable half-smile.

When I remind him that, ready or not, it'll be brought, he just laughs. "Totally worth it, though."

And you know what? He's right. I can't think of any better reason to be up all night.